W9-AUI-075

NO FIREWORKS

NO FIREWORKS

Rodge Glass

faber and faber

First published in 2005
by Faber and Faber Limited
3 Queen Square London WC1N 3AU

Typeset by Faber and Faber Ltd
Printed in England by Mackays of Chatham, plc

All rights reserved
© Rodge Glass, 2005

The right of Rodge Glass to be identified as author of this work
has been asserted in accordance with Section 77 of the Copyright,
Designs and Patents Act 1988

*This book is sold subject to the condition that it shall not, by way of trade
or otherwise, be lent, resold, hired out or otherwise circulated without the
publisher's prior consent in any form of binding or cover other than that in
which it is published and without a similar condition including this condition
being imposed on the subsequent purchaser*

A CIP record for this book
is available from the British Library

ISBN 0–571–22627–2

2 4 6 8 10 9 7 5 3 1

For Alasdair

Her Final Power

Jews bury their dead quickly. Twenty-four hours after her last breath my mother was in the ground, mourners crowding greedily round the hole she was about to be buried in, peering into the nothingness. The casket was lowered into the space, and my son Nathan and I were called forward to be the first to scoop soil onto it from two piles at the graveside.

'You don't need to cover her completely,' whispered the Rabbi. 'Just a little, then pass the spade on. A line will appear behind you.'

'And make sure you pick from the good pile!' added my mother. 'Don't lock me in here under stones and weeds!'

Evelyn was always full of surprises. In life she went to extraordinary lengths not to raise us as Jewish, but in death expected us to form an orderly queue and shovel quality earth onto her in the company of an Orthodox Rabbi. Nathan threw the spade deep into the dirt and thrust a great heap angrily onto the coffin, quickly turning away in disgust. I hit the target the second time, on the first attempt drunkenly missing the hole and muddying the Rabbi's shoes instead.

Back at the house, we waited in the lounge for the vultures to arrive, each of us pacing nervously while caterers worked quietly in the kitchen making sandwiches. Evelyn was not a popular woman and we had tried to explain that it would be a small gathering – the funeral itself was embarrassingly quiet – but they'd brought enough salmon and cucumber for hundreds.

'Death attracts,' said the caterer gleefully. 'Just you wait and see.'

And, amazingly, people began to arrive. They were a curious bunch, mainly acquaintances of Evelyn's attending out of a misplaced sense of duty, but there were also a couple of teachers I had worked with and one or two people my mother may have called friends, though I hardly knew them at all. Their names escaped me. We rarely saw Evelyn's associates, even in her last days. People did not rally round.

The average age in the room was around sixty, close to mine, though I felt young in this company. These people moved slower than me, complained of aches and pains, and seemed attached at the hip to their spouses. They nodded timidly as they arrived, shaking my hand and muttering, 'I wish you long life,' as some had done at the funeral, moving quickly on to others close by for easier, lighter conversation. Some of them looked half dead already. They came with their own black silk head coverings and shawls in blue velvet bags with gold-coloured Hebrew lettering on the front and seemed to be quietly enjoying themselves, though of course they could not say that to me.

I looked around our living room, usually so empty, now half filled with mourners. The ones I caught glancing at me did so mostly with pity, but some with disapproval. A few men discreetly consulted mobile phones for football scores; others arranged their dress in preparation for prayer. The women were not expected to do anything, except stay separate from the men. Soon there was an invisible line between them, with the small glass coffee table acting as the centre of the divide.

I was shown to a low chair that had been brought in earlier in the day by a busy-looking woman from the synagogue who said she was there to help. I sat bewildered, my eyes searching the room for ways to escape between the knees of my guests. A black silk head covering lay unhappily on my head, a borrowed white shawl hung loosely from my shoulders; a child's, thin, small, the tassels at the tip hardly reaching the bottom of my tie. It was all they had to spare.

2

'There you go,' said the woman. 'Perfect. As soon as the Rabbi arrives we'll begin.'

At the back of the room, just in my line of sight, stood Nathan, my daughter-in-law Arabella and granddaughter Lucille, both with their arms crossed, sternly tight-lipped. Arabella had suggested we burn the will or just ignore it; Lucille had wanted to conduct a service of her own, which she had been working on since before Evelyn died, and was mortified when told she was not allowed to. I said we'd do one of our own later in the week if she liked. A serious, super-intelligent fourteen-year-old with a thin frame and piercing dark eyes, Lucille had been devoted to my mother right up to the end, spending much of her free time at her bedside, bringing her tea and listening to her talk long after the rest of us had stopped paying attention. Sometimes she'd just sit there next to her, reading, while Evelyn wrote the letters that took up so much of her time. Last night, after they took her body away, Evelyn and Lucille had continued their discussions in secret at an altar of old cushions and teddy bears arranged in the corner of Lucille's room, while I listened in through the wall. This was a ritual previously reserved for Lucille's conversations with her own mother, ten years deceased.

'*The whisky, the whisky,*' Arabella mouthed to me.

The flask was poking out from the inside pocket of my suit. I popped it out of view while watching Arabella and Lucille whisper unhappily, arms still locked tight in front of them.

Though they weren't related, they might as well have been. Lucille's mother was weak and unremarkable compared to the woman who replaced her so quickly, and she was rarely talked about. Even Lucille didn't ask questions about her any more. Dressed in an almost identical all-black outfit to her stepmother, fine shoulder-length brown hair perfectly combed in the direction of the floor, Lucille was Arabella in miniature, not her mother. For so long Arabella had been like glue, keeping us all together somehow despite everything. No more though. That time was long gone, eroded by a series of betrayals which had slowly turned her love to resentment. We no longer deserved her.

A steady hum rang round the room as our guests waited for the Rabbi to turn up, exchanging pleasantries, asking after each other's families, mumbling cautiously about the rumoured circumstances of Evelyn's death. The Rabbi was the last to arrive.

'What's he like?' one of the visitors asked another as the Rabbi rang the doorbell. 'I've not been to Shule since Old Chelm died.'

'One of the new breed,' came the whispered reply. 'They call him The Advertiser. Once he gets his claws into you, you can't get them out without a *significant* donation.'

This received a stifled laugh from the group as I sprinted to the front door to get there before anyone else. A pale-skinned, bearded, fat man of middle age wearing a large black hat with a thick rim and long black coat, the Rabbi clapped his hands together and smiled softly as he greeted me and crossed the threshold. He sweated hard in the heat, breathing heavily. He seemed completely other-worldly to me, a strange, almost historical anomaly against the backdrop of our decaying sixties-style front room with its long-abandoned fireplace, foul-smelling and ugly, its mantelpiece cluttered with cheap, modern, porcelain farmyard animals (pigs included), directly behind the seat he was about to be asked to take.

'Did you find us all right, Rabbi?'

'Oh yes, no problem at all.'

A button on his coat dangled precariously, threatening to drop to the floor. He had cleaned his shoes since my earlier faux pas; they now sparkled in the artificial light. A couple of crumbs nestled comfortably in his beard. Speaking in deep solemn tones, talking and moving slowly as if out of respect for the dead, articulating as much with his hands as with words, almost like a magician, everything the Rabbi said and did was fascinating.

'Much traffic?'

'I walked.'

'Of course.'

I gestured towards his hat and coat.

'Thank you,' he replied, 'but I keep them on for prayer.'

We both hovered momentarily; he kissed his forefinger, then the scroll on the side of the front door.

I showed him to the lounge, wondering through my haze what this large and impressive man was really doing in our house, what he would think of to say to all these strangers and why he was wearing so many layers in such heat.

'Your mother was a special woman, Abe,' he said sympathetically. 'You may know we were in contact by telephone quite regularly in her last weeks.'

'No, Rabbi, I had no idea. What did you talk about?'

'Oh, you know,' continued the Rabbi. 'Theory, Jewish history, the peace process. She was not one for light conversation, as I'm sure you know.'

We laughed. Nathan approached.

'She asked a lot of questions,' said the Rabbi acknowledging Nathan, shaking his hand softly and letting the other hand fall gently on his shoulder.

'Are we ready?' he asked him.

Nathan nodded. The Rabbi went to his space, ushered by the woman from the Shule, and turned to address the growing crowd, which was somewhat larger than I had expected. It fell silent almost immediately. (Behind him, the caterer was grinning broadly, vindicated.) The Rabbi greeted his audience with a simple 'Shalom,' and then started a call-and-response prayer.

Few in the room were able to join in with it. Those who could mumbled rapidly in Hebrew, rocking slightly forward and back, forward and back. Lucille gaped at them, open-mouthed. Like many of the non-Jewish majority present, Nathan and I sat dumbly with our books open at the first page, occasionally looking up to see what everyone else was doing, apart from when we were called upon to recite short prayers ourselves. The Rabbi had written these out in

5

conveniently numbered phonetics for us, large capitals on synagogue-headed paper, to save us the embarrassment of struggling with the Hebrew, though this was more for Nathan than for me; sober, I should have been able to cope. Nathan's expression as he mechanically read from the script was as I imagined mine: numb. He had hardly spoken to me all day. He and Arabella were not talking either, though that was no longer unusual.

The service passed slowly, each prayer or half-slurred tune sounding like the last, the long minor notes suiting the bleak atmosphere perfectly. It was strange, this faith. Watching the few religiously inclined amongst the group – none of whom I recognised – lolling back and forth, eyes closed, deep in prayer, and seeing uninitiated friends and acquaintances copying the movements out of an odd respect, I let out a stunted half laugh. Several people turned their heads to look at me, embarrassed, while my mother barked in my ear:

'Where are your tears, boy? Make like you love me!'

I had been hoping Evelyn might leave us alone in death; at the icy-clear sound of her voice, I half jumped out of my chair and let out a small cry. The woman from the Shule bolted from her spot by the Rabbi, pushed through the crowds and came to tend to the bereaved, pushing me lightly back onto the chair.

'It's OK, Abe,' she whispered in my ear. 'Don't be ashamed to grieve.'

As the prayers continued, I felt less obliged to join in. It had very little to do with me. Instead, I looked past everybody and into our garden, through the gap in the hedge that lead to the road, where as a child I had watched my wonderful first wife, then just ten years old, pass by. She was the smallest part of her mother's proud troupe, which marched by each Saturday on its way to synagogue, heads held high and bright skirts matching. I loved her even then and used to wonder whether I was Jewish in the same way she was, in

Shule every weekend and on festivals, or whether Jewishness was something that might wear off if ignored for long enough. 'I wish it bloody would,' Evelyn said, when I asked her. I hadn't wanted Wife Number One to leave me. I loved her increasingly as the years passed, showered her with kisses when we were together, loved her habits, her little faults, our secrets, but though I tried to show I cared, it was never enough. I couldn't rid her mind of the things she thought I was doing with others when she wasn't around, and in the end it was our undoing.

Presently the mumbling stopped and the Rabbi kissed his prayer book, laying it down carefully on a nearby seat.

'I did not know Evelyn Stone well,' he began, 'but I knew her well enough to be sure of this: she was a believer in *life*.'

He turned his heavy head to smile at me.

'Ladies and Gentlemen, Evelyn Stone *lived*. Her ninety-three years on earth were remarkable. Who among us can claim to have had a life like hers? Raised in one of the poorest parts of Jerusalem, Evelyn educated herself in the Torah and Talmud, as a teenager moved to a kibbutz, where she worked in the fruit fields and factories, and then came to England, building up a successful international company from nothing. She was a fierce intellect, a dedicated professional, a smart businesswoman and a fighter, but also a devoted mother, grandmother and great-grandmother – an example to us all. Evelyn raised Abe alone in an age when such a thing was much less common and less accepted. Her family was what she lived for – she told me that herself.'

Nathan slowly raised an eyebrow. Behind him an attractive woman looked at me and smiled. Not with desire, just with kindness. Things were changing.

'Evelyn gave kindly to the synagogue over a great many years,' continued the Rabbi. 'She believed in the value of Jewish community. Though she often felt it difficult to take part herself, this didn't stop her supporting others more able to. Yes, sometimes she had inner struggles, but she told me that belief was always there, even in her darkest moments. If she wasn't in prayers – and prayer was difficult for her – then it was because she was always wrestling with her Judaism, as many of us do, as we all *should* do. Like our forefather Abraham, she was always asking questions of the Hashem, Blessed Be His Name. Sometimes, He does not mind answering. On the contrary, He has been known to find the openness refreshing.'

The crowd laughed politely. I had drunk just enough to feel anaesthetised and so could not join in. Nathan was beginning to perspire. My temples throbbed agonizingly. Everything else was as nothing.

'The Talmud teaches us to ask questions. Indeed, surely Judaism is all about going in search of what we do not yet know. Evelyn's life taught her to do just that, and she encouraged others to do so too. Like the great Rabbis of the past who argued about the tiniest detail of Jewish law, like the youngest child of the family who, on Seder night this week asked, 'Why?' and like the wise son, always asking, always wanting to understand, always grappling for meaning, Evelyn Stone spent her life searching for deeper knowledge. We can all learn a great deal from her.'

At this the Rabbi stopped for a moment to let us all consider what we could glean from such a life, while he wiped his brow with a handkerchief. Nathan's face was now bright red. Arabella could be heard climbing the stairs, the distinctive clip-clop of her high heels disrupting the hush, while I had begun to drift into thoughts of whether I had enough money in my wallet to pay for the drink I would undoubtedly need once everyone had gone.

'This week, at the Seder table,' said the Rabbi, 'we each heard the story of the exodus of the Jewish people from Egypt, and were instructed to act as if we were freed from bondage all those years ago as we go about our daily lives. Evelyn's life was much like the history of the Jewish people – a story full of tragedy, full of mistakes, a struggle to be free, but a struggle that allowed her to emerge stronger. This is how we should remember her. This week, in the spirit of Evelyn Stone and in the name of Hashem, King of the Universe, let the story of Pesach, as the Torah commands, go from generation to generation. Let the word of Hashem survive, as it does in our synagogue, where, in acknowledgement of her generous donations and her commitment to Jewish life, I am proud to announce that our new hall will be named the Evelyn Stone Memorial Hall. Now let us say, Amen.'

'Amen,' said the congregation.

Evelyn had wanted to die and had talked of little but her determination to do so for many months. She had been slowly shutting down little by little. Her bowels had given up, her eyesight and hearing were almost gone too, and her heart was not far behind. 'If you were a real man you would kill me off,' she had said, holding my hand in her bony grip. 'But you're not. I fear I shall have to do it myself. A son who really loved his mother would not stand by and let her suffer so.' But she had made me suffer too, and was still doing so. With money enough to build a memorial hall I could have paid off all my debts; walls with her name on them were more important to her than her only child's financial security.

Evelyn was preoccupied with her own impending death and the consequences of it, and protected her will fiercely at all times, keeping it locked in her bedside drawer, the key round her neck. Its contents were to be kept secret until the day she stopped breathing and started to rot; until then, we would just have to wait. It was her final power over us. Once, I tried to slip the key from its string necklace while she was sleeping, only to have my hand almost bitten off when she suddenly awoke and sank her teeth hard into it, leaving deep marks that still remain today. I didn't try again.

When she finally did die the first thing we did was open the drawer: as well as her generous donations to the synagogue,

Evelyn had left her savings in equal parts to Lucille and to the Rabbi's good judgement, though she had not actually been to his place of work in decades and openly talked of both the curse of Judaism and her dislike of Israel, which she called an oppressive state run by war criminals. Though she knew I desperately needed it, she left me no money at all; instead, I would retain my rights to half the house, if it was ever sold – what Evelyn could do with her half now she was dead was unclear. Nathan and Arabella didn't even get a mention. In the will, Evelyn demanded a full Orthodox funeral, this traditional service of mourning at home (one night only – the customary full week would have killed us all), and even specified the caterer, though paying for that was to be my privilege. She had fallen out with another, cheaper, local company twenty years before.

Another prayer followed the end of the Rabbi's speech and then people prepared to leave. Salmon and cucumber sandwiches lay hardly touched by anyone; half-finished drinks were left everywhere. As soon as was polite I went to the downstairs toilet, needing water, but was sick immediately on getting there, struggling to crouch in the tiny boxed space as it all fell out of me. A watery yellow stream slipped through without difficulty. I got up, checked the lock was secure on the door, then knelt back down, face in the bowl, arms resting on the rim, remembering my mother. For so long she was the old woman who cried suicide; it didn't seem right that she should actually be dead. I swilled, spat out hard and stepped back into the breach.

In ten minutes the house was empty, the Rabbi the last to go.

'May Hashem keep you in the company of Zion,' he said on his way out, solemn and genuine. 'Your mother will be sadly missed. And take care of yourself, Abe, you look pale. Remember, you can always call me. You are never too far away to come back. Evelyn was a shining example of that . . .'

He placed his card in my palm, smiled and was gone, his grand coat tails flapping in the wind behind him. I read the print – RABBI J. M. TAYLOR, AVAILABLE 24 HOURS (APART FROM SHABBAT!) NO DOUBT TOO BIG OR SMALL – and slipped it into my wallet.

Once the caterers had left, Nathan made quietly for the door as well.

'Where are you going?' I asked.

'Nowhere.'

'Mind if I join you?'

He shrugged. I grabbed my coat and followed him out of the door and down the path, wheezing and struggling to catch up. My son showed little concern as I waddled up alongside him, puffing on my inhaler.

'Why so quiet?' I asked.

'Why so talkative?'

Silence. My breathing became more regular as the ventolin got to work and my airways opened. I sighed.

'OK then. What's wrong with Arabella?'

No answer.

'Nathan, is everything OK?'

No answer.

'Is there something you want to tell me? Is this about the will? Or . . . have you been . . . unfaithful?'

At this he stopped, zipped up his jacket irritably and said:

'You of all people have no right to ask me that. Or anything. Go away.'

Nathan waited for me to leave. I didn't. I was grateful for the rest. Instead, I said:

'Why do you treat me as if I have somehow ruined your life?'

Now he raised his voice, the acid tone echoing right around the close.

'Why don't you show me you haven't?'

At a very young age Nathan had decided to become a psychiatrist rather than simply book an appointment with one. He put his hands in his pockets and continued walking, now even faster. I tried again.

'Strange that no one ate the sandwiches, don't you think?'

'Not really, Dad. Passover starts today. You're not supposed to eat bread. If you'd listened properly to the Rabbi's speech you'd know that.'

'Yes . . . you're right. I forgot.'

We carried on.

The walk was instantly sobering, the afternoon's heat having been replaced by light rain and a cool, bracing wind. Nathan and I circled the quiet, affluent suburb together in silence, our brisk pace identical, left and right feet in step, shoes scuffing the pavement rather than gliding over it. I'd never spotted that before, how we walked the same way, hurried and ungainly, but suddenly it seemed important; we shared a trait.

Nathan had always been more like his mother, Wife Number One. He inherited many of her physical attributes – the little snub nose, big, questioning eyes, pallid skin, thick jet-black hair – but also her mannerisms, opinions and values. Nathan was sullen too, always silently aggrieved, rarely telling you what was wrong. The detail wasn't important, really: all that mattered was that all of it was my fault. The way his mother died, the two women I failed to replace her adequately with, the drinking, the pretence; he would never forgive me for it. Not properly.

Nathan had become even more pessimistic about life since his suspension from work. His house was repossessed and he, Arabella and Lucille were forced to move in with me – the ultimate humiliation. The proud graduate I knew had been replaced by an altogether sadder figure, defeated by conspiring forces only he could see. That young man was still in there somewhere not too far away, but he refused to come out. Perhaps if Nathan knew how little money I had as well, it would make him feel better. I thought about telling him, but stopped myself. Nobody else needed to know, not yet.

We stopped again. Nathan's voice lowered as he turned to me and said quietly:

'Dad, do you think other people's lives are like this?'

'I don't know . . . what are ours like?'

A low brick wall was behind us, opposite the playing fields. We sat on it.

'You know . . . just so . . . *hopeless*. Stupid. Tragic. Senseless. Do you ever feel that everything's just . . . completely out of your control? That you might as well just let it all go . . . people's expectations . . . your own . . . all that worry?'

I couldn't reply. Nathan kept talking, but slower, looking at the pavement.

'I saw this documentary a few days ago . . . about the Buddhist centre in the city. You know, how its members got involved, what it meant to them, that kind of thing. And everyone on it . . . the people they interviewed, they just seemed so . . . I don't know . . . *calm*. This one guy was talking about how he used to get road rage and how it just disappeared when he started meditating. I quite fancy some of that . . . *peace*. I'm sick of everything else.'

'Me too,' I replied weakly. 'Do you think you'll be cleared on Thursday?'

'Absolutely,' he snapped, defiantly back to his old, familiar self. 'I have done nothing wrong. It's the only thing that can happen.'

I watched the movement of our feet for most of the short walk home, considering their shape and size, the way the rain splashed off our shoes while we walked, listening to the grunting sounds my son was making, avoiding eye contact. Nathan has X-ray eyes; sometimes I can't look at him. The rain got heavier as we walked, large droplets crashing off my Sunday-best black boots and the shoes Nathan had worn to work every day until so recently. Our feet took us home, both of us exhausted. On the way back we passed the church at the bottom of our road where I noticed the sign on the door: a picture of a wild green labyrinth above which was written: 'Jesus: A-Maze-Ing. Solve the Puzzle – Details Inside.'

The signs were always changing; I rarely paid attention to them. We walked past the church and up the hill to the house, where Arabella and Lucille were supposed to be waiting.

174

The old house is not special any more; nobody's taken an interest in how it looks since the late sixties. Apart from the overhaul each new wife or live-in girlfriend has given the walls and carpets to erase the marks of the last, number 174 has been decaying for years. Even when Evelyn was still active, she didn't care. 'Decorating is the pastime of idiots, Abraham. Read a book! You'd never catch Charles Darwin in overalls!' she'd say, battering the floor with her walking stick. So it's not surprising the neighbours pass and shake their heads, lamenting how it brings the price of the area down. Ours is the house children leave rubbish outside: crisp packets, sweet wrappers and cans, littering the garden and the area around the bus stop. The hanging baskets in the cast-iron porch are just that, baskets without flowers, filled only with crusty old soil and the dangling remnants of dead weeds, and the plant pots by the front door are cracked beyond repair. In the past few years, many of the surrounding homes have been extended upwards or outwards or both, some housing several expensive cars. The Hagstroms next door have just bought another sports car, which, along with the others, is protected by high iron gates connected up to modern security systems. Our whole house sags and I wish I'd attended to it. At any time in the last thirty years I could have done so, but now it's simply not possible.

If 174 ever passes to Lucille, she'll have to spend a fortune redecorating or else sell for a lot less than it should be worth. But it still has one spectacular feature. Sometimes you arrive home, step inside and feel you've wandered into a forest. When all the doors are open and the light is right, the conservatory at the back seems to enclose the whole house and the effect is magical. Despite tall French windows it's a light-starved space surrounded by willows that seem to merge with the shrubbery inside, with tiny shafts of light poking through. Unlike the other rooms, the conservatory has weathered well. It's the room in which Wife Number Two told me she was leaving me, the room in which Wife Number Three said she'd marry me, but just sometimes I am able to forget and the whole place seems mysterious, outside history, full of possibility.

Arriving home with Nathan after the service, I forgot about everything for a second. Looking straight through the house to all that green, through the hallway strewn with plates of half-finished sandwiches and coffee cups, I felt certain that everything would be fine. The warmth, the magical familiarity and the knowledge that Evelyn wasn't there any more – briefly, it was all OK. I touched the old wall and smiled. Crumbling yes, but hanging on. That feeling disappeared quickly.

'Arabella? Lucille?'

Nathan's call was desperate.

'What's wrong?' I asked.

But Nathan ignored me, instead going through to check the kitchen and the back garden.

'Arabella? ARABELLA!'

No one was home.

Without further discussion, we filtered into separate rooms. As we no longer had other homes to go to, the two of us gravitated towards the corners of the old place instead, not wanting company, shuffling about, heads down, hands in pockets, making tea and coffee, returning to our rooms. Nathan's mood had darkened again; I left him to wallow alone. I went upstairs to my room and threw my wet coat over a radiator, first removing the whisky bottle – a cheap malt. I half-filled a small glass, unlaced my boots and sat on the tattered old chaise longue by my window, sipping and listening to Nathan heavily pacing the floor. Perhaps knocking on his door and suggesting a spot of meditation might be a good idea. Perhaps not. He was still sensitive about even living here at all.

174 has a strange history. Evelyn and I moved into the house on arrival in England in the early fifties. I have lived here most of my life, and Nathan was born and brought up in the house too. After a twenty-year hiatus in a bungalow of her own nearby, I had taken Evelyn back into the house a year ago rather than put her in a home where she would have drained the goodness from the nurses, and the rest of the family followed after the financial troubles began. My home was once again Nathan's, Arabella's and Lucille's; we were all now living off the dead woman's hospitality.

When Arabella and Lucille returned, Nathan and I moved instinctively towards the front door, drawn to it like boy scouts wanting our next instruction. We met in the hallway in time to catch Arabella kiss Lucille on the forehead, tap her conspiratorially on the back and send her up to her room. Looks were exchanged.

'It's all right, I wouldn't take her with me,' said Arabella. 'You should know that.'

Her face was ashen and she looked unsteady on her feet, not the first to make a dramatic exit from that hallway. I had watched three women leave through that door. Nathan had watched Lucille's mother collapse for the last time in front of it. Perhaps we were about to lose another.

I had never really warmed to Arabella, but Lucille loved her and I was tired of departures and tragedies. She was a good example to us, a far better teacher than me (not much of a compliment), a hard worker, good organiser and probably the only proper grown-up ever to have given Lucille much care and attention. She was also the only one in the house who could cook and the only one prepared to clean.

'For God's sake stop it, woman. Leave me alone,' Evelyn used to say when Arabella fussed around her bedside. 'Cleaning's for the proles.'

But Arabella was as sharp as my mother.

17

'Well, I'm the working class in this house, so shut up and move while I change your sheets.'

She liked directness, order, common sense. Maybe she wasn't so bad after all. Watching her stand in that doorway, crying now, tears falling silently down her cheeks and onto the dirty wooden floor, suddenly I wanted her to stay, wanted Nathan to make her stay, but in his wife's presence Nathan had lapsed into a kind of trance again, or had pretended to, turning away from her and climbing the stairs without comment. Lucille was safe; he had done his job. I put an arm round Arabella's shoulder, sat on the bottom step of the stairs with her and waited.

In just a few moments she had collected her thoughts, regained her composure and set about explaining the situation clearly. Though sometimes the masks slipped in our family, they were usually hastily put back as if nothing had happened.

'Abe,' she began, wiping away her tears, 'you haven't been here much recently. The pub landlord has seen you more in the last month than any of us have. Not only has your son gambled away our home and apparently lost his job in circumstances he will not explain, but he has now accrued so much debt that I am no longer able to support him. I will not protect a liar. Also, since Evelyn's death, I have had to reconsider my financial position. None of us, apart from God, has received what we hoped for.'

This last sentence she spat out.

'Though Nathan himself seems to feel little loyalty to me – as you can see, he feels no obligation even to talk – I have not decided to leave him or you or Lucille, at least not yet. But if I am ever to return after leaving today, there a number of conditions. If I walk through that door in a week, I want none of them questioned. Otherwise, I shall just pick up my suitcase and go again. OK?'

By now Arabella was facing me, fingers intertwined, talking as if to one of her students.

18

'OK. What are they?'

'One: I take complete control of Nathan's finances. I take over his accounts, I sign the cheques, I cut up his credit cards. He cannot be allowed to haemorrhage money any longer. Perhaps you could grant him an allowance of some kind until his disciplinary situation is resolved, something appropriate for a thirty-five-year-old psychiatrist on the verge of bankruptcy. Two: make sure he gets another job. It doesn't matter what it is. Make him stack shelves for all I care, but as long as he's doing something he can be accounted for. Three: get him some counselling of his own. He will fight it, but you must make him. And four: I need never cook or clean in this house again.'

Arabella took a deep breath and kept going:

'Abe, I am taking a holiday, alone. If hundreds of pounds can go missing out of my husband's account overnight, I can certainly spend a few days in Bournemouth, especially now Evelyn does not need looking after. I'll return if and when I'm ready; you will not contact me.'

'That seems reasonable,' I told her, rising to my feet. 'Though Lucille won't like it.'

'She knows what I'm doing.'

'But I don't understand. Why do this now? Why today? We need you . . .'

'Evelyn no longer controls the events in this house, Abe. Now, anyone can. You should understand that. It is my turn, and I will not come back until I am ready, if at all. I don't want to hurt Lucille, but she is Nathan's daughter, not mine, and I have to do something for myself now. She knows I love her, whatever happens.'

'How can she when you're leaving her?'

'If it were not for Lucille,' she continued, 'I would have gone a long time ago, but I am more responsible than that, and for some reason I still value my marriage. Others may consider marriage something only to be borne when it is easy. I do not. And I don't do this lightly. I have kept to my responsibilities, Abe. Now it is someone else's turn.'

Arabella was beautiful. Though still only twenty-nine, to have a face unspoiled by creases after ten years negotiating my son was no less than incredible. I remembered the day she arrived at the house, barely nineteen, tears streaming down her face and a suitcase in each hand. She was there to see Nathan, who had moved back in only weeks before. 'You only have to look at parents to explain the actions of children,' she said when I asked her what on earth she was doing at my front door at midnight, though I had never seen her parents. She had always been feisty.

Now, I kissed Arabella on the forehead, said, 'OK, whatever you want,' and went back up to my room to hide, crossing Nathan, who was coming down to make tea, on the stairs.

Sitting on the chaise longue by my bed, surrounded by clothes, mugs and plates I had not put back in their proper places, I wondered how we would be able even to go shopping if Arabella controlled Nathan's money. It had been a long time since I had attempted anything so complicated as drawing up a shopping list or cooking a meal, and Nathan was incapable of either. Perhaps Arabella considered the situation to be my fault and Nathan still, ultimately, my problem. A spasm of rage at the idea of her thinking this subsided too quickly for me to do anything about it. Instead, I counted the cash in my wallet: just enough for a couple of drinks, to last me until the next instalment of the money came through, now just half of my old wage. The school let you claim the full salary for a while, then suddenly take half away as if you've done something naughty and don't deserve it any more.

Standing to reach for the bottle, I poured another drink and enjoyed feeling the weight of my body taken from my feet again as I sat back down in my favourite chair with a small glass in my hand. Ah, the soft pattering of whisky into finely cut glass; a sound preceding peace with less guilt than sex and a purer rush than a hundred-yard dash. Tinkle tinkle splash and straight down my throat, lighting up my insides on the way down. No fireworks, no fireworks, as always.

Nathan was standing at my door with a cup of tea in each hand.

'Gremlins. The bank gremlins are in the kitchen,' he said.

I took both cups from him and handed one to Arabella, who was standing behind him, keeping the other for myself. It was a long, twisted road ahead of us.

3

Arabella

When Arabella said she was going on holiday immediately, I was stunned but didn't argue. No space for negotiation, no staying one more night and thinking about it in the morning. My third wife must have said she was going ten times before she actually packed a bag. Arabella set about preparing unopposed, and for half an hour I hovered by her bedroom doorway watching her: suitcase out on the bed, being steadily and neatly filled with a selection of jumpers, jeans, T-shirts, underwear and swimwear. She was calmer now. A bit of swimming might help her relax, think, decide to come home quickly, I hoped. I wanted to go with her, hug her, do something to keep her. Folding a map of Britain, she shot me a look of unexpected disdain, while downstairs her husband seemed to have shut off from the world entirely, blankly looking out of the window into the back garden like a man lost.

Lucille came out of her room and stood beside me, surprisingly composed.

'Got everything you need? Want my teddy?'

She held it up to Arabella.

'No, darling, you keep it. I'll be home soon.'

Lucille clutched the bear close to her chest, making a babyish face.

'Will you?'

'Of course I will. I'm just going on holiday.'

'Who with?'

'Shouldn't you be getting ready for bed?'

'Nobody goes on holiday on their own.'

'I do.'

'No, you don't. Who are you going with? Where are you going to? Can I come?'

'No, darling, you have to go to school.'

'I hate school.'

'You're too old for teddy bears. Perhaps I *will* take it with me.'

Arabella snatched it.

'That's fine. I've got loads more.'

And she did. Mountains of them. Big brown bears, talking ones, squeaking ones, every type of teddy you could imagine. We were always buying her worthless things. Arabella added the teddy to the suitcase and, followed by Lucille and I, carried it to the kitchen table where Nathan sat, red-faced, nursing a full glass beside one of my bottles of whisky. Nathan didn't even drink whisky usually; I would have to start watching my stash. Arabella packed some tins and packets from the fridge into the suitcase, picked at a salmon and cucumber sandwich, said goodbye to Nathan as if she was popping out to the corner shop and, hugging Lucille, told her she would see her soon and to be good for Grandpa. Not for Dad, for Grandpa. She left, lifting the suitcase with one hand and clutching bank statements in the other. We trailed behind her to the front door.

'The wilderness,' she said, pausing to look me deep in the eye, 'can be powerfully curative of city ills.' Then she stepped theatrically through the door and across the porch to her waiting car. She was very melodramatic sometimes; Bournemouth was hardly the wilderness.

'Remember to wrap up warm!' called Nathan from the kitchen, innocently or sarcastically. I followed her to the car.

'I'm OK. Go inside,' she snapped, lifting her suitcase into the boot.

I wanted to kiss her, but instead said:

'You hate me for having this house.'

'Because you didn't work for it, yes,' she replied. 'But there is still hope for you. The single greatest thing you can do in your lifetime is begin to understand what you are. There is nothing nobler, or more worthwhile, or more rewarding. I think it was Wilde who said that, or Mark Twain. Think about it.'

I hated her again.

'People attribute all kinds of crap to those two.'

'That may be so, but I am going to try to understand who I am anyway. I suggest you do the same.'

'Stop this. Are you coming back?'

'I can't tell you something I don't know.'

'Why don't you know?'

'You're horribly weak, Abe, it's suffocating.'

She was suffocating too. As she said it, Arabella looked away from me, fishing for something in her pocket that wasn't there. She got into the car, started up the engine and left without another word, while I returned to the house with the words 'I'm changing' still lodged in my throat. Nathan and Lucille were sitting on the stairs.

'I wonder if they'll have lights this time of year,' my son said when I returned.

'Dad, that's Blackpool,' replied Lucille, deadpan.

And with that, as if in direct response, though it was still early evening, Nathan responded, 'Right then, I'm off to bed.' He rose, picked up a newspaper and the betting form, said, 'Goodnight, all,' and was gone, back to his imaginary world of tranquillity.

Lucille and I sat on the stairs. My thin hands trembled, as they had been doing more often recently. Lucille's contrasting calmness was almost unsettling. My little girl, so strong, so self-controlled. Arabella would soon be back from holiday, Dad would be OK, Granny Evelyn wasn't really dead. Everything was fine.

'Read to me,' she said, pointing to the book on the coffee table. 'What's in that one?'

It lay under Arabella's list of demands.

'It's sad. Don't you want me to read one of yours?'

I got up and made my way to the bookshelves, scanning for something suitable but finding nothing, only some children's stories Lucille had devoured years ago and stacks of battered school textbooks for my old Year Seven and Year Eight classes. Seeing the schoolbooks made me think of whether I'd ever go back and of the long drive there I used to enjoy so much every day, twisting through country lanes in the early morning, listening to Elvis and tapping the wheel. It was almost worth returning for that alone.

'No, they're all for babies. They're boring,' said Lucille, bringing me out of my daydream. 'I want something with real people in it. That one looks good, what's wrong with it? What's it about?'

She pointed once again to an old book that had been lying on the hall table since I took it off the shelf to re-read a couple of weeks earlier. It had been decades since I'd read it, and months since I'd read anything, though I'd had plenty of time for it. The front cover of the book depicted an angel blindfolded with a white bandage, holding wilting flowers in one hand and being carried solemnly on a stretcher by two young boys with swastikas on their arms, one looking out at the viewer like a Nazi Mona Lisa. Insolently? Sadly? Numbly? I picked it up.

'It's about a man living in Germany in the Second World War,' I said. 'An aristocrat; a kind of lord. He keeps a diary of how he feels about all the things happening around him, writing down many things he wasn't allowed to say out loud at the time because he disagreed with the Nazis about how to run Germany. He stays in a big house he's lived in all his life, scribbling in his diary, burying it in his back garden between making entries and then digging it up when he wants to write. Isn't that amazing? He's afraid of Hitler, but brave too. Do you know who Hitler is?'

'Of course I do! How stupid do you think I am?'

'Sorry. I didn't think you covered him until Year Ten.'

She screwed her face up in mock disgust and then giggled. 'He had a funny moustache!'

'And wasn't so great to us Jews either.'

25

'Us? You're not still Jewish, are you? I thought you'd given all that up ages ago. Rebecca says that if you don't go to synagogue and do Sunday dinner or Jewish Christmas and everything, then you're not Jewish, and we don't do *any* of that in our house.'

'Ignore Rebecca. Look at what happened in our home tonight! If those aren't the actions of a Jewish family, then what is?'

'You didn't even understand it.'

'I understood plenty! And I used to know a lot more too. It's just . . . faded a little, like when you learn something for a test at school but can't remember much a few years later. Anyway, the point is you're always Jewish, whether you want to be or not. That's what the Second World War was all about, right? Getting rid of all the Jews, homosexuals, gypsies, blacks, everybody, whether they chose to be what they were or not.'

'I thought it was about money.'

'Oh, very clever.'

Lucille wrinkled up her nose and forehead, half in concentration, half out of suspicion. I started again.

'You're Jewish just because you are. Somebody said, *I am a Jew because I am a Jew because I am a Jew*, I'm not sure who. I used to know, but anyway, there's nothing else to it. You just choose whether you want to learn about it or not. Your father chose not to and not to pass it on to you, but it's still there. It never goes away. And it's Friday night dinner, not Sunday; the Jewish Sabbath is from Friday night until Saturday night.'

She was looking down at the carpet now, but suddenly I didn't want to, or couldn't, stop the lesson.

'On Friday nights you eat special bread called Challah, drink special Kiddush wine, and the women light the candles as the sun's going down to bring the Sabbath in. It's quite beautiful, really. By Jewish Christmas you mean Chanukkah. You're Jewish too, you know. You can take it up whenever you like.'

26

But I was talking in a language she couldn't understand, a language *I* hardly understood. There was a brief, awkward quietness between us. The Hebrew words sounded strange to me and were misleading for her. It made it seem like I had access to this whole other universe, when in fact I'd just told Lucille most of what I remembered myself from my first few years of life on the kibbutz and my first and only Jewish marriage. It's amazing how quickly it all just disappears. Lucille's face glazed over in a way I had never seen before.

'Or you can drop it,' I said, finally.

We laughed together at the thought of having a religion of some kind. How ridiculous. But the laughter faded quickly.

'If you wanted me to be interested in being Jewish,' she said, 'you should have showed me what it was like. Granny Evelyn says the Jews are hypocrites and that's why she hates the Jewish army. "The indigenous population of Palestine has been systematically discriminated against since the Balfour Declaration in 1917." I learnt that one off by heart.'

'Look, I'm not saying I want you to be Jewish or to agree with everything Jewish people do; only that it's there for you to pick up if you want.'

'Why would I want to pick it up if you haven't ever shown me that it's mine?'

'But you've just said somebody has!'

'I said *you* hadn't showed me, that's all.'

'When did you two do all this talking anyway?'

'All the time. When you were at the pub, mostly. Granny Evelyn says I'm going to grow up to be a genius, and it's important for a genius to take everything in. She said when she was fourteen she knew she was going to be one too. You just know, apparently. It happens all the time in families of idiots.'

It was so hard to believe Lucille was only fourteen. A surge of pride rose inside me.

'Come on, get back to the book,' she said. 'Read me a good bit.'

'Do geniuses get stories read to them?' I said, smiling. 'I thought they all did it themselves . . .'

We moved through to the lounge, where I lit the fire and threw her a bar of chocolate, which she ignored. Bit by bit I translated the German in my head before reading aloud from 18 July 1944, chewing on some chocolate myself and thinking about how exciting it was to have something so important to say that you would risk your life to put it on paper. As I read aloud about the author's fear of the Nazis, his attachment to his grand home, the library he had worked hard to build up and was afraid to lose, I felt our own big house closing in around us, our own little library to our left groaning with the weight of books on its shelves. Lucille was concentrating but fading; I kept going for a while until she fell asleep on me, exhausted, a Buddy Holly record cooing in the background, the fire blazing. I woke her, took her up to bed and tucked her in. It was still only nine o'clock and with Nathan in the house I was free to go to the pub and burn the last of my money, just like I used to as a teddy boy all those years ago, blowing my week's pay on a Friday night like everyone else. It was all so much easier then. But I couldn't go yet. Something stopped me. Instead, I went up to my room and sat, not moving, trying to get my breath back. Climbing the stairs seemed a lot harder these days. The house was quiet, Nathan alone in his room, Lucille in hers, and the sun only just beginning to set. Arabella would be out of the city by now.

Lucille was awake again, already. Through the wall I could just about hear her talking, asking Evelyn if she had enjoyed the service and saying she didn't think much of it herself – not very personal, she thought. Though I could hear few words, Lucille sounded as if she was talking to Evelyn like she did when she was alive, the old woman listening to her theorising while poking at a bowl of soup, only without her characteristic grand replies. I pressed my ear to the wall but could make out less and less; she was talking more quietly. Eventually, apart from the faint rise and fall of Lucille's voice, the rhythms of her speech, so confident, almost like a politician making a speech, I could hear nothing.

I'd only seen Lucille's set-up for these sessions once before, and we'd never talked about it – even over the subject of Lucille's mother, we preferred to pretend – but it formed an incongruous image in my head. A clutch of my old cushions brought down from the loft, book-ended by a couple of her favourite teddies, at which she knelt to pray. The confident, intelligent, strong teenager, crouching in the dust, talking first to her dead mother and now to mine. Why wasn't she outside playing with friends? Where were her friends? I took my ear away from the wall, embarrassed, ashamed, and sat back down on my bed, taking another puff on my inhaler and peeling up my shirt sleeve to scratch my arm. If I could just get well, I could do anything.

I knocked on Nathan's door and entered, finding him sitting up in the middle of the big double bed he and Arabella had shared, legs crossed in a meditative pose, reading the betting form and humming.

'Come in! Plenty of room in here!' he shouted.

Either side of the bed, which was cluttered with pull-out sections from the weekend papers and details of the week-end's races, were things Arabella had not taken: make-up applicators lying on the bedside table, a half-filled suitcase she had decided to leave behind still open on the floor, the clothes she had worn for the service abandoned on her chair. A card sat propped up on Nathan's side of the bed.

'Can't you hear Lucille?' I said. 'Aren't you concerned?'

The muffled sound of one-way conversation coming from her room filled the silence between us. Nathan dropped the paper onto the duvet and again his manner changed.

'It's her first real experience of death, Dad; for God's sake let her have it.'

'Pardon?'

He got up from the bed, irritated, and started packing Arabella's things away into the suitcase.

'Just turn the music up and forget about it. *Relax.* What do you know about children anyway?'

'I don't understand . . . are we supposed to let her keep believing in this? Isn't there some gentle way to explain?'

'Explain what?'

'What death is.'

'She *knows* what death is, Dad. We all do.'

'But she's deluded! This has been going on for years, and it's getting worse! Don't you think this is dangerous?'

He slammed the suitcase he had been packing back down on the floor.

'Dangerous? It's the least dangerous thing I can think of. It's not half as dangerous as that farce you put us all through today.'

'It wasn't me . . . it *wasn't* . . . That wasn't my fault,' I stuttered.

'Then whose was it? If *you're* not responsible, who is?'

Nathan left the suitcase on the floor, got back into bed, legs stretched out, and lifted the paper between our faces to show me he had finished. I left.

I passed my own room and chose instead to go into Evelyn's, a small box-like space that some years earlier she had turned into a spare room for visitors (before they stopped coming). It even had a small en suite bathroom fitted, so everything she needed was there. It was comfortable, though a little bare; not the ideal place to end a life. The television was placed in one corner, her bed tilted in its direction. Her meals were taken up and we took turns to keep her company; she never left the room in the last six months before they finally took her away cold. Creeping inside, I wondered if her death might all have been a hoax, if she could still be sitting up in bed, waiting to see how long we would wait to start clearing out her things, but no. The room, still spinning a little from the drink, was just cold and empty, smelling faintly of the disinfectant used to clear the smell of the dead.

Evelyn had been remarkably prepared for death, tidying up and dividing her possessions into conveniently labelled boxes, though perhaps Lucille had done that for her. I got down on my knees and rummaged through them. One box contained things I recognised, classic highbrow novels Evelyn had entertained herself with in her last years: Chekhov, Dostoyevsky; she liked the Russians. Other boxes were less interesting, full of knitting needles and sewing equipment. No old boxes of photographs or letters, no evidence of the varied and dynamic life the Rabbi had gushed about. You had to be impressed by her thoroughness; we would only know what she wanted us to. I took out the whisky flask, added to it from a new bottle in Evelyn's cabinet, took a swig and began to hunt through her wardrobes and drawers. She was no longer able to stop me.

The floor was soon covered in old rubbish. I became increasingly desperate to find something of interest, but there wasn't a single thing worth keeping or even selling. Evelyn had been obsessively secretive in life and seemed to have taken everything with her into death, but just as I was ready to give up I noticed a white envelope on the bedside table, face up.

The front of the envelope said 'Abraham Stone' in my mother's familiar elaborate handwriting and was sealed with red wax. Inside, there was no explanation or introduction; nothing but a short note headed 'KNOW THYSELF':

So, here we are – and maybe you'll pay a little more attention to me now I'm dead. You may think you know me, Avraham – you always considered yourself very clever – but you're about to find out there's a lot you don't know about us both. The question is, do you have the courage to listen? Because of what happened to me, I brought you up to believe in nothing, but it has made you less of a man. And I'm sorry. Be patient, though. If you give me a chance, I will show you it's still possible to rescue your life from the gutter. Listen to my story, and open your eyes.

And there, halfway down the page, it stopped. I got into her bed, turned over, tucked the sheets under my sides to protect me from the cold and re-read the note repeatedly, looking for clues, once, twice, three times before returning to my room. Though I'd never heard her actually say the words 'I'm sorry' when she was alive, Evelyn's voice was nevertheless clear, the breaths and pauses familiar, the accent, a mesh of Israeli and English, stinging with every syllable. I heard her ghostly voice in my head, picking the spittle out of each language and piling it high for melodramatic effect. Everyone was like that in our family. Arabella had been a worthy admission.

4

Encounter

I had been ill on and off for a long time – months, years, my whole life really, but nobody properly knew what was wrong with me. All my doctors had agreed it was connected to my asthma and eczema, and also nervous stress, depression and insomnia – perhaps a combination of all five of these – and that it might become serious, maybe even quite soon. That's why I had been off work on sick leave for so long, nearly six months now. But when I pressed them for details on my condition they withdrew into metaphors about the mysteries of the universe and the boundaries of science being pushed every day, Mr Stone, and how you never know when they might come up with a cure or even a definition. Over the years I had often wanted to demand to know who this great 'they' was, this mysterious medical élite working tirelessly away on a cure for my unique illness that was not quite this and not quite that and, crucially, not quite treatable, but never had the courage. I'd stopped paying the condition close attention after finally realising I'd never be able to get rid of it and that while I was complaining about my symptoms the doctors were just trying to get me out of their offices with minimal fuss. What the thing was didn't matter to me any more; I only knew that it was constant and horrible and oppressive, that it made me tired of life, often too tired to take part in it at all, and that I wanted nothing more dearly than to destroy my body. I wanted to scratch, bite and rip at my flesh until I was nothing but a pile of pain-free organs.

I sat up on the bed, walked over to the mirror and made a quick inspection, spotting new grey hairs, I was sure, right at the front, at the hairline. I'd been more than lucky so far, requiring only minimal trickery to hide the ageing process, but that luck was starting to cave in on itself rapidly. In the last few months my bathroom cupboard had quickly come to contain an embarrassingly large collection of hair-loss treatments and wrinkle cream among the usual medicines. They say that's how it happens, like with the Italian women Henry's always talking about. They're all stunning from birth, until one day in their mid-forties they are stripped of their beauty, withered old hags slung onto the slag heap of society, unattractive, old, replaced.

My hairline – was it further back today? It never seemed to get less surprising that I was actually losing my hair. I sat at my desk, where piles of old books littered the once tidy space where for years I had marked papers while my favourite rock'n'roll records played in the background. Half-finished packets of pills I had lost patience with spilled over the desk and onto the floor by my bedside. What was I supposed to be taking this week? The last appointment with the doctor seemed so long ago. Never mind. Perhaps I could do some work now, but what? There was no work to do. I rubbed my eyes, picking a little sleep out of the corners. A cool pint, foam dripping over the sides of the glass onto the bar, that's what I needed, and a quick warm shot of good whisky to dull my memory again. It was still only hours since they'd carried Evelyn out of the house and put her in the ground.

I decided to go to the pub but didn't want to go out the front door and have to pass Nathan's room on the way down. The floorboards creaked, his hearing was sharp and his questioning obsessive. You don't get any space here, nobody leaves you alone. He'd be out of his room in a flash, although Arabella had been allowed to leave without objection. 'What's wrong?' 'What's the problem?' 'Where are you going?' 'Why?' 'When are you coming back?' Or perhaps he wouldn't even notice me. He had become unpredictable, childish, and children miss things. I stood up, took a deep breath and opened the bedroom window. Of course I could have crept out the front door, but somehow that seemed less exciting.

My clumsy jelly legs struggled to find their grip – the pipe seemed smaller than it used to be – but that aside it was much as I remembered from when I used to escape to The King's Arms as a teenager, calling for Henry on the way. Not shaving for weeks just to look old enough, rolling in drunk after closing, trying not to wake Evelyn for fear of the belt. (She continued to beat me long after I had outgrown her.) As I hit the ground with a thud, I felt the old rush of adrenalin I used to get from creeping around unknown. Still pretty spry for an old man! But then the pangs in my chest started, and the regret. Asthma would surely kill me in the end; at least then they'd know what to put down as the cause of death, something nice and clear and understandable. Cold northern winds rushed about me and the smell of fresh black suburban tar on the new roads stank. I walked to The King's, breathing heavily, headache throbbing, no longer young, no longer middle-aged, and more aware of the heaviness of my body than ever before.

The King's Arms was much like its customers, lazy and unremarkable, and was arranged to look what the brewery imagined to be old and authentic, like many other pubs in England. And what a dead place England is. The wood was too shiny and the early-twentieth-century framed photos of long-dead local dignitaries looked as if they were plucked from a catalogue. The whole place was fake but had been getting steadily more so for nearly half a century, and I'd hardly noticed the changes. In my own way I liked the routine. Liked hating it, liked complaining. Henry had the right idea – seeing the world, getting out. It must be a lot easier to enjoy your home when you've seen everyone else's. I had never even left England since arriving fifty years before.

Brushing the rain off my coat with my hands at the entrance, I noticed a woman in her thirties smiling at me from behind the bar, the bar manager pointing at me and laughing with her as I walked towards them. She couldn't have been much older than Arabella, but I was flattered, so I took a stool a few yards away and called the manager over to find out who she was as she served someone else. Gary was a cockney temporarily marooned in the north; nice, but a bit of a troublemaker. Always on the lookout. Nobody took him seriously. The kind of person you could know for twenty years and then not notice pass out of your life.

'Evening, Gary. Pint please. And a JD, straight.'

'That's a young man's drink. I've told you that a hundred times.'

His broad grin seemed to cover his whole face.

'Just serve me, will you? Who's the new girl?'

'No girl that, Abe, a *woman*. That's Rachel. Started this week. She's a businesswoman actually. Quite classy. Owned a couple of shops in town, selling fabrics, till her husband left and took all the money. Said the leases were in his name, and they were. Lost the house as well. Shame for her, really.'

'Kids?'

I prefer women who haven't experienced childbirth.

'None. Only married five minutes – makes you look like a trooper! Couple of years tops, three maybe. Anyway, I don't think she'll be staying long. Going places, she is. Very smart woman, knows what she wants, not afraid to go after it. That type. Still, nice to look at while she's here, eh?'

'Why did you employ her if you don't think she's going to stay?'

'No such thing as long-term staff round here, Abe. You should know that. Anyway, I'd rather have Rachel for one month than some lazy student for six. She might not have anywhere to lay her head at night, but with some people you just know it's gonna be worth your while to take them on, you know? She's a survivor, and survivors always seem to find a way out of trouble; they see an opportunity and take it, and fuck everyone else. I like that kind, so she's staying on the couch for now. Sort of reminds me of myself when I was young.'

'Is she single?'

'Oh yeah, and looking, I reckon. On the rebound, big time. I've already mentioned your name, pointed you out when you came in and everything!'

'Yeah, I saw. Lucky me!'

'You could have at least shaved, Abe. You look terrible . . . I'm trying to talk you up here . . .'

I smiled mischievously.

'Anyway, best keep your coat on. I said you was easy to reel in, and loaded, so you might be getting some attention!'

'Well, *easy*, yes, but loaded?'

'Yeah . . . why not?'

'Actually, Gary, I had my wallet stolen yesterday. It had everything in it – my cards, money, even a couple of cheques. I haven't got a penny on me. Can you let this one go?'

'No problem. Only 'cause it's you though! What would I do without my best customer?'

Gary winked.

'I'll, er, tell the young lady you've got a tab tonight. That should do it.'

'Thanks, Gary, I really appreciate it. I'll give it you as soon as I can. You know how these things are to sort out . . .'

'Yeah, like I said, don't worry about it. Just don't die on me!'

Gary went away, grinning.

The barmaid approached. A little too made-up, perhaps a little too skinny, but she definitely looked interested. These days, when I meet a woman I forget who I am, what I look like, how old I really am. I'm a teenager again, greased hair, cocky.

The barmaid leaned over to me as if we were facing each other across a small table, so close I could clearly smell her perfume. The King's was dead; ten, perhaps eleven people in the whole place. That's Sundays for you. She spoke first.

'No company tonight?'

'Oh, I find my own company far superior to anyone else's. Besides, what would we talk about, me and this hypothetical company? I don't have anything to say.'

I was away.

'Oh, come on, I'm sure you do . . . Can I get you anything?'

'No thanks.'

We looked down at my full pint and Jack Daniels.

'Well, let me know when you do. I'm Rachel.'

'I'm Abe.'

Her hand fell lightly on mine.

'Hi, Abe. Gary's been telling me all about you, that big old house, what a difficult time you've been having . . . You must be terribly lonely up there all on your own . . .'

'Well, actually, I'm not strictly alone . . .'

'I'm sure you could do with some company. I know I could.'

She held eye contact for two, three, four seconds in the silence, and then walked away, the heat of her hand still warming me.

I let my eyes drift casually towards the football match on the screen just to look at something until she returned, but I knew it was already decided. How though? Experience, sixth sense, predator's instinct – I just knew. I recognised those looks, those cheap lines, the unspoken pact. Then I noticed my hands holding the pint: like Evelyn's, grey and ugly, wrinkled, no longer the hands of a teddy boy, and that bite mark, ever-present, like a prison number. I was getting old quickly, too old for this, but you don't question, do you? You just take, or else get nothing. The reason doesn't matter. My heart beat fast and hard; the thrill was still as great as ever. Just like my early meetings with Wife Number Three. She was a barmaid once, not far from The King's. It must have been fifteen years ago and nothing's changed. No bloody change.

Newcastle were playing on the TV. I wasn't interested – I can't watch anyone apart from United and England, just get bored – but I had to do something in case she looked over. The rules of engagement never change. It's crazy. 3–0 now. The game was as good as over; there was no point in watching, but it didn't matter. She mustn't see me watching her, that was the main thing. I downed the JD and pretended to be engrossed, though I was really thinking about how long it had been since I'd been in this situation or anything like it, whether I was still up to the task, whether I'd ever get the chance again. One drink soon became two, then three and then four. The barmaid returned intermittently to serve me; we chatted a bit, and then about an hour later she returned holding a short message written on a beer mat.

'Abe . . .' she whispered, her lips brushing against my ear, 'have you ever done anything *bad* in *public*?'

She slipped the beer mat into my palm, closing her hand around mine.

'How . . . how do you mean?'

I thought these days were over.

'Oh, I don't know, say, in an alleyway or a cinema or' – and now her voice became even quieter – 'a *car park*?'

'Well, never a car park . . .'

'*Would you like to?*'

'When?'

'How about *now*?'

Before I could reply she was gone, handing over a set of keys to Gary while reaching for her coat off a hook behind the bar.

'Back soon!' she shouted at him, running to the door and flashing me a look. 'I'm taking my break!'

I went into the Gents to check myself, read the note – BLUE FORD SIERRA – and, after a couple of minutes hesitating over whether this was too good to be true, followed her outside, thanking God for my extraordinary good luck.

Trying to keep the gear stick out of the way, clawing at each other, I thought of Evelyn and how perfect it was, on that particular day, to be grabbing at a young woman I hardly knew the name of in a twenty-year-old car, shaming myself yet again outside The King's, scene of a thousand shames. For her part, the barmaid seemed possessed. I couldn't under-

39

stand it. It was shocking, strange, wrong almost. I was used to a bit of a warm-up, the old gentleman in me, I suppose – women were different in the old days – but there was no time for that. Instead, we grabbed clumsily, in too much of a rush, hands running over each other quickly, checking each other out – backside, legs, chest – my hands touching her face, fingers not brushing her neck but clutching at it, then finding their way down her back, under the tight black top of her uniform, fumbling with a bra strap while her hand went straight for my trousers, first squeezing my jeans hard, then forcing a hand down to where my erection was peeping out of the top, grasping it so tight I gasped.

'How long have you got?'

My left hand was caught in the fastened cuff of my shirt.

'Not long, be quick.'

I went to kiss her softly but almost had my head taken off with the power of the one I got back. I should have just keeled over and breathed my last there and then. It would have been perfect – my final asthma attack, my last words: 'Don't tell my mother how I died!' – but I was still breathing, just about. That was when the panic started. Where was my inhaler? It took all my ingenuity to manage to hide the wheezing, even heading downwards simply to get far enough away from her face to conceal my struggle with my chest. I wasn't much use when I got down there though.

The barmaid was now winding back my seat as far as it would go, then hers, pushing up my T-shirt and starting to kiss my chest, licking up and down fast, flashing her tongue in and out of my belly button, too quick, then moving downwards. She crouched underneath the seat and ripped off my trousers. Could she see the grey hairs on my chest from down there? Her car was round the back of the pub; it was too dark, it had to be. Was she disgusted? Don't the aged smell different? And how old was her ex-husband now? Thirty-five maybe, forty at the most. Was he better looking? God, how low she'd stooped. Gary was probably lying though; what does he care? Everything's a laugh to some people. She's probably my age, a product of plastic surgery; it's amazing what they can do these days. The bloody gear stick though: if you could just put it down flat. Bump, bump went my head on the side window, then the roof; her leg on the steering wheel as she tried to straddle me (having given up on the under the seat approach). Meanwhile, those old hands of mine grappled with her jeans, still not off properly, while she negotiated my trousers, pulling them off my legs, leaving the socks. I hadn't done this for years – Wife Number Two had a thing about socks during sex, said it was wrong to keep them on, disrespectful, and used to go crazy if I tried it. She had a point maybe; it made it seedy somehow. And Evelyn, who made me wear shoes with no socks for school when I lost an old pair. No appreciation of money, she said. School in winter, no socks, it's chilly. I had to buy new ones on the way to the bus stop, take them off before coming home and hide them. Frustrated, the barmaid took off her own top and unclipped the bra I'd struggled with.

Now she was naked and straddling me, her hot body writhing maniacally as if drunk, rubbing her pubic bone back and forth hard up against my poor cock, half cold from exposure, half sizzling with anticipation. My head was at breast height, so close I could have touched them with my tongue just by flicking it out of my mouth, but still, despite all the excitement, despite the fact I had no right to be in such a situation at my age and had done little or nothing to encourage this madness, watching her releasing her breasts from the cheap cotton cups I was amazed to find myself disappointed. *I didn't know I was alive!* Kissing like a kid in the back of an old Sierra with a woman half my age I didn't even know, disappointed at the look of a 32B! The nerve! I buried my head in her anyway, enjoying the soft warmth rubbing against my cheeks. My divorce papers needed to be signed. What was it about sex with strangers that reminded me of outstanding administrative work?

'What time is it?' she said abruptly.

I removed myself, trying to find some light to check my watch.

'Twenty to. Got to go?'

'Fuck, yes. Hand me my jeans. Look, I'll see you later, OK?'

Henry says bar staff are amongst the worst treated, lowest-paid workers in Britain today, often only receiving a fifteen-minute break for a seven- or eight-hour shift. He always tips well.

I could hardly breathe, but disguised it as best I could as I reached for the jeans, which were sprawled on the back seat, letting one hand fall on a naked thigh as I passed them back. Smooth, hot. My own skin is so coarse, flaky, unattractive, at least to me. Other people don't seem to notice it as much. The barmaid – what was her name again? – hurriedly dressed, reapplied her make-up in record time, brushed her hair and kissed me before leaving.

'I like you,' she said, and was gone.

I sat there, stunned.

I dressed, stalled for a while, briefly considered leaving but quickly changed my mind, deciding another drink was need-ed to recover. Another pub? No, too far away, and besides, I wanted to keep looking. Five minutes later, I re-entered and ordered the same again as if nothing had happened. Still sweating, I rolled up my shirt sleeves at the bar, revealing arms cut from several punishing nights spent scratching. I stayed until the bar shut, eyeing her casually, her doing the same, me flicking my eyes to the TV screen and back in-between. The pub was getting busier; she couldn't or didn't want to stop to chat now. The sound was turned off after the game, but you could still see pictures, though they were get-ting blurrier as I drank more: a music channel, playing a cover of an old Elvis song, it said at the bottom of the screen. Nothing changes there either. Elvis is always in the back-ground somewhere.

I was so drunk by closing time that I nearly lost my balance getting up off the stool and trying to walk to the door. Two men who had been deep in discussion near me came and offered to share a taxi. I'd seen them around a couple of times; perhaps they were worried. I was OK, just a little dizzy. Maybe Gary had asked them to make sure I got home OK; it wouldn't have been the first time. The two men virtually carried me while the barmaid finished her cleaning duties, managing eventually to haul me outside, though I didn't want to go. She was enjoying this. The men hailed a taxi, pushed me in it with them and, after finally getting me to tell them my address, ordered the driver to take me home first. They dropped me off and I thanked them, loudly vomiting part liquid, part salmon and cucumber sandwiches over the brick wall in the front garden as they drove away into the black. I had lost track of how often I had been sick since finding my mother slumped dead in bed. Three, four, perhaps even five times. My body was like an empty sewer.

5

Nathan

When I stumbled in, gagging for water, Nathan was sitting in his dressing gown at the cheap foldout kitchen table, still drinking. The room was starting to spin for him too, I could tell. He sat with one foot half off the floor, facing the door and with both hands occupied, one around the top of the bottle, one around the base of the glass, perhaps so he could move easily if discovered. However, he must have been so preoccupied that when the moment came he'd missed his cue. Bills and betting slips surrounded him. He sat immobile, guilty, like a kid with one sweaty finger on the remote control, ready to change the channel should Mum come in. Seeing him made me sober up again, sharply.

'How's that eternal calm coming along?'

I ran a large glass of water, drank it and poured another.

'It's . . . been a long day,' he sighed, eyes fixed on his finger, which was now circling the rim of the glass. 'There were a few things to go through . . . I thought it was still early. Where have you been? I didn't hear you go out.'

Even drinking *my* whisky out of one of *my* glasses he still somehow managed to sound condescending.

'The King's . . .'

'Oh, there. Lucille's asleep, exhausted. She was at it again with the cushions earlier. Too young to get drunk, I suppose.'

'Hmm. What you got there?'

Nathan picked up a sheaf of papers and held them close. The silences between our speech were getting longer – massive, gaping, stupidly so. I half expected him to make a joke or just get up and leave, but he was still stuck to the seat when he finally spoke.

'Stuff from the bank manager: polite requests, requests, demands, threats. You know . . .'

'Yeah.'

'Hardly the stuff of enlightenment.'

He passed me a single page of a statement, which I scanned. Most of the withdrawals were in cash from the bank or cashpoints around the city; everything else seemed perfectly normal – credit-card payments to supermarkets, high-street shops, betting shops, a couple of massage parlours, nothing out of the ordinary – but the cash withdrawals were huge. Two or three hundred at a time, most days, until the money had run out, more than run out, all in the space of just a few weeks, mid-March to the beginning of April. Nathan's fall had been swift and dramatic.

'I don't remember half of these things.'

'I know, son, I know.'

I wanted to lean over and hug him, tell him I understood, that I had nothing either so we could have nothing together, but Nathan wouldn't have wanted that. As far as Nathan was concerned, he was innocent. I was just an idiot who went to the pub instead of paying his bills. Nathan continued his defence.

'According to this letter, I went to my branch on Monday and tried to take out £500 I don't have any more. How could I have forgotten that? My account is littered with these things. I'm going to see them tomorrow morning about it.'

Another awful pause. Nathan's shoulders drooped, and the rest of his body seemed to follow as if folding sadly in on itself.

'She confiscated my cards before she left, cut them up in front of my eyes. Did you know that?'

'She's been promising to for weeks.'

'She doesn't believe me any more. She doesn't trust me. It's all over – I know it.'

A tear crept out of his eye and trickled slowly down his cheek, getting caught in three-day-old stubble on its way.

'Dad, I just don't know what's happening to me . . . it's hard to feel anything. I just feel so strongly that it's not my fault, that someone else must be to blame for all this.'

Yet more horrible silence. A space, perhaps, for a father to say something reassuring. Nathan remembered something and panicked.

'Can you buy Lucille a new uniform for school? She's grown out of the old one. I should have done it weeks ago. She looks ridiculous. And a new bag, she needs a bag . . .'

His eyes were still looking at the floor, fingers now hovering above the glass, hesitant. It all seemed to hit him suddenly.

'Oh God . . . how am I going to look after her alone?'

'I'll be here to help.'

I almost touched him.

'Will you? *Always?*'

'Always, I promise.'

Nathan thought for a second and then replied flatly, without bitterness:

'Well, that's one thing I'll say for you. You might have fucked things up between us, but you've always been good to Lucille.'

A thank you, almost. How peculiar.

'Thank you, Siddhartha,' I said quietly.

I watched my son's features keenly for what he really meant, but nothing offered itself up. I did find it easier to love Lucille. She was young, bright, a joy to be with. Nathan was sullen and bruised, like me.

'Today was our tenth anniversary – and I forgot. Can you believe that? You know how women can be about these things. There's just been so much happening . . . I told her I was sorry, but . . .'

Nathan's tears were now in full flow. There was no sign of all this in their cheery light-hearted goodbye a couple of hours before; I missed so much of what really happened in my own home. I looked away, for just a moment, to stop

46

myself from having to see Nathan cry, but within seconds it was over anyway. His head resting on the table, one hand still clutching the bottle, completely still, Nathan was fast asleep.

I drank my glass of water, poured another, plucked the bottle out of his limp hand and went upstairs, leaving him snoring in the kitchen. But still I couldn't go to my bed. I bypassed my own room, Lucille's and Nathan's, and climbed the steps to Evelyn's room with her letter in my hand. Paper in hand, I fell asleep, fully clothed, surrounded by her things, staying there until the doorbell woke me the following morning. It was the first good night's sleep I'd had in months.

6

Visit

I didn't expect to hear from the barmaid again, so I was genuinely surprised when she came to the house early the following morning with my wallet. Swinging it suggestively in front of my bleary eyes, she stood in the doorway dressed in light blue jeans and a black top worn off the shoulders, carrying a small rucksack and smiling at me suffering with my hangover in last night's clothes. I was pleased to see her and let it show.

'What time is it?' I barked, playfully.

'Time you got up, you old drunk.'

'But I am up!'

'Only just.'

Twenty years ago I wouldn't have let a woman into my house so early in the morning, before I had washed, before I had even focused properly, but a granddad must take beauty where he finds it. He never knows when he might next find some more. So I stood aside and took her coat and bag, inviting her to come inside and make herself comfortable. She did.

'Thanks for bringing the wallet. I'm always losing that thing,' I said, shouting through from the kitchen, not quite knowing where she was.

'Oh, it's no trouble . . .'

I put the coat on the hanger and laid the bag down underneath it.

'This is heavy. What's in it?'

'Oh, you know, just a few things. It's an overnight bag, really. I'm kind of like the lonesome traveller right now; I carry my world on my back. What's the pantomime with the boy who runs away?'

'*Dick Whittington*?'

'That's the one.'

'Is that who you are then?'

'Just better looking.'

There was that voice of hers again; like Gary had said, very sure of itself, unashamed.

'I like your place,' she said. 'A bit battered, but homely. You must be very happy here.'

'Well, I'm used to it.'

The barmaid wandered around the house, checking out all the rooms like an estate agent valuing them, while I stood at the kettle rifling through my wallet to check nothing was missing and trying to remember her name. Rebecca? Rose? Rita? I used to work hard at being a romantic, but over the years the need seeped away thanks to death and divorce; instead, I learned to get what I wanted by saying and doing what was strategically important. And so it has continued.

I wasn't much attracted to the barmaid in daylight – she had a slightly bent nose, which was off-putting, and was too thin to fit my normal preferences – but I put the kettle on anyway and wondered whether there would be time to have some less hurried, more penetrative sex before Nathan returned. (There was no way of telling: Nathan had taken Lucille to school as usual but had been disappearing for hours at a time recently.) But first we talked, while she looked at the photographs crammed onto the kitchen windowsill.

'Gary says you're not married,' she said, peering at a recent one of me hugging Wife Number Three. 'You aren't, are you?'

'No. Any particular type of tea you'd like? My mother was a tea snob. We have them all. Earl Grey, English Breakfast, Assam . . .'

She pointed at a woman in the photograph.

'Earl Grey's fine. Who's this then?'

'Ah . . . I didn't say I was *never* married. I have been . . . three times. That's Number Three; recently departed. This house, anyway. Not the world, sadly.'

'What was she like?'

'Oh, the worst of a bad bunch, by far. Currently taking me for every penny I don't have.'

'I see.'

'I don't really see how you can . . . I have upset many women in my time, and many have had the right to be very annoyed with me indeed, but this one's a complete mystery. She has no right to be upset, but seems to be chasing my money and possessions with the vigour of all the others put together.'

'Perhaps its delayed karma.'

'Perhaps.'

The barmaid was still looking at the photo, taken in the garden the summer before, lingering a moment before turning to face me, close up. She seemed smart and was easy to talk to. Strangely forthcoming – I liked that in younger women. I pulled her towards me.

'Were they all so awful?' she said.

'What, the marriages? No . . . I loved my first wife very much and even thought I loved the second, for a while anyway. But that was a long time ago.'

The barmaid giggled.

'It's not funny!'

'Three marriages? Oh, it is. That's just . . . careless. You've got to laugh . . .'

'Well, I hear your record isn't exactly clean either. And you're a lot younger than me. Many of your mistakes are still ahead of you. I might be one of them. How do you take your tea?'

'No milk, no sugar. And what about this little madam? Who's that?'

The photo was of Lucille and I on the day she started school. I ushered the barmaid away from the window and towards the settee, smiling proudly.

'Oh, that's my granddaughter the genius. With some idiot.'

'I've been picked up by a lot of those,' said the barmaid, sitting down. 'Of all shapes and sizes. My love life is a never-ending saga of turning away fools. And chasing them.'

I finished making the tea and turned round to hand the barmaid her cup, but suddenly she seemed upset, and we weren't having fun any more.

'I just feel so gullible, you know? I'm just looking for someone to finally love me for who I am.'

'I can't imagine finding someone will be a problem. There will always be plenty of available men for women like you. Good and bad. You just have to pick the right one.'

'That's the problem.'

'You don't appear to lack confidence.'

'You're not looking hard enough.'

'I'm not looking hard at all.'

We put the mugs of tea down on the table, untouched.

Kissing her was a miserable business, an expression of sadness, but this didn't stop us continuing from where we left off the night before. Though at first she seemed reluctant, she allowed me to take her clothes off right there on the settee. This time I unclipped her bra expertly with two hands, and once she was naked she began to undress me. The thrill of doing this in the full knowledge that Nathan could walk in at any moment was almost too much for me, but just as my jeans hit the floor, exposing my boxers from which Bugs Bunny grinned, winking at us, carrot in hand, the phone rang. Turning away I answered it, expecting it to be Wife Number Three about the divorce papers. If she thought I was going to sign my own financial death warrant she was sorely mistaken.

Actually, it was the headmaster of Lucille's school, insisting somebody come and pick her up immediately. He said she was in very serious trouble and that it was most urgent that a family member go straight to the school. With Nathan unaccounted for and Arabella gone, I would have to go, so I assured the headmaster someone would be there soon, reluctantly making my excuses to the barmaid and putting my clothes back on sheepishly. She was not offended. On the contrary, she seemed to find this apparent dedication to my granddaughter endearing. She cheerily declined my offer of a lift home, saying she was staying at the pub till she found a more permanent home, and enjoyed the walk there anyway.

'Don't go forgetting Rachel now, OK? My number's in your wallet. Call me.'

She winked and left, almost springing out of the door and down the path, past Wife Number Three's car, hopping over the shrubs Wife Number Two first planted twenty years ago, over the road and away from me. I winked back to nobody and smiled, muttering the name Rachel under my breath, noticing that she had left her overnight bag behind. There had been several Rachels over the years, some fine to look at, some even fine to be with.

Picking up the post on leaving the house, I noticed a second note from Evelyn among the bills and letters of condolence, none of which I opened. My name had been written across the top and it had a local postmark dated the day before. I slipped it into my pocket as nonchalantly as if it were one of Henry's postcards, but with my heart pounding inside my chest. The letter would have to wait, whatever it said. I was needed now, and was glad to be.

7

Nayborough Grammar

As I turned off the main road into the school car park, I felt sad that I'd never visited the place for anything nice. Lucille had spent seven years at the preparatory school on the same grounds, graduating three years ago to the seniors, but I'd never crossed the gates before, not even to watch her take part in a concert or play, since she refuses to get involved. She only does what she has to and nothing more, never joining the after-school clubs, taking part in performances or trying out for one of the sports teams. Sport is silly, she says. Instead, Lucille spends her spare time at home searching the internet or immersed in a book or, more recently, talking to her mother and Evelyn. I parked, got out of the car and walked towards the grand arched entrance, its Latin motto gleaming above me like a threat.

Nayborough Grammar was very different to the school I taught at, or used to. Here, the affluent paid to have their children groomed for exams, in cold classrooms that were more like factories. Every day the kids were told how lucky they were to be there. My school was more ordinary. I knew these institutions well and recognised the smell from my regular visits when I was young and in better health. I accompanied many school football teams on Saturday mornings to places like this, where we were usually soundly beaten. With all those tests and rules, I never understood how the teachers had the time to make their children so good at sports. I waded through the sea of little uniformed bodies, which shuffled quietly and efficiently between classrooms, and went in search of my little girl.

Eventually I found the headmaster's office. A very solemn secretary lead me in, taking my coat from me and placing it on a hook in the hallway while I took a sly puff on my inhaler to alleviate the tightness in my chest. It was a large oval room filled with evidence of success. Every space on the mantel-pieces and tables was utilised, and the walls were adorned with certificates and medals: 'Head Boy, Nayborough Grammar School, 1958', 'Tennis Champion, Cambridge University, 1961', 'Tennis Runner-Up, 1962', and a black-and-white photograph of a fighter pilot, perhaps the headmaster himself, in pride of place on the desk. There was also a large cabinet of silver trophies. The secretary showed me to a seat at the far end of a space where the headmaster and Lucille waited, him shuffling papers on his desk and her, head bowed, stick legs swinging sulkily, in a massive wooden chair close by. Neither acknowledged me. I sat with hands deep in coat pockets, fingering the morning's letter with a shaking hand.

At over six foot, thick set, with a jet-black thatch of hair combed impeccably back over his skull, the headmaster cut a frightening figure. He was about my age, with the body of an ageing, sagging athlete and a dark, shrivelled face that looked as if it had been too long in the sun. Over his suit he wore a full black robe pleated at the shoulders. A minute or so passed before he spoke, and I wanted to defend Lucille over whatever she'd done, but could say nothing.

The headmaster stood up and leaned over the desk, wiry fingers propping his body up like little buttresses on each side of the desk.

'Mr Stone,' he said in a fierce baritone, 'let us get to the point. This morning, at first break, your granddaughter was caught trying to escape from the school grounds via the back wall, while an innocent boy lay in the first-aid room with blood pouring from a significant knife wound. Reluctantly, he has named Lucille as the perpetrator of this crime, and, when accused, she has not denied it.'

'So she hasn't admitted to anything?'

'She has not denied it, and we are not detectives here, Mr Stone, we are teachers. Children need to learn that if they can't speak up for themselves, then no one else will. An education is not just about times tables, it's about learning how to conduct yourself. That's why Nayborough Grammar has been at the top of the educational tree for five hundred years.'

I bristled at this but tried to keep quiet, for Lucille.

'And as I'm sure you appreciate, we would be doing your granddaughter a great disservice if we did not punish her severely,' he continued.

Lucille looked up at me briefly but, though I searched her expression for what she wanted me to do, there was nothing in it but contempt.

'But she has a great future!' I cried. 'Don't high marks count for something?'

At this the headmaster raised a hand to stop me, resumed his seat, pondered over his answer for a few seconds, sighed and said:

'Lucille, leave the room.'

The frail little monster sloped off unwillingly and, with her departure, the headmaster became calmer.

'I would like to share your enthusiasm, Mr Stone, but am not absolutely sure if she does have a great future, at least not the way things stand. Let us put today's incident to one side for a minute and look at the wider picture.'

He turned back to the window and gazed out onto the school grounds.

'Undoubtedly, she is a bright girl – her marks are, as you say, often high – but that's not all one needs to be a success. This is by no means the first time Lucille's behaviour has come to my attention. Several teachers have reported her to my office for disrupting classes, and I have noticed her inappropriate behaviour at break time myself more than once. It is not just the number of incidents that is alarming, Mr Stone, it's their nature.'

'What are you talking about?'

'Well, last week – and this is just one example – she complained to her English teacher that what her class was studying was boringly juvenile. The teacher recommended she buy something by Jane Austen, a fourth-year text. Next day, the teacher concerned found a copy of the book in her pigeonhole with "Jane Austen is unreadable" scrawled in red block letters across the title page. And the week before, despite being the youngest person in the ensemble and only third violin, she suggested to the music teacher that the orchestra should not be playing Glenn Miller! And she called the *Star Wars* theme *rubbish*! Does nobody teach *respect* in your home?'

He waited for a reply, but I couldn't give one.

'Well, obviously not. But we expect more from Nayborough's young ladies. Lucille does not seem to comprehend the importance of fitting in or working as part of a team – she resents the very existence of Games and Home Economics classes – and is generally the opposite of the well-mannered, studious, ambitious young people this school is famed for producing. And on top of all this, violent assault! I have been left with no choice but to suspend her, pending an investigation within the school, though you may choose to withdraw her completely first, saving us all a lot of bad publicity, time, effort and cost.'

The headmaster checked himself, readjusted his cloak and briefly changed tone.

'I fully understand how difficult it must be for Lucille . . . losing her mother so tragically to cancer at such a young age – my own mother suffered the same fate – but we all suffer, Mr Stone, we all suffer. It's no excuse. And such a tragedy makes the support and discipline a father provides more essential, not less. I don't know where he had to be so urgently this morning . . .'

'Actually, he's going through a . . .'

'I don't care really, but I recommend that, if you can find him, you discuss what arrangements you wish to make as soon as possible. If that is what you choose, there will be plenty of schools in the locality happy to take Lucille, though perhaps her father may prefer to send her to a psychiatrist first, one of his colleagues perhaps. Until the matter is settled, it would be unwise for her to attend school. Keep a close eye on her at home, for your own safety.'

I thought of Lucille waiting for us in the corridor, no more than a pile of girlish bones, neither trouble nor danger to anyone in her fourteen short years, until today at least.

'Will the boy be all right?'

'Eventually the boy in question is expected to make a full recovery, though he will not be able to write in his examinations in May and will be a great loss to the rugby team this season. I doubt there is another prop forward as talented in the whole school.'

He pondered this for a moment, perhaps considering possible replacement prop forwards, and then dismissed it. A smirk appeared on his rubbery face, packing the spare folds of skin together at the ears.

'One girl does not a great institution make, Mr Stone. I think that is all.'

And with that, he made to open the door for me, but, overtaken with anger, I blocked his exit, doing my utmost to pull myself up to his height – chin to the skies, cheeks red.

'Is that all you have to say? Then I must find the answer to some questions of my own.'

I opened the door.

'LUCILLE,' I barked, shocking her into swift movement, 'come back inside and sit down this instant.'

The headmaster, shaken too, sat down.

'Mr Stone, this is most unorthodox. I'm going to have to ask you to . . .'

His hand reached towards a bell push.

'Summon your secretary if you wish. I won't mind.'

Lucille arrived, hovering by the door, petrified. The headmaster folded his arms and there was a silence, a hush no one was prepared to break. Lucille's eyes stayed pinned to the floor, the headmaster's remained fixed on me, burning with indignation, and both waited for me to speak. With another rush of adrenalin, every courtroom drama I had ever seen came back to me and I became someone else, someone courageous and clever. I breathed deeply, and made the room mine.

'I must say, sir, that your story does not add up. I think you are using this as a convenient excuse to get rid of exactly the kind of girl your precious institution should be treasuring. I have three decades of teaching experience myself and recognise an untrue story when I hear one, whether from a child or a teacher. Let us summarise the facts. Tell me again: you questioned Lucille thoroughly about what happened?'

'Mr Stone, you should save your eloquence for a worthier cause. If you insist, I will repeat what I said, slowly. Lucille will not answer the charge and we are not here to draw information from her that she is unwilling to provide.'

Lucille could see me shaking, I was sure. And Evelyn and Nathan and Arabella, even Lucille's mother, all of them shaking their heads. I trembled, overcompensating for nervousness with volume.

'So she neither denies nor admits anything!' I boomed. 'Has the boy said why she did it?'

'He says they were having a purely verbal difference of opinion. He was joking, and she lost her temper and attacked him.'

'Joking about what? Do small fourteen-year-old girls carrying knives lash out in this way at every kind of joke by a rugby-playing athlete? Have you even established who the knife belonged to?'

'She refuses to say. He also refuses to say and is too ill to be pressed on the matter. Children often argue about silly things, as you seem to have forgotten. And this incident, which you are turning into a fiasco, has culminated with a real victim.'

I pressed on.

'You have said this took place during a break time, yes?'

I looked at Lucille, and she nodded.

'Surely there were other pupils present. What do they say? Or are they dumb as well?'

The headmaster stood up and slammed both fists, clenched, onto his desk.

'They refuse or claim not to have seen. There is such a thing, Mr Stone, as *esprit de corps*! Your granddaughter – as I was trying to subtly explain to you without her being present – is generally unpopular because she has no sense of it.'

I approached the other side of his desk, leant over it and shouted.

'Until now! From what you tell me, a conspiracy of silence surrounds this crime, a conspiracy involving all the children present, Lucille included. But since you tell me Lucille is an outsider in your school, and since I know she has always been well-behaved at home, perhaps there is a chance she was being bullied in a jocular way she could not share. Did that boy call you names, Lucille?'

I asked the question while still facing the headmaster.

'Yes,' came a squeak from behind me, after a short delay.

'*Dirty* names?'

More silence. I turned round to see her legs bunched up in the chair, face hidden in her lap.

'One was, but I didn't know what it meant.'

'Then how did you know it was dirty?' asked the headmaster suavely.

'Because of the dirty way he said it.'

The headmaster shrugged, looked back at me with raised eyebrows and a crooked smile.

'TELL US THAT WORD!' I ordered, but she kept an obstinate silence. Why would she not help herself? My mind took a flying leap.

'Was it YID?'

And for the first time, she looked straight at me, startled. I grabbed her and was out of the room before I could think.

'You can stuff your Nayborough ladies up your arse!' I screamed, unsure quite what I meant but already on my way out, snatching my coat from the hook. As we walked away my nose began to bleed hard, staining the front of my shirt.

'It wasn't "Yid",' said Lucille, yanking my arm. 'He called me a leper.'

On returning from the nearest toilet, tissues stuffed up both nostrils, I found Lucille in the corridor, holding hands and talking in whispers to a slight ginger boy of similar age wearing thick glasses and holding a brown briefcase. Neither headmaster nor secretary were anywhere to be seen. When I approached Lucille she turned from the boy without a good-bye and ran towards me as if she had been alone, and we walked to the car without a word. At the thought of Lucille keeping a prop out of the rugby team for a whole season, I threw an arm around her, smiling. She wasn't talking, but clung to me tight and that was enough. Once safely in the car, she ripped her tie off.

'Woo hoo! I'm free!'

Lucille tossed the tie around her head like a lasso.

I borrowed Lucille's phone and called Henry, arranging to meet him as soon as possible in a nearby restaurant; he's the one adult I know who can be relied on, and there's nothing he loves more than a good, meaty drama. Usually he paid for our meals together anyway, but today he would have to.

8

A celebration

Henry is my only remaining friend, and also the oldest and most reliable since the departure of wives who were also my friends. He's lived all over – Romania, South Africa, Zimbabwe, Strangeways – so contact was sometimes difficult, especially before the days of high-tech communication, but he always sent a card or a letter wherever he was. In over fifty years, we have never been out of touch. While I stayed in England he dealt in silver all over the world, making money by moving things other people made between countries until taking early retirement nine or ten years ago, saying it was time to stop running. He's hardly worked a day since, though large sums are still added to his account from time to time. These additions are usually followed by gold necklaces for his wife Beryl and lengthy, extravagant drinking sessions for us. We've been friends far too long for me to ask where they come from. Evelyn asked me once how he benefited from having someone like me as a friend – less successful, less charismatic, less charming, less good-looking – and I struggled to answer her (though the less good-looking part could be disputed), but this never seemed to occur to me when we were together. I always continued unthinkingly.

As he walked into the restaurant I noticed that, though we were born in the same year, Henry seemed so much younger than me these days, virtually unchanged in appearance since he retired. Compared with my wrinkled, jaundiced skin and grey, thinning hair, his healthy tan and flowing blond locks looked like vigorous maturity. Lucille, who had been quiet since we left the school, smiled and perked up at the sight of him. He has a maddening habit of calling me Henry, saying I need only three more wives to equal Henry VIII.

'Good to see you, Henry,' said Henry. 'I've been bored off my fucking tits this past week.'

He hugged me warmly.

'Do you mind?'

I pointed to Lucille.

'Oh, sorry, sweetheart. Didn't see you down there! Ignore those words you just heard – *banish them from your mind for ever!*'

He wagged his forefinger wildly at a giggling Lucille, who always enjoyed it when he swore. Henry says I'm due for another marriage this year, because so far they've come in twelve-year intervals: '67, '79, '91. Could Rachel be my Anne of Cleves?

Lucille waved back at Henry.

'Watch your mouth and get on with choosing what you want,' I said, smiling at him. 'We've already ordered.'

Henry ordered a large Hawaiian pizza. I was having spaghetti bolognese and, despite gentle encouragement otherwise, Lucille insisted on the chicken Caesar salad without dressing, croutons or chicken. The drinks arrived and I gave my account of the affair.

'We must decide what to do now,' I said, after briefing Henry on the major developments. 'The first thing is what to do about school tomorrow.'

Lucille suddenly sat up straight and said proudly:

'Don't you want to know if I did it?'

'We should concentrate on what you're going to do now,' I replied. 'Tomorrow your father will wonder why you're not at school, and I'm not going to know what to say. I hardly know what to say to him when I *don't* have something to hide. Don't make it any more complicated for me than it already is.'

'Well, I *did* do it. And I enjoyed doing it. There's this boy, Jonathan Cairns, who's always picking on me for no reason. He pushed me into the boys' toilets, waving this big ruler around, calling me names, and I was really scared. So I grabbed my knife from my bag and put it right through his hand. I didn't mean to, it was a mistake, but it felt great. He ran away with the knife still stuck in his hand, and I ran too. Nearly got away as well. One of the teachers caught me halfway over the wall by the sports block and pulled my leg till I fell down.'

The waiter hovered by Lucille's shoulder, waiting for the right moment to put the plate down.

'Did he physically attack you?' I asked.

'Not really. And anyway, he can't now, can he? Because I don't have to go back. I heard Mr Foster say so. Mr Foster's an idiot though. You shouldn't listen to what he says.'

'What about Jane Austen? And orchestra and Games? Should I not listen to what he says about that?'

'Charlotte Bronte thought that Jane Austen was unreadable – it said so on the internet – and that's what I think too. I bet he doesn't even know that and he's supposed to be clever. Anyway, it doesn't matter now, does it? We'll find some-where else for me to go, or maybe I won't go anywhere. I hate school anyway. You don't learn anything. Dad won't mind – he hardly even notices what I do.'

'He hardly notices anything.'

'Don't worry about all that nonsense now!' cried Henry. 'We'll work it out later. Come on, you two, on your feet! A toast. Lucille is free!'

'Hold on a minute,' I said. 'Where did you get the knife from?'

'Granny Evelyn gave it to me. For emergencies.'

'*Emergencies?*'

'Yeah, it's a dangerous world out there you know . . .'

'It is when you're carrying a *knife* . . .'

'Come on,' interrupted Henry. 'Never mind that. Charge your glasses, I say!'

So the three of us raised our glasses, standing round a tiny table in an empty restaurant before midday only yards from the school, to celebrate Lucille's expulsion. Henry always seemed to know when a situation needed something extra and was a master of providing it, puffing out his chest and preparing for one of his infamous speeches. His voice quivered with mock emotion as he first addressed Lucille and then the grand audience in his head, growing louder all the time. As Henry summoned the spirit of Churchill, I caught a whiff of my own armpit and retched. I had not washed since before Sunday's service.

'Lady and gentleman,' he roared, 'Join me in this celebration of freedom, of independence, of the Stone family spirit! Of the fact that, even in this cruel modern world of the corporate devil, David can still beat Goliath!'

He turned to a smiling Lucille and placed a hand softly on her head.

'This is a victory not only for you, little one, not only for the Stones and not only for England, but for JUSTICE! JUSTICE! JUSTICE! Damn these idiot headmasters! And if this is not over yet? We shall continue. We shall go on to the end, we shall fight them in the school corridors, we shall fight on the playgrounds and in the classrooms, we shall fight with growing confidence and growing strength, and defend our Lucille, whatever the cost may be' – and here his voice became soft and tremulous, his fork waving in his free hand – *'we shall fight on the beaches, we shall fight on the landing grounds, we shall fight in the fields and in the streets, we shall fight in the hills; we will never surrender! To Lucille!'*

We clashed glasses and he sat down to laughter and a round of applause, with the waiters joining in too. My friend Henry, I loved him. And then he was back to normal, talking to Lucille through mouthfuls of pizza, pointing at her mobile, which lay by her plate.

'How would you like a new mobile, sweetheart? Give that old brick to your grandpa.'

He picked it up and threw it at me.

'There you are, Granddad, welcome to the twenty-first century.'

Lucille laughed.

'I tell you what,' he said to her, 'after lunch we'll go and choose you something a little more up-to-date, then all three of us can keep in contact about this new school thing wherever you are, *and* you'll look *cool* as well.'

At the word 'cool' Henry waved his cutlery around as if he couldn't take it seriously.

'It'll be our little secret. We can take you to see a couple of other schools, tell the teachers that Grandpa looks after you, and if you ever think of something you want to tell us, you can. Let's leave Dad out of this; he's got enough to think about. Grandpa Abe and I will sort it out.'

'Can I get a special ring tone and a cover and a little bag to keep it in?'

'Sweetheart, you can have *whatever you like*.'

Pleased by his contribution, Henry tucked heartily into his meal, while Lucille toyed distractedly with her lettuce and I sat sadly between them, panic quickly returning and permeating my whole sweaty body. It was the panic that had ruined me. Whatever you do, in the end the adrenalin goes, leaving behind a hole. Whatever you do to try and make it go away – drink, sleep away your life, pick on elderly headmasters – it all goes. I felt faint, realised I was sweating horribly and desperately needed the toilet. The bladder and bowels – they were changing too. I didn't seem to be able to hold it in like I used to. I excused myself with a murmur and almost ran to the Gents.

I settled in a cubicle, pissed sitting down and took Evelyn's second letter out of my pocket as the rest fell out. This seemed the right time to open it, with my trousers round my ankles, literally shitting myself because of my recent outburst. The first time in years I'd stood up for anything. I broke the seal, unfolded the paper and read. Again, the heading 'KNOW THYSELF' was at the top.

'Hello, Avraham – were you expecting to hear from me so soon?

Though it may be painful for us both I have decided to tell you everything. You may not recognise much of what you think of as your mother in the content of these letters, but you must accept that it's true, all of it, and that you will feel better when this process is all over. Ready?

'Yes,' I told her. 'Let's go.'

Deep breaths, Abe, deep breaths. I turned the page and continued, wishing she'd just get on with it.

So now we're being honest, what have you done with your life, Avraham? Nothing. What have you learnt about this world in sixty-one years of existence? Nothing. And what do you believe in? Nothing. You will be annoyed at me for saying this, but if you think about it I'm certain you know it's true. It is time to learn a little more about who you are, but first you must know about me, beginning to end. Avraham, much of my life has been a compromise I didn't want to make, and I have resented everything for too long because of it; that can't be altered any more, but you can. I don't want you to feel the same when you take your last breath as I know I will. A mother has to keep trying, in her own way.

These past months have taught me what it is like to be alone, to regret and no longer be able to do anything to make it all right again; when she can't even choose when to go to the toilet, there is little left a woman can accomplish in this world, apart from in her mind, with her God, with her family. And so I turn to you. Consider the evidence: you have drunk away most of your adult life in anger at me, you don't exercise and you fret about even the slightest thing, which can't be good for your heart. You don't THINK enough, that's the problem, and that's what all THIS is for. Don't waste the time you have left and don't ignore me – you may have escaped the cold hand of God so far, but you're lucky to still be alive. Every day He picks more victims, and one of these days He's going to pick you . . .

And that's when I knew she was enjoying herself, at least a little, and that there would be a lot more to come: the three dots, the promise of more, said more about her than she could ever tell me. When Evelyn was still alive and rambling, too weak or too bored to leave her bed, I thought she was just confused, but no, she knew exactly what she was doing, leaving the beginnings of sores for us to scratch once she was gone.

It was all too much, too much. Perhaps better to do nothing, pretend the letters weren't there, pretend I couldn't hear her. I hurriedly drew up my trousers and returned to the main restaurant, trying to stay calm.

'Everything's fine, Lucille,' I said. 'I'll see you at home, OK? Henry, take Lucille to get the best phone out there. I'll pay you for it tomorrow.'

Lucille had seen and heard enough recently to know I was hiding something. Calmly lied to again and again, she knew when loved ones weren't telling the truth. But I had to leave. Henry had seen my sudden departures many times before and knew to do nothing about it. Also, I knew he would treat Lucille to something else as well as the phone because he knew I couldn't: a book maybe, something she'd really want. I had no money for those kinds of things any more. He put a big, comforting hand on my shoulder, thinking he understood, but how could he? The thick fingers attached to Henry's strong palms were like big sausages tightly packed together in cling film, soft and pink and comforting.

'Call me,' he said, and I left.

I stumbled out of the restaurant and down the road, turned a corner and entered the nearest pub, a place I hadn't been in years. A couple of pints, a couple of JDs to steady the system, that's what I needed. There was still that change in my pocket, just enough for a few drinks. Special circumstances. Your dead mother following you around can be a bit of a shock. In life, yes, all the time, every minute, whispering in your ear, calling your name, telling you off for the slightest thing, that's fine.

You get used to the hatred, the disgust, the disappointment, but you hope to be free one day. As if the nightmares aren't enough. Her near-skeletal frame, weak but still with that venomous tongue, threatening to the last breath every night:

'Pay attention! Take notes, darling, take notes! It might save you from your next marriage!'

That one was an old favourite. A bitter sense of humour right to the very last half-breath. The brittle, shrill voice, condescending, still so clear.

'I will decide when to die,' she had said to me. 'I will decide. You'll find me dead one of these mornings, then you'll be sorry.'

And then you do. But now she was six feet under and was still worried I might be ignoring her. We'd had her buried, yet still she was alive, somehow. I walked back home, a mile maybe, no small distance for a man of my age, one who was sometimes barely able to walk a hundred yards. Just trying to clear my head, get a little peace, I pressed on through the streets, head bowed to protect myself from the rain. Evelyn followed me: *What have you done? Nothing.* I could picture her, as clear as the road in front of me, spitting the words out, quietly and coldly from her bed.

I don't know if anyone was awake when I returned to the house. The rest of the day vanished in a bout of more drinking and self-abuse, locked in Evelyn's room, smashing up bits of furniture with a hammer. After that I fell into a deep asleep. All I remember about the night is waking into half-consciousness in the darkness with my feet up by my head, scratching my thighs with my nails like a crazed monkey, dreaming of slicing a perfectly straight line down the middle of each of my forearms and watching all of my insides falling out through the slits. My dreams were getting more vivid and more frightening; the next was even more so.

9

Memories of Evelyn Disturbing the Quiet

Even late on, when she knew death was ready to pounce, or when she knew she was about to pounce on it, Evelyn still rarely talked about herself or the past, but I could not stop myself from wanting to know. Our conversations had always been about me or the whole world. There was no in-between. To her they were one and the same. When I tried to question anything she had done or press her for even a snippet from her own life, I was usually angrily dismissed.

'A son has no business knowing personal details about his mother, Avraham,' she'd say, shocked. 'How can he respect her if he knows her darkest thoughts, what she thinks about in her idle moments, what colour underwear she prefers? *I swear I shall die before you know the colour of my undergarments!*'

So when she began to talk about herself, I absorbed every last detail.

It was the day she died, and I sat at Evelyn's bedside, waiting for something to happen. The room was beginning to smell of that stench of the dying, as she was effectively starving to death (she would only drink soup) and the curtains were drawn, though it was daytime; Evelyn didn't want anyone to see what was happening to her. It was a great exertion for her to talk, but she managed it through regular pauses for breath.

'It all started with that bloody song . . .' she said, still struggling to contain her anger after so long, while the news bleated away in the background. 'Your eyes were like spinning plates when you first heard it, I remember . . . You knew it was bad, and *loved* it . . . On that day your mind blew out of your ears and never returned.'

She thought patiently for a second, as if thinking of the answer to a question I had just asked.

'But you know, the thing itself wasn't dangerous. A couple of verses and choruses don't threaten me, not that you could understand anything as subtle as that. No; I knew you were bound to turn on me – all sons turn on their mothers – but I hoped you might do it in a way I could respect. Join a movement, make money, do *something*. But not my boy. That wasn't the sound of true rebellion. It was a call to dance and forget, because you were too afraid to break loose and actually change the world. My *god*, Avraham, where was your *courage*? What kind of a generation takes a song like that so much to its heart? *Rock around the bloody clock.* A generation of cowards, that's what.'

Holding her spoon in mid-air, waiting for the right moment to swoop, I replied:

'I still like that music. It moves me.'

'I know, and look at you . . .'

In went the spoon. My mother spoke through a mouthful of soup, some of which tumbled out the sides of her mouth as she did so. I had never seen her so pathetic-looking, so defeated.

'You're a catastrophe, Avraham. Three times divorced . . .'

'. . . not yet . . .'

'. . . but soon, a signature away, and penniless too. You have no savings; you could have had a great career . . .'

'You blame one song for all that?'

'Forget the song . . . you wasted every opportunity you were given. What are you going to *do* now, Avraham?'

'What do you mean?'

'What are you going to do after I die? How are you going to survive? Is that school going to give you enough to get by? And for how long?'

I wondered if she had taken the overdose yet, whether this was the final speech. I wanted to feed her soup for ever.

'I have a few ideas,' I lied, pushing the spoon between her lips again. She swallowed reluctantly. 'There are many things I could do.'

'You can get a proper job. It's not too late.'

'I *have* a proper job.'

'Yes, but for how long? How long will they let you keep picking up the sick note and cheque and going straight to the pub?'

She shook her head in shame.

'You talk like I have slept through life,' I said. 'You forget my struggles with health, the tragedies this family has had to endure. And what about my achievements?'

'Ha,' she spat. 'You have no idea what real work is. Nobody does any more. Life is too easy for people – there's nothing stinging them into action. Say what you like about the Nazis and the communists, but at least what they did reminded decent people about the value of life.'

Evelyn coughed hard, swallowed and coughed again.

'It's too late for Henry VIII and Charles II now, Avraham. You have to think of yourself . . . they have plenty of others to worry about their legacy.'

'But I love them! They need me!'

Evelyn sighed a deep, deep sigh, as Lucille walked into the room. She turned to her for support.

'You see? Still acting like a stupid teenager. Can you believe it? Sixty-one years old, he is. *Sixty-two nearly!*'

Lucille nodded in assent.

'Why don't you become an accountant?' said Evelyn. 'Or a barrister? Now *there's* a real profession. Oh God, what does it matter? I tried! I tried! But what's the point . . . there's nothing left for me now . . .'

'How can I be too old to teach History GCSE but young enough to retrain as a barrister? I'd be the oldest in the classes by about four decades! I don't understand you. I could be in good health for many years. I should do what I *want*, surely. Besides, you always said I was getting old, even when I was a teenager.'

'That's because your life has always been running out much quicker than you realised. I was trying to make you see that.'

71

'Why are you so keen for me to *live*, as you say? What is that anyway? It's my life, mother!'

'You sound like a boy. You cry out for independence while clinging on for dear life. You talk and think in dreams.'

'What's wrong with dreams?'

'Nothing. I have had many myself . . . but I have chased after them, not waited for them to realise themselves. Honestly, Avraham, I couldn't care less what you do any more, but for God's sake do *something*.'

Evelyn seemed so crushed. It made me want to make up, finally, for ever. I could have reached into the drawer right then to check whether the stash of pills I knew she had not been taking was still there. If they were, I could have removed them; if not, I could have called an ambulance.

'I am happy, mother,' I pleaded. 'Is that not enough for you?'

'Maybe you are, maybe you're not,' she said almost in a whisper, turning away. And then, even lower, shaking her head once more: 'You stand for nothing; that's what breaks my heart.'

The bowl of soup lay in my lap getting cold, the spoon resting in it. There were many things I wanted to say to Evelyn before she died – and perhaps it was my last chance to do so.

'How did you decide what to do, when we got to Britain?' I asked. 'Where did you get *your* direction from?'

'Things were different then,' she replied weakly. 'People didn't value choice as much as they do now . . . we didn't expect anything . . . how can it matter now anyway?'

'I want to know.'

Evelyn took a deep, wheezing breath and finally told me a scrap of something I didn't know. Perhaps she should have been stopped from talking, but it would only have been postponing the inevitable. What was the difference if she died today or tomorrow? It was more important to me to keep her talking than to preserve her energy for more silence in a possibly extended future.

'I got a job in a factory making children's toys,' she started wearily, 'but found being an employee disagreeable – the boss always acted as if he owned you – and after living on a kibbutz for so long I was too proud for it. So I saved until I could afford to leave. I became my own boss and employed others – not easy, I can tell you – but didn't like that either. It was awful . . . suffocating. When you have something of your own, however small, everyone else likes to think it is rightfully theirs too.'

She was taking more pauses for breath now. I didn't stop her.

'They get too close . . . take advantage . . . steal . . . lie . . . They hate you for being in charge, so take little revenges . . . everything from pens and pencils upwards – they pretend what's yours is theirs so much that they finally begin to believe it. In retaliation, you begin to distrust them . . . mistreat them . . . and in the end feel you own them, just like you felt owned in the beginning. The whole thing was a waste of time. I would have been more comfortable quietly resenting somebody else.'

'Why did you do it for so long then?'

'No more questions, Abe. I'm tired.'

'And why did you sell up so suddenly? What happened to the money?'

Evelyn ignored the question.

'I am determined to somehow make you into a man,' she said slowly. 'Perhaps when I am gone you will listen to me. Now bring me some tea – I'm thirsty – and don't leave the teabag in the cup too long. It doesn't live in there, you know.'

Her dulled green eyes looked me over while she decided what else displeased her. Finally she came up with an ancient complaint.

'Stop slouching, Avraham, you look like a hunchback. And no sane woman wants to wed one of those. Now go.'

Lucille was just returning to the room but turned round to leave when she heard this.

'No, not you. You stay,' she said. 'There's something I want you to write for me.' Now she pointed to the TV. 'Oh, look at this . . . I saw this report earlier . . .'

I left the remaining soup on the bedside table and went as far as the other side of Evelyn's door.

'Turn it up,' I heard her say to Lucille, a little strength returning to her voice. 'Can you believe this?' And then, after a few seconds, 'To understand anything you need to understand America, my dear. She is the vulture of the world. See that fellow on the left?'

Now her voice fairly trembled.

'A thousand plagues on his head.'

As we took away her other pleasures one by one, the television became more important to Evelyn and she became increasingly possessive over it. After years of mistrust she had finally made her peace with the machine, at last discovering that there were many channels she could disapprove of, newscasters she could despise, faceless conglomerates she could criticise for their interpretations of world events. Television fuelled her. Sky, CNN, ITV, the BBC, these were her enemies now, and Lucille was there every night to receive what she had to say. I walked away and down the stairs in despair on my way to the kettle. An hour later she was dead.

I know Evelyn loved me because she never stopped trying to make me a better person. 'Each new day,' she used to say, 'is another chance to make it right.' Even, as on that day, when she was so ill she could hardly move, she was still trying, but seemed to be completely certain that I would not pay attention any more – and maybe she was right. For some time, elements of her behaviour had become increasingly childlike – she often sent meals clattering against the wall as soon as we'd put them in front of her, Arabella's carefully prepared meals sent flying time and again without a thought – but right at the end, when she couldn't even sit up, that seemed to have been replaced with a kind of simple agitation at the business of still being alive. There was a marked change in her behaviour, but it wasn't that Evelyn was at peace or even close to it; more like she knew that soon she could be, and that in the meantime even the smallest thing became so much more difficult because of it.

10

On Call

When I woke again it was four o'clock and my whole body was sore from scratching. I got up off Evelyn's floor, staggered through the hall to the sink in my bedroom, splashed my face with cold water and collapsed on my bed, still fully clothed.

'Go on, do it,' said Evelyn. 'Call him.'

Without thinking, I took the Rabbi's card from my pocket and reached for the receiver.

'Hello?'

A woman's voice groaned in the background:

'Whoever it is, tell them to go away.'

'I think it's Abe Stone . . .'

'Well, does Abe Stone not have a watch? *You think Rabbi Gamliel took calls at this time of the morning?*'

I cleared my throat:

'Hello? Are you there?'

'Abe, I'm going to take this in the office . . . hold on . . .'

I wondered if the Rabbi would dress before moving rooms or sit at the desk in his underwear, all that weight spreading happily out over the sides of the chair. Perhaps he slept in his hat and coat. He returned, still sounding groggy but more business-like.

'I'm in the office now,' he said. 'And all yours.'

'I'm sorry for calling so late . . . I didn't know what else to do.'

'Don't worry about it,' he yawned. 'It's my own fault for putting it on the card, after all. What seems to be the problem?'

I rose from the bed and carried the phone over to the chaise longue by the window, lying back on it with eyes closed.

'It's Evelyn. She's . . . talking to me.'

'How do you mean?'

'Well, not talking exactly. More . . . *communicating*. I'm afraid, Rabbi. I thought this was over . . .'

'What's she saying?'

'She said she'd turned me into nothing, that I'd done nothing with my life. That I don't believe in anything.'

'And is that true?'

'. . . I don't know. I just hate her for saying it.'

The Rabbi thought for a moment before answering.

'You have good reason to be angry, Abe, but try to forgive her if you can. You know, Evelyn may actually be trying to help you. Have you thought of that?'

His voice was soothing, like medicine. I pictured him in a large leather seat, fingers intertwined.

'Your mother and I talked a lot,' he continued. 'Remember that towards the end she was a very ill woman, very mixed up, and much of what she said and did cannot be fathomed out. By anyone. However, she did seem to be certain about one thing. She wanted you to understand your Jewish roots . . . and I'd be happy to help you look into it if you want to . . .'

I remembered with a jolt that I did not believe in God, and if I was going to consider it, I wasn't entirely sure if I wanted him to be Jewish. Suddenly I was annoyed. I sat up.

'But why should I do what she wants me to do? She's dead! And I'm sixty-one! Anyway, how can I just *start* to be Jewish now, after all this time? I want nothing to do with it . . . and she never wanted me to touch it either . . . I just want to be left alone . . .'

'Well, *you* called *me*, Abe.'

We were both more awake now and talking much louder. The Rabbi considered the situation carefully before steering the conversation back round, and it occurred to me that I too should think about what I was saying rather than just let it all fall out of my mouth uncensored.

'You have mezuzot – that is, scrolls – on the insides of your doors, yes?' asked the Rabbi. 'I've seen them . . .'

'The last owners of the house had them fitted . . .'

'And there are Hebrew books on your shelves . . .'

'Yes, but Evelyn never read them . . .'

'She spoke Hebrew though?'

'Only to swear . . .'

'But she called you Avraham, didn't she?'

I didn't answer.

'It sounds, Abe, like you have been part of a Jewish household, whether you knew it or not.'

'I *am* circumcised, I suppose. That's hard to forget.'

'Right then!'

'But when I was a child we never went to synagogue, didn't celebrate the festivals, didn't socialise with other Jewish families. Mostly it was as if I wasn't Jewish at all, until I got married the first time. And when my wife died, it all just . . . went away . . . completely . . . until now. For God's sake, my third wife was a Catholic! Not that there's anything particularly *Christian* about the divorce settlement she wants . . .'

The darkness made it tempting to keep on talking. I tried to imagine what the Rabbi was doing, whether he was really worried on my behalf or, like the doctors, he just wanted to get rid of me.

'Abe, I'm just trying to show you that Judaism is, and always has been, a part of you. An important part. And that you will always be welcome as one of us, if that's what you decide you want. I can't force you to do anything – and neither can Evelyn. You have to choose for yourself. The Jewish people are survivors, Abe, and so are you. You'll be fine, I'm certain.'

He laughed.

'As long as we're all still breathing, there's hope. And isn't that what Evelyn has left you with? Hope?'

'Not really. I just feel . . . dead.'

'Abe, go to bed. Try and relax. Forget about Evelyn for an hour or two. I'm sure whatever is unclear now will become clearer in time: she never left *me* guessing for long. And remember, you can do nothing about the past, only tomorrow and the day after that.'

'That's very saccharine, Rabbi.'

'A lot of Jewish teaching is, but it doesn't make it any less useful.'

I sighed deeply and lay back on the bed, phone still at my ear, wondering how many sighs I had left inside me. I was being pulled in all directions by forces stronger than I could ever be.

'Evelyn was right to be ashamed of me,' I said. 'I *am* nothing. I don't understand . . . *anything*.'

'No man is worth nothing, Abe.'

'Isn't he?'

'Look, all I'm saying is you should value yourself a little more and not be afraid of a bit of good old Jewish syrup. Tomorrow, will you do something for me? Go somewhere you've never been, read, talk to strangers, eat food you've never tasted. Get out into the world – it'll make you feel much better. There are many worse men than you, Abe Stone. Sleep, and rest, and see what the morning brings.'

'Rabbi . . . do you really think I can change?'

'Of course, if you want to. But what do you want to change into? Do you know that?'

'I think I can work it out.'

'Well then, that's your first job. Goodnight. We'll speak soon.'

Though it must have been in my head already, waiting to be brought to life, the idea that I could start again seemed so new and exciting that I completely forgot to say goodbye before putting the phone down. All the lethargy, the irritation, the confusion just seemed to fall away, and the future was already better. Not clear, exactly, but better. It might not have been what the Rabbi or Evelyn was trying to say to me, but I suddenly realised that it didn't have to *matter* what I did. The important thing was that it was big, and dramatic, and mine.

Some time later, with my clothes hung neatly in the cupboard, empty bottles safely in the bin and the window wide open to let the air in, I finally lay down to sleep, still buzzing. I pulled the duvet covers tight around me and dared to hope for a little peace.

11

A Surprise

The morning after the bad night before, despite the lack of sleep I felt able to do anything. I got up, dressed, walked to the local shop, bought a different paper to my regular one and got as much food as I could with the change left over from what I'd spent in the pub. (There were still a few days until the next sick-pay cheque came through.) I walked up the drive, ingredients for a hearty breakfast under one arm and newspaper under the other, and felt great, better than I had in a long time. I could do anything I wanted to, whatever plans Evelyn had. I opened the door, picked up the post, removed her third letter from the pile of demands and began to cook for the first time in months, rolling the crackling sausages around in the pan and humming old-time rock-'n'roll songs as I went. When the food was ready I read the letter at the kitchen table over a large plate of sausages, eggs, beans and toast, while Lucille got dressed and Nathan slept on upstairs.

Dear Avraham – (And there was my first mistake. Father of a multitude, indeed. Leader of the tribe. You can hardly lead yourself to the bar and back!)

You will be unsurprised to hear I have lied to you for many years about my life. I thought you might be interested in hearing the truth. I was not born on a kibbutz in Jerusalem, but in Berlin, into a family of fear: of the depression, of the communists, of the Nazis – everybody. My parents were experts in it. I have lied about them too.

We were a practising Orthodox family. My father was not a kitchen hand but a dentist, and my mother a housewife, not the great pioneer you have heard so much about.

I based her character on what I myself would like to have been. We had been wealthy but were fast becoming less so, many people choosing to go elsewhere to get their teeth seen to. Life was muted. I had no siblings. Though not all Jews lived like this, I grew up among fatalists who taught me to be morose also. My parents were not idiots; they were just afraid for the future but not practical-minded enough to do anything to change it.

From the age of ten I was included in the house chores, taking pride in everything I was given to do. I was bored, had no friends to play with and wanted things to occupy me. By thirteen I had taken on jobs in other people's houses, helping neighbours and friends of my mother, doing whatever work was available and stealing from their precious stashes that were so inevitably under the mattress in a shoebox. (How unimaginative the oppressed are.) Sometimes I was paid as well. I would hoard the money I received, counting it again and again under the covers at night, saving up for my escape, already dreamed of. Each passing year was worse for us while I was growing up, and as I turned into a woman my resolve only strengthened – I had to leave, as soon as I was able.

For all their fretting, my parents were unprepared for the political upheaval in '33. I promised myself I would always be strong, depend on nobody and never turn into one of the quietly righteous like my father, who was killed along with the rest of the family sometime during the war, in the concentration camps, probably Buchenwald or Ravensbruck; I never found out for certain . . .

Do not be sad for them, Avraham. It is foolish to mourn for people you never knew. Concentrate on the family you have now. My parents should have got out of the country sooner but chose instead to be silent, trying desperately not to draw attention to themselves, hoping that nobody would notice them and that nobody was listening to what was being written in the papers about us, said openly in the streets and at rallies. They may have seemed comfortable to jealous eyes, but were far too afraid to be. They were Little Jews, afraid, huddling, stupidly waiting on the Messiah. For them, every night from then on was the same, spent in dull panic, dreading the following day but doing nothing about it. I had read about worlds far away, the promise of a different life; Germany was not interesting to me any more. Its people were consumed by mistrust; I did not feel like one of them. I had heard about Israel and wanted to live there, where Jews were supposed to be strong; I thought I knew it all. I did not. If only somebody had explained to me then, as I have tried to explain many times to you, that, though you may not feel like you belong at home, you will never truly belong anywhere else, I might have been saved some of the terrible mistakes I was about to make. I prepared to leave.

I turned over the last page but there was nothing more. Lucille appeared.

'You coming?' she said, whispering while peeping round the door. 'Dad could be up any minute. We need to go.'

The breakfast had gone cold; I felt ill and couldn't eat it. I got up, put the letter in my pocket, left the food on the table and walked out of the house to try, once again, to forget her.

12

The Great School Search

Henry's home was a grand old place we used to play in as kids, tormenting the poor family that lived there for a whole summer, breaking into their home and even pissing on their Persian rug one time when we knew they were away on holiday. 'I want that and I'm going to get it,' Henry had said proudly, pointing with one hand and zipping his trousers up with the other. 'You just see if I don't.' Thirty years later, he returned to make the owners an offer they couldn't refuse. Naturally, he had the carpets replaced before he moved in.

'Come on in, you two,' he bawled. 'I'm on the phone – just a bit of business. I'll be done in a minute. Sit down. Beryl will make you a drink. Beryl! See to Abe and Lucille will you? BERYL! BERYL!'

Henry and Beryl always seemed to communicate by shouting, whether pleased or angry with each other, and I'd always wondered if they shouted like that when they were in bed. 'OI, DARLING! PASS ME THE WATER! I'M BLOODY PARCHED HERE!' I wouldn't be surprised.

Beryl appeared from behind him and shunted us into the house, chattering about the weather, and soon we were standing by their couch holding massive mugs of chocolate.

'Well, well, well, got the day off school, have we? And what about you, Abraham? How have you been?'

Beryl gave me a long, warm hug, cradling the back of my head in her hand as she did so.

'Are you looking after yourself?'

Her hand now held mine, tightly.

'I swear you've lost weight again. You're nothing but an empty shell!'

She turned to Lucille.

84

'Learn from that, young lady. You don't want to be a bag of bones like your old granddad! Nobody wants to kiss a skeleton. Men want something to grab onto!'

Lucille blushed as Beryl clutched my right buttock with a sturdy fist, shaking the bony flesh and making a disgusted face.

'Ugh!' she exclaimed, pulling her hand away suddenly.

Beryl is a wonderful woman, a woman from another time, one I secretly miss. She's one of life's grafters, wonderful to be around. A plump, red-faced mother of four and grandmother of twelve, seemingly always cooking, eating or entertaining, she wears a permanent smile and never passes judgement. Mere circumstances don't seem to get her down, and after nearly forty years married to Henry she has certainly experienced the good and the bad, often in quick succession. The heavy lines on her face show life has not always been easy, but it's clear she has lived, and lived well; besides, the lines are often deepened with laughter as she is seldom serious.

I envy Henry for his wife. To Beryl, the smallest things are funny, the simplest things marvellous, and her house is always buzzing with activity. She dotes on all her grandchildren but is nevertheless always excited to see Lucille; she and Henry are the closest thing Lucille has to extended family. Today the house was empty but for the two of them, a rare thing indeed. Usually there were children everywhere, not necessarily relations of theirs. I dreaded visiting their house for fear of mistaking one small member of the clan for another.

'So what's the occasion? Day out? The pictures?' said Beryl. 'I hope you've got a sick note from Granddad!'

'Actually, I'm going to be looking for a new school.'

'Oh. Really? Well then . . .'

Henry appeared, pen in mouth, paper in hand, silencing his wife before she could say any more. He wore a loud checked shirt with sleeves rolled up as far as they would go and an equally brash flat cap, back to front, speaking like an old-style race commentator.

'Sorry for the delay, laddies and gentlefolk. From now on everything will be running smoothly and exactly to plan. This morning we have a tight schedule, and top of the list of things to do is . . . *The Great School Search!*'

He brought out a map of the district, upon which he'd put large red circles round the local schools, and a sheaf of information about the schools printed off from their websites, which he presented like a rabbit from a magician's hat.

'Ta da!' he bellowed. 'Righto, my little Samurai, we'll soon find you a new house of learning. Now, I want you to give marks out of ten for these places, and once we've got a shortlist, we'll go visiting. We're not going to every centre of excellence, you understand. Your granddad and I are old men and we haven't got time to spare. And besides, we'd be searching till you're twenty-one, and there's no point in that is there? So, you're looking for three you like and if it turns out those places don't want you, we don't want them either. We'll bloody well teach you here!'

By now we were all sitting round Henry's big wooden dining table, inspecting the map for ourselves, laughing along with him. But I was laughing out of fear.

Lucille's eyes sparkled: she revelled in the attention. Yes, Uncle Henry no, Uncle Henry. He really was a magician, getting you to see what he wanted you to see, distracting you with his clever charm, a charm that still had Beryl and me spellbound. As he talked I felt a lump appear in my back pocket and, touching it, found it to be a small roll of notes. Apart from Evelyn, Henry was the only one who knew I had virtually nothing to live on, and would soon have less. Nobody made me feel wanted and looked after like my old friend.

Henry and Beryl's place was a house of laughter, where no comment seemed loaded with mistrust or sarcasm and no one seemed to do anything they didn't like. In short, heaven. A place I would happily go to in death. I needed to talk to Henry and make him understand, come up with a plan of action for *me*. *I* needed print-outs and maps and to be the centre of attention. I wanted him to tell him about Evelyn's letters, about her voice in my head. The room went black.

'Abe? Abe? Are you all right? Lucille, go and get a damp cloth and some water for your granddad.'

I had fainted. When I woke I was on a couch surrounded by Lucille, Henry and Beryl, all fanning my face with tea towels and blowing on me.

'Abe, wake up, wake up.'

I had tissues at my nose too; the bleeding had started again. I looked up.

'Henry,' I said, 'she's trying to ruin me. She doesn't want me to be happy or settled or calm. I think I'm losing my mind.'

'Nonsense,' he replied, 'there's no such thing. It's just the shock of finally getting rid of that old bitch. Your body can't cope. But look at Verdi! He reached his mental peak in the last ten years of his life. You're *white*, man. Are you all right?'

'Mmm,' I said, fainting again.

Beryl drove me back to my house and put me to bed, while Henry and Lucille went looking for schools. When she left I made her promise to get Henry to bring her back in school uniform, at the time she would be expected back from school, just in case Nathan was home. No matter how ill I am, there always seems to be enough energy left in me to remember what I need to lie about. Nathan might have been madly irresponsible, but he still had his moments of clarity. I wouldn't want to be caught out.

Surprisingly, when I awoke some time later I felt refreshed once more, completely forgetting the reason for my fainting and bounding out of bed like a young man in full health. It was Tuesday, mid-afternoon. My room was tidy, though I didn't know why. Everything was going to be all right.

13

The Walk of My Youth

I showered, dressed smartly and left 174, almost bouncing down the road, for the second time in one day. 'No Jewish boy is free until his parents are dead, Abraham. This much I know. Prepare yourself for a lengthy sentence,' Evelyn would say, before beating me with her belt. But I was more determined than ever that she would not be in my thoughts. I was a new man, unbound now, starting life with a shot of fresh air and a brisk walk in my home town, far away from school and responsibility and children asking me why they hadn't seen me in class for so long, off to try new things and talk to new people and live the life I always could have had. I used to like walking, going to little shops, searching out cobbled streets and untouched corners of the city, though even the untouched parts are not so untouched any more. (God bless those corporate executives, they know a good spot for a coffee shop when they see one.)

I used to go walking all the time as an adolescent, whistling my favourite rock'n'roll songs as I walked, simply enjoying movement, being alone. I liked my own company in those days. But after a while I settled into a regular route, which I took every night after dinner – the repetition was comforting: through the passage by the golf course, down the high street, back on myself at the war memorial and home through the football pitches. There wasn't any aesthetic reason for going that way; I just knew how long it would take and had learnt that if I didn't stay out too long Evelyn didn't complain. I'd make some minor excuse and have my coat on before she could ask questions, feeling so much freer outside than in the house, stewing, with Evelyn clouding everything. She had become so bitter. With every passing year, her ability to participate in the outside world shrank: you had to be careful not to catch it off her.

I wrapped myself up in my old coat and took a deep breath, drawing in the fresh air. Though it was spring, it was a cold day. I scuffed my heels on the paving stones, kicking frozen leaves and just thinking. Surely there had been some men in history whose most satisfying days had come in the twilight of their lives? So Verdi reached his mental peak not long before his death, did he? I tried to think of others. Michelangelo? Shakespeare? Wordsworth? I liked to think so. The thought warmed me.

I decided to repeat the walk of my youth step for step, but had gone no more than a couple of hundred yards when I passed the church at the bottom of the road and stopped to have a look, hovering nervously by the entrance under the small archway. Somehow, the old place was more appealing now, and I wanted to stay a while. Above the entrance it read: 'Jesus said I will never turn away anyone who comes to me,' the words hanging over a picture of a pair of outstretched arms. I sat down on a bench in the church gardens, part of which was a graveyard, and stretched out my sore, tired legs. The church was something of an anomaly, really – quite different to anything else in the bland suburban landscape around it – and I wondered lazily what the area might have looked like a hundred years ago, before any of the polite brick oblongs, grey pathways and numerous identical round-abouts that now characterised the place were so poorly designed and executed around it. The church was so much higher, so much more colourful, more ambitious than any of its neighbours, yet it was ignored by most, me included. I had passed it thousands of times, usually on my way to The King's, but never even given it a thought. The tall, narrow spire of the church, the clock face reading FORGET NOT GOD, the sad figures on the stained-glass windows – it all looked so welcoming. *I will never turn away anyone who comes to me.* My back twitched, my chest tightened. I pulled out my inhaler, took a long, deep puff, and sat immobile while the peaceful feeling of my airways slowly reopening took me over. Perhaps some things were about to change, in a way neither the Rabbi nor Evelyn could predict. I left the church behind and headed along my old route, through the quiet streets of the estate and into the town.

The main road was busy, much more so than I remember it being in the past. A great deal seemed to have changed: the smells were different – cheap pub food, coffee, beer – and the colours were all brighter; brash double yellow lines, dazzling signs, red cones. Even the council bins had changed colour. The place now looked like almost any other British high street, and less appealing for it. Many of the shops and pubs I expected to see were no longer there and new, cruder versions of them stood in their place. The old pubs had become style bars and most shops had either changed owner, become part of a chain or been turned into modern flats. Why is it that newer buildings are always less pleasing than old ones? I missed the old places, though perhaps Rachel would not have cared for them, and Lucille was too young ever to lament their disappearance. Had I even properly remembered the old streets? Was it ever really like that? They say the elderly exaggerate the good old days and quietly forget the bad. I had always prided myself on not being like that, keeping with the times, embracing the future – computers, the internet, new language, none of that fazed me – but perhaps age was finally beginning to take over. You have to keep alert, stop it happening. I slowed up in front of an unfamiliar charity shop and looked in the window, where there was a large poster, reading:

'For God so loved the world that he gave his only begotten son, that whosoever believeth in him should not perish, but have everlasting life.'

Looking in the window at customers idly scanning the shelves and racks, it seemed like an oasis of calm. 'The JESUS SAVES Charity Shop,' said the sign above the door. In the cartoon underneath, a long-haired white man in a swishing robe dived to rescue a football from going in the goal behind him.

Everlasting life. Evelyn used to say faith in an afterlife was an insult to man's development. She hated the religious (or at least we thought she did), and Christians particularly. The Evangelists, she called them. The great mistakes of world religion was one of her favourite topics and we often quarrelled about it in her last years, even when she was too weak to get out of bed. We never stopped arguing – the need to be irritated never left her. When making a point she sat up as much as she could, croaking and waving her index finger about as if standing at a lectern talking to a large crowd of followers. It was the recruitment she despised the most.

'"God shall have a witness in every nation," it says in the bible – you can't deny that's what they really want to do. They can't keep it to themselves. There's no point in being a Christian if you aren't going to go out and convert others. That's what you can blame for British colonialism, some of it. *Oh, we must go and let the little black children know about Jesus.* Shame on them, Avraham, and shame on us all for tolerating it. *You are all wrong, except my lot* – that's what Christianity has to say. That's what all religions say! Where's the one for people who think their leader *isn't* special? Where is that community who believe they haven't been chosen at all, the cult where the followers don't believe their leader is the Messiah? Christians – ha! They're worse than the Jews. Bring me my soup.'

Evelyn was very pleased with this. But for all her faults, at least she always reminded me not to consider myself chosen. 'Neither Jesus nor Mohammed nor Buddha cares for you, boy. Nobody does. Now go and brush your teeth!' That was the party line in my house.

My eyes were suddenly drawn to the door of the charity shop. A smaller, handwritten poster underneath the larger one said:

'Jesus wants YOU! To help out in this shop, Mondays to Thursdays, 12 until 5. Call in and speak to Maureen for details.'

A teenage girl appeared behind the poster and began to put up another next to it. 'Campaign for the people of Ethiopia – while you've been watching the war, one million people have been trying to get your attention.'

Spotting me staring, she smiled innocently and suddenly I felt forty years younger, but awkward because of it. I scurried away in shame. I completed the rest of the route without taking in much around me, turning back on myself at the war memorial just as all those years ago. Though it took me longer and was more tiring, I enjoyed the old walk. If I could have taken the past I remembered and cloaked myself in it, I would have.

On the way back I was sure to pass the shop again. 'Jesus wants YOU!' – I liked that, and decided to pop in for a look around. Maybe Beryl might like a present for looking after me earlier, or perhaps there might be something in there for Lucille. Thanks to Henry, now I could pay for it. Already the quote from before about everlasting life was gone, but it had been replaced with the same one I'd seen at the church earlier on:

'Jesus said I will never turn anyone away who comes to me.'

I didn't ever remember seeing that quote before today, and there it was twice in one morning. I opened the door and walked in.

The walls were covered end to end in artwork – one painting was from Uganda, wherever that country was, another was by Maureen herself – and local children's drawings were pinned up on a noticeboard behind the till. The children had mostly drawn pictures of their families and Jesus performing miracles, but one or two snowmen had survived from Christmas. It wasn't a stuffy place; it seemed a shop for young people. Decorations for the upcoming Easter celebrations covered the other walls, bunting hung from the ceiling and Easter eggs were stacked in all corners of the shop. A boy and girl chatted at the counter – the girl I'd seen putting up the poster and a young lad of roughly the same age wearing a T-shirt advertising a rock group. (A skeleton was devouring the insides of a young girl in a red dress.) My favourite song, 'Rock Around the Clock', was playing quietly in the background; second-hand racks were filled with old videos, DVDs, tapes and some vinyl. I flipped through the videos, chose a couple of old black-and-white films for myself (an early Hitchcock and one with Elvis in it) and made my way to the counter, noticing a poster of a tiny, starving child standing in a desert that hung on the back wall, accompanied by yet another quote underneath, which I couldn't quite make out. I was looking for symbols everywhere. The young girl saw me trying to pick out the message and stood in front of it.

'We're changing things around at the minute,' she said firmly. 'Actually, I'm just taking that one down; it's one of Maureen's. We think the image is a little out of date. Customers feel guilty or angry when they see it. I certainly don't think it converts anyone.'

'Why would it make people angry?'

'Because they want to know what a starving child has got to do with Christianity in England. They think you're trying to make them feel bad and so don't want to spend money here. They're right. That kid needs food, not Jesus. Can I help you with anything?'

It seemed like a long time before I could respond. It wasn't that I wanted her – even an old letch like me knows to stop at teenagers – but still, something about her was spellbinding. I pushed over the video boxes dumbly.

'Good to hear that song,' I said. 'It's been a while.'

'I hate it,' she replied bluntly, pointing to the young man. 'It's his thing, not mine. Rinkety-dinkety nonsense, if you ask me. That boy listens to *anything*.'

The girl went through to the back to get the videos while I pottered around, waiting, strangely unoffended by her slight on my musical taste. I picked up a leaflet hanging from a carousel on the desk:

'Acceptance: the way to serenity and peace of mind.'

I turned to the first page and absent-mindedly read a passage on what to do when life seems too much to cope with, about getting life back into focus and needing to know who we are, while in the background 'Rock Around the Clock' faded out and was replaced by 'Chantilly Lace' by The Big Bopper. (Nathan was conceived to the sound of The Big Bopper. That still makes me smile.) The girl returned.

'What do you think you're doing?' Evelyn whispered in my ear.

'I'd like to apply for the job please,' I said, surprising us all.

'Well, Maureen's on holiday just now,' said the girl, a little taken aback, 'but I'm in charge while she's gone. You can talk to me. I'm Gilda.'

She held out her hand and shook mine vigorously.

'Hilda?

'Gil-da,' she repeated, slowly. 'It's Italian. From Verdi's *Rigoletto*, you know it?'

I shook my head.

'No, but I understand he reached his mental peak rather late in life . . . which is comforting.'

'Really? They say Michelangelo got wiser with age too. Anyway, *Rigoletto*. Not a happy ending I'm afraid. I get murdered. Have you got a minute to talk now?'

'Yes, now's fine,' I said, still not sure whether I meant the offer. I considered putting the leaflet back on the carousel, but she saw me looking.

'Take it,' she insisted. 'There's hundreds of them.'

'Not bloody surprised!' said Evelyn smugly.

The price rung up on the till. I fumbled in my pockets and, removing a crisp note from the roll Henry had given me, handed over the money, smiling shyly. Cheerfully, Gilda took it and popped the money into the drawer.

'Come through to the back then. Follow me. Nas!'

Gilda called to the young man and indicated he come over, asked him to watch the till, kissed him lightly on the cheek and led me towards the back room. Nas smiled at me, then her. As I followed Gilda through the short, narrow corridor, I watched her backside lilting from side to side in her jeans and felt, much to my relief, nothing. Once through the door, she bent over, picked up a bowl from the floor, cleared a pile of papers from a chair and patted it, indicating for me to sit.

'Welcome to my office.'

The office was more like a student's bedroom, notes and books scattered all over the floor, half-opened drinks and crumb-filled plates blocking the doorway, but Gilda was not ashamed.

'Sorry about the mess,' she said matter-of-factly. 'The boss isn't back until next week. You know how it is.'

'Of course, of course. My room's no different, actually.'

I liked her. We sat.

'So, are you a Christian?'

'No, I'm not actually. Just curious, I suppose. Is that a problem?'

'Not at all.' Gilda smiled.

Suddenly I blurted out:

'I'm Jewish.'

A pause.

'Sorry about the Christ-killing thing . . . that may have been a mistake.'

She stared at me coldly for a second. Evelyn cackled in the background.

'Is your name Judas? Or Pilot?'

'No, it's Abe.'

She chuckled.

'Well then, Abe, you're in the clear, aren't you? It is rare, admittedly, but we've always been mixed faith in this shop. Mohammed's a devout Muslim, and he's worked here every Thursday for months now. Sue is a Buddhist. We're all friends from college. Of course, for most of us Jesus and his teachings are the key thing, but really we're just here to do good. Most religions teach the same thing essentially, so instead of fighting about it we pool our resources and do as much for the community as we can.'

'I see.'

'In fact, sometimes I wonder whether what religion you finally choose is important at all! You can just be . . . spiritual . . . and make a difference that way. Don't tell Nas you heard me say that though! He'd kill me!'

The room was tiny, and we were so close that I could smell Gilda's body odour – musky, but not unpleasant – quite clearly. She was not wearing perfume and, I noticed, hardly any jewellery at all. Were all young girls like this now? She looked me in the eye and spoke politely but directly. Being treated as an equal – almost like one of them – seemed strange, but then all young people appeared to talk to everyone the same these days, like they were making an arrangement for a Saturday night. Henry says it's a great leveller. Gilda retrieved a pad and pen from under a magazine and scribbled a small heading, underlining it three times and adding an exclamation mark at the end. She had big bright eyes that shone innocently and wore a cross around her neck.

'So you're looking for the twelve till five slot then,' she said. 'We're very relaxed around here, as you can tell, but don't be fooled by the mess – we're pretty dedicated too. Now, *chores*.'

She counted them on her fingers.

'Like the rest of us, you'll be responsible for manning the till, checking stock, taking in donations and keeping the shop looking nice, that kind of thing. Sound OK?'

I nodded.

'If you like you can get involved in fund-raising, too, but it's not compulsory. And all the work is, of course, voluntary.'

She seemed suddenly to remember that she was supposed to be asking questions. 'Anyway, what makes you think you would be good at the job?'

'I hadn't really thought about it like that,' I said, shrugging. 'It was more about what the job could do for me. I'm sure I could do the shopkeeping though.'

'What qualifications do you have?'

'Three degrees – English Language, History and German – and I can operate most computer programmes.'

Gilda was laughing again.

'I was thinking more along the lines of a maths O-level. Why on earth do you want to work *here*?'

'I like it. I was just passing, and . . .'

'You must have done a thousand more challenging things . . .'

'If you will have me,' I replied sheepishly, 'I'll accept the challenge here.'

Gilda looked down at her blank page, embarrassed. I too was surprised to hear the sadness in my voice.

'Of course!' she said, trying again. 'We need help and you want to provide it: that's good enough for me. Welcome on board.'

She thrust her strong hand out once more and this time I shook it more firmly, smiling too, her good humour infectious. We walked back through the short corridor and again I found myself looking at her firm body and her exposed belly button, but I was not aroused by it. She was somehow very comforting, but her glowing sexuality did not touch me in the usual way.

'When would you like to start? Monday?' she asked, leading me through the shop and holding the front door open.

'I can start before then, this week if you like.'

'Fine,' she said, grinning. 'Come in Thursday morning – Nas and I will be on duty – and I'll show you around properly. Things may be a little hectic because of Easter, but I'm sure you can handle that.'

So that was it then. After three decades of thoughtless continual service, I was so easily no longer a teacher. I was a shop assistant. Gilda picked up a dazzling red modern-looking Bible from a bookshelf and popped it into my bag with the videos.

'Here's a little something to read in the meantime. I'll pay for that one,' she said softly. 'Don't look so afraid. If you don't like it, all you have to do is shut it to make it go away. Oh dear – Abe, you've got blood on your arm. Would you like a tissue or something?'

'Oh God . . .'

I looked down to see a slow red trickle meandering down my forearm, between the cuts and bruises that divided the paleness around. She returned quickly with a clutch of toilet paper.

'Are you OK?'

'It's nothing. I'm a little fragile, but fine. Thanks.'

I dabbed at my arm, soaked up the blood with the tissue and left, waving at Gilda on my way out.

Not looking where I was going, I back-pedalled onto the pavement still gazing and bumped straight into Rachel, who was carrying a slew of bags and talking on a mobile phone.

'Careful, old man! You want to watch where you're going.'

'Sorry, I'm in a rush . . .'

'Hold on a second,' she said to the phone, and then, in my direction, 'Me too. Do you want to meet later? Your house, in an hour?'

'Can we make it later?'

She grabbed my wrist with her hand and rattled it affectionately.

'Fine, three hours. It will still be light then. There's somewhere I want to take you, not far out, in the country. We'll go there in your car. I just know you'll love it! Was everything OK at the school yesterday?'

'Yes, fine.'

'Good, good, tell me all about it later . . .'

Before I could tell her she'd left her things at my house, she was gone, almost skipping up the high street, bags swinging happily from her shoulders and talking hurriedly into her phone. Though she was much older than Gilda, she seemed more juvenile, and I disliked her for it.

Still standing on the pavement in front of the shop, people with places to go to hurrying past me in both directions, I picked the book Gilda had given me carefully out of the plastic bag to have a look. It was a little worn at the corners, obviously second-hand, but otherwise it was in good condition. It said *'The Good News Bible'* in large, elaborate Gothic lettering across the top of the page, above a picture of a harbour scene at sunset, red blob sun falling behind the clouds and boats bobbing contentedly on the water. I opened it. On the inner sleeve, next to the price, was a handwritten note:

Some people buy pets for company, but they cost a lot to feed and can run away. This book is better than all the furry friends in the world. It too is alive, but instead of you feeding it, it feeds you. And it will never run away.

God Bless, Gordon xxx

P.S. READ ROMANS 10:13

I didn't understand the message, but that too was something that was becoming quite regular and it no longer alarmed me. I rifled through the pages, found Romans 10:13 and read:

'As the scripture says, "Everyone who calls out to the Lord for help will be saved."'

I wasn't yet sure I could risk calling out but hoped he might spot my new job and take it as an indication of good intentions. It was only a short walk to The King's.

14

Back in The King's Arms

I sat at the bar, drink in hand, sulking silently, listening to my mother and hoping she would soon leave.

'Sit up straight,' she barked. 'Why sit on a stool with a back to it if you're going to slouch like a schoolboy? Get yourself a bean bag or something!'

It was time I learnt to be alone. Since Wife Number Three's messy departure some months ago prospects had been barren for me anyway, until Rachel. Soon that arrangement would become permanent: no hope of twin plots, so no need to tag along this evening in some little park pretending that I was with someone whose name I was still learning. Gary poured me another drink and smiled, happy to have my debt repaid, with interest, so quickly. The fresh ice cubes bobbed and clinked around the glass.

Somehow I couldn't forget what she'd said – *I just know you'll love it, Abe, I just know.* Winking at me like we were old friends, touching my arm, assuming. She *didn't* know me; nobody did, so how could she be so sure what I would love? I loved old-time rock'n'roll, George Best, Spike Milligan, boxing, my first wife, getting drunk with Henry and talking about the fifties, my first Norton Dominator motorbike, the tiniest insignificant details of royal history, sleeping with strangers. You've got to be careful with women who think they can tell you what you want. Let them get comfortable and before you know it they're straightening your tie, buying your clothes and taking you out with people you don't like to places you don't like, dressing you up like a doll for sale. I hate the outdoors. The countryside bores me. I'd much rather be in the pub with a pint and the paper, or teaching bored fourteen-year-olds about the last Tsar of Russia. Why was

Rachel even interested in me? And what could be the eventual outcome? Another marriage? *'Wandering Abe Stone – fourth time lucky'* teased the gravestone in my mind's eye. I looked at my watch; late already. Why didn't I just say I was busy? Well, it was too late for apologies. She'd just have to wait for me or go home. I downed my JD.

'Go on, drink yourself to death,' said my mother. 'What else are you good for?'

Gary was on hand straight away to pour another as I grimaced into the bottom of the last. He knew not to ask what had happened with Rachel. I twirled the ice cubes round my glass, watching them get slowly smaller and eventually evaporate into the black, my mind then drifting from the glass to the other customers, to Gary, to my greying hands, the imprint of Evelyn's teeth on the back of the right one, and then back to the glass again. Memories of nights I'd spent hunched on that stool fell in and out of my mind. That's how forty years have passed, wasted, but still I didn't want to leave The King's. I was happy there, though the alcohol was playing with my moods. We said six o'clock, it was nearly seven forty-five and already I was very drunk.

'Hey, Gary, know why I became a teacher?'

Gary strolled over, washing a clean glass with a dirty towel.

'This again?'

'Henry VIII, that's why. At the beginning at least. I even remember the teacher who taught me to love him. Some things you never forget.'

'Henry VIII? That guy didn't know what he was doing half the time.'

'Exactly! And people bowed down to him anyway, just because of who he was and because he *acted* like he should be in charge, even when he didn't have a clue what to do next. That's why he survived for so long. Lesser men would have been overthrown or manipulated into more sensible behaviour. But not Henry. It wasn't just him, of course – you don't make a career choice because of one fat dead Englishman. There were others too. Elizabeth I was quite a character. Charles I, too. It was mainly royals though, that excited me . . . That's the thing about teaching English history, Gary. Spending a lot of time teaching the royals means you don't have much left to talk about all the bad things we did abroad. Clever, eh? Keeps kids interested, all that marriage and divorce. Anyway . . . what was I saying? Oh yes. That's why I became a teacher.'

'So you could be an idiot?'

'So I could *dream* about being one – tell the stories as if they were mine. All that Anne Boleyn stuff . . . it's magical . . .'

'It's probably not true you know . . .'

'. . . It's the greatest story ever, don't you think? A man leaves his wife of twenty years for someone the whole country hates, sets up a new religion, proclaims himself God's messenger on earth – *Jesus*, basically – and then one day just . . . changes his mind about the whole thing and hangs the woman he'd done it all for. And he gets away with it! Amazing! They even let him marry again . . . *four times.'*

'Like I said. An idiot.'

'You never knew who he was going to turn on next. He changed his mind repeatedly but seemed at the time to have complete faith in whatever he was doing at that minute. Incredible.'

Gary left to serve a customer. I finished the story, quieter, so Evelyn could hear it.

'I want to do and say what I please and then switch course without warning. I want the power to be a fool and be lauded for it.'

Evelyn chose not to reply. I stopped talking to her and picked up my drink.

A man I vaguely recognised approached me – a middle-aged, bearded gentleman, thin as a rake, wearing a head covering clipped onto his hair and smiling. I couldn't place him, but this was no longer unusual. The man waited for a second and then broke into a smile. I didn't know many Jews any more.

'You don't recognise me?'

He dusted the bar stool with his hat and sat down.

'I didn't expect you to. I just thought I'd come over and see if you were all right.'

'Oh, I know – you carried me to the cab, right?'

'And took you to your front door!'

We both laughed.

'The name's Lenny – I took your left side; not too roughly I hope.'

He put his hand out, and I shook it.

'No, no, you were very gentle, I'm sure. Thanks.'

'Not at all. Don't feel bad.'

'Well, thanks. And I was fine, really, I promise.'

The man grinned, mock bowing, slipping effortlessly into character.

'Well, sir, I must have underestimated you. I mistook your quietness in the taxi for ill health. You must have been deep in thought.'

'Ah, yes, I am one of the great philosophers. Let me get you a drink . . .'

But the man held up his hand to stop me.

'Come and join us! My brother Benjamin is with me – the one who held your right side. I'm sure he would love to hear you talk in sentences!'

This comment amused Lenny greatly. I decided to join them, hid the Bible in an inside pocket of my jacket when Lenny turned away, and took my drinks over to their table.

The man's brother looked similar to his sibling, only a few years younger and heavier. Not so much a paunch yet, more like a paunch in waiting, and his beard was wispier, like candy floss compared to the rich, thick, dark one his brother sported. Both men seemed to be constantly smiling through their beards. Their tone of voice, wiry, soaring and dipping, was everything I understood to be Jewish and everything I'd been taught to be suspicious of. Somehow they were not quite as I'd come to expect though, not cartoonish at all.

'Self-haters, cowards, narrow-minded idiots,' cut in Evelyn. 'We're not in Vilna now!'

Many years ago, when the family next door moved house Evelyn frothed at length for weeks about our prospective new neighbours. She had feared the area was becoming more Jewish and had heard the new family were ultra-orthodox – Beards, as she preferred to call them. 'I tell you this, Abraham; if I see a Beard coming up that driveway I shall chase him all the way back to Poland! That's not religion, that's fear of the world! Give me anything but a Beard. Black-hatted fools; it makes me ashamed to share a race, never mind a postcode!'

But I was no longer listening to her . . . and anyway, maybe she'd changed her mind on that now.

'So what brings you two here twice in a week?' I asked. 'The orange juice?'

'Serious business,' said Lenny. 'The orange is just a bonus. My son's bar mitzvah is on Saturday and there's a lot still to be done. My wife is in an awful panic and will not give us a moment's peace in the house. So here we are, every night, drinking The King's Arms out of soft drinks!'

The man giggled, high-pitched, and held up an almost empty glass.

'I think it's beginning to kick in!'

His brother, more anxious, interrupted.

'We've done hardly anything. I'm supposed to be making a speech and can't decide what to put in it. There's so much I want to say, but I'm afraid I shall be very boring. I've never given a speech before, not even at my own wedding.'

He made a show of the scribblings in front of him.

'Nonsense,' said Lenny, 'you'll *kill* them.'

Benjamin continued, unconvinced.

'In public I get nervous and sweaty and start to stutter ter-ribly. We might be there all night before I g-g-get to the end of my first sentence!'

Lenny could barely control his giggling.

'Why don't you try your speech out on Abe?'

Benjamin shook his head.

'Please, go on,' I said. 'Pretend I'm an audience of hundreds.'

I tried to steady myself, holding the underside of the table lightly with both hands.

'All right, but you should know Lenny just wants me to tell a couple of old Jewish stories and sit down! So there'll be no tales of cute things my nephew did in the bath. I wrote down a couple of stories my father told me.' Benjamin rearranged himself in the chair. 'This is one he told at my bar mitzvah, way back in '52. Needless to say, back then there was no marquee to organise and no live band. Things were different then.'

He clapped his hands together and started as Lenny left for the bar. I was transfixed. I sat and listened while Benjamin practised his speech, his tranquil, deep, worldly voice, just like the Rabbi's, calming me with every word.

'One day many years ago, an Israeli fellow – Shmuel – a restless, angry young baker, is cycling down a road in Jerusalem on his way home from work when he comes across a Siddur, a prayer book, lying in the gutter on the side of the road, front cover hanging off to one side and dirt caked on the pages. He picks it up and dusts it off, shaking his head at the sad sight of it. Checking for damage, he decides the book can be salvaged and puts it in his satchel and takes it home for repair. That night, Shmuel painstakingly cleans and sews up each part of the Siddur until it looks almost new and then sleeps well for the first time in years. A new peace comes over him. His wife thinks he's a fool. Anyway, that night he's visited in a dream by the voice of God, telling him his mission on earth must be the love and restoration of scriptures, so in the coming weeks and months Shmuel seeks them out – Torah, New Testament and the Koran, which he notices tend to be more well-thumbed. He seems to notice books everywhere on his route to and from his job at the bakery, just lying there for him to pick up, and rescuing them from the roadside quickly becomes a habit. Over the years Shmuel comes to be a greatly respected man in Jerusalem. Some say he's a prophet. People start to go to him with their damaged and old books for repair, some leaving them with him afterwards, which the Rabbis say is a great mitzvah, a good deed. His house becomes a holy building, a shrine of words, where he works unceasingly, inspecting and repairing. He has to give up his job at the bakery to cope with the demand. Many years later, when the war comes to Jerusalem he decamps to the hills in the north, needing the strength of thirty men to transport all of his books into a large cave, his new home, which well-wishers from all sides decorate with carpets and flowers. Some say that Shmuel no longer needs any food but the love of God, and they come to visit him, some wanting advice, some hoping for miracles, some travelling for many days to reach him. A rumour goes round that Shmuel once took the ashes of a burnt Torah and assembled them one by one until it was complete again, more beautiful than ever before. He is not only righteous, but famous too. Soldiers let him be. More years pass. In his old age he works less, but still he repairs what he can. Then, one day, a journalist comes to the cave. The journalist asks how Shmuel started out and why, about his huge collection of prayer books and his eating habits. He says, "How do you occupy yourself all these hours in the cave when you are not working? Do you read the scriptures? Do you pray?" Well, Shmuel blushes scarlet, looks up at the journalist and replies: "I work and pray all the time but cannot read. The Lord has created shapes for me only."'

Benjamin sat back and smiled, satisfied.

'That's beautiful. But what does it mean? And why would you tell that story at a bar mitzvah?'

He beamed.

'When my father first told me that story I didn't understand what he was going on about either. Probably trying to get me to work harder at school. It couldn't have sunk in though. I failed everything!'

Lenny returned from the bar.

'He liked it, right? I don't know what you're worried about. All you've got to do is spin a yarn, face the boy, tell him to work hard, marry Jewish and grow up to earn a lot of money. What can be so hard?'

Lenny patted me on the back like I was an old friend, plonked a pint of lager onto the table in front of me and settled himself.

'*L'Chaim*, to life!' he cheered.

We all held our glasses high, clinking them roughly. Had I mentioned I was Jewish? Lenny turned to talk some more about arrangements with Benjamin, while, drifting from them, I began to feel myself getting giddier, almost outside my body, looking in on another night of drinking taking hold. The King's was filling up, afternoon turning into evening. The night staff were just arriving – joking with each other as they did so – and outside the sun was just beginning to dip into the horizon. I could feel the panic coming on again. I coughed, trying to still the hotness swelling inside me by putting a hand to my chest. There, there, said the hand, there, there. My new phone bleeped. A message from Henry. I excused myself and read it.

LUCILLE HOME AND SAFE. SCHOOL SEARCH GOING WELL: CALL BERYL TOMORROW. JUST GETTING ON A FLIGHT TO JERUSALEM. WILL CALL. H.

Jerusalem?

'Excuse me, gentlemen,' I said to Lenny and Benjamin. 'I'll be back in a minute.'

They nodded and returned to their conversation.

Outside it had started raining, so I stood in the pub's entrance hallway to make the call, one finger in my ear to help me hear over the music. I dialled Henry's number frantically.

107

Henry had amassed over almost five decades a great deal of experience in my problems, particularly with women, but had developed a sophisticated, offhand cynicism, treating all my dramas as if they were mere continuations of the last, forever getting confused as to which one was which and dismissing all non-female-related issues as unimportant. But despite this, I kept going back to him. I had no one else. Henry had always been convinced that all I needed was to settle down and everything else would neatly slip into place, as it had in his life. The phone trilled many times before he answered.

'What?' he said in his familiar boom.

'Can you talk?'

'Henry! I'm getting on the plane.'

'Henry, please . . .'

'Ah! Let me guess. Anne of Cleves! The Flanders Mare!'

I could picture him, waving his arms dramatically about in the queue, and wished he was closer.

'Poor, poor Anne, a meagre substitute for Jane Seymour. You want to skip her and Catherine Howard. Go straight to Katherine Parr! Look, I can't talk. I'll call you from Jerusalem.'

'What are you going there for? I need your help.'

I hoped he could hear the crack in my voice. Henry sighed.

'Henry, I'm in an airport lounge. They're going to call the flight any minute. Is it about Lucille?'

'I don't think so . . .'

'Right then. Unless someone else has died, I'll speak to you on the other side.'

The rain splashed down hard onto the window pane in front of me, the night's drink starting to take hold. I looked back into the pub at Lenny and Benjamin laughing happily and missed my friend.

'Well, have they?'

'Have they what?'

'Is anyone dead?'

Henry sounded irritated, like an executive interrupted in

an important meeting by his daughter just calling for a fun chat with Dad.

'I'm too old for this,' I said, almost shouting into the receiver. There was a long pause, the airport noise humming in the background. I heard Henry sit down, his bags clattering down around him, and then nothing, so I hung up the phone, went back inside to thank Lenny and Ben and made to leave. Both men insisted I attend Little Lenny's call-up in synagogue on Thursday morning, and I said I would if I could. Lenny said of course I could and that his son's voice would make the angels sigh with gladness. On the walk home my clothes became drenched, the downpour unrelenting. I wrapped the Bible in my coat to protect it.

It was late when I walked up the pathway Wife Number Three had paid for only a couple of years ago with her Christmas bonus. At the time I'd grumbled about the cost, so we'd bought something cheaper than what she wanted; now I was left with it, she was long gone and there were cracks in the paving already. Poking at them with a stick, lamenting my decision as I hovered outside the door, I wondered how long Rachel had waited for me, if perhaps she had waited all evening and whether I'd ever see her again. I hoped not. If it was the last time, perhaps I would give up women for good. I shook my head side to side in the porch, trying to dry my hair a little, Bible still under one arm, hidden. Just having it there made me feel stronger.

Rachel's attachment despite my outward indifference was curious and apparently powerful, but I didn't know her well enough to guess how she might respond to my non-appearance. Stepping inside, still dripping from the rain, I was surprised to see her and Nathan rolling back and forth on the floor, half naked and kissing passionately. I stood there aghast. The door swung open and hit one of Rachel's discarded high heels, resting there and letting an icy draft come in through the hallway.

It wasn't possible that they hadn't heard me come in, but both continued as if I wasn't there, even more keenly, perhaps to make it look more plausible. Goosebumps appeared on Rachel's back, while Nathan's old sweater hung limp over a chair. The bookcases rattled. Though I tried not to look closely it was obvious that Rachel looked good: sexy, commanding, hunched tight over Nathan's torso, legs astride him in the same bra and pants set I remembered from Sunday night. He looked like a flattened mouse. The passage of only a few seconds, amid exaggerated grunts and slurps, limped slowly by. Dumbfounded, with my house keys dangling from one hand, I wondered whether to bother putting my coat on the hook behind them, but in my panic could not move at all. I finally decided to let my jacket dry on a radiator upstairs instead, passed them by and climbed the stairs quickly, wincing at every squeak of the stairs, echoed by their forced squealings in the background.

'Oh!'

'Oh God!'

'Oh *God*!'

'Oh *Gooooooood*!'

In one sense my problem was solved, but as is so often the case, it's disappearance only served to make way for another, bigger, uglier one. Out of earshot of the grappling couple, I passed Lucille's room on the way to mine.

'Today has been better,' I heard her say to Evelyn, 'if a little strange.'

15

Early Morning at 174

In the dimness of early morning I lay in bed wondering if Rachel had stayed over or run for home as soon as I was gone. Though no noises in the night had suggested it, I hoped so, for Lucille if nothing else. She would be devastated when she woke up, and we would all be to blame. I put on an old dressing gown – a hole-filled, grey, scabby thing Wife Number Three bought me one year for my birthday – and decided to go downstairs, tiptoeing to my bedroom door, listening for noises from across the hall on the way.

Though I heard nothing, I ventured out quietly anyway just in case Rachel or Nathan should appear. One hand lightly pressed on the wall, I crept over the landing painfully slowly, past Lucille's room, my heart broken for her, then the bathroom and eventually down the stairs opposite Nathan and Arabella's room, at each creaking step expecting someone to let out a scream of ecstasy or pain or alarm. There was no movement; only more silence. Not even the sound of Nathan's nightly elephantine snore. Perhaps, peacefully wrapped in Rachel's warm body, he had, for once, stopped doing it. Perhaps he lay awake, watching her, afraid to fall asleep. Arabella had been gone since Sunday. It was Wednesday morning. I ran a large glass of water in the kitchen, my throat parched from another night's heavy drinking, and imagined Nathan lying in bed upstairs entwined in Rachel, basking in a comforting half sleep, and sighed, walking over to my favourite chair in the conservatory. I pulled the chair opposite towards me and hauled my feet up onto it, making myself more comfortable and thinking about when Nathan was born.

Nathan, meaning 'gift'. I didn't like it. Wife Number One named him, but I let her, thinking he would be the first of many. I always wanted a large family, but did not say so until it was too late. Before everyone moved back in so recently, the house always seemed bare, as if there weren't enough bodies for all the space. I hoped one day to have many grandchildren, like Henry and Beryl – and this place would have been perfect for it – but Wife Number One died not wanting any more children with me, the second refused outright and the third wouldn't even let me in the bedroom. (Unfortunate, since she was entitled to hefty discounts from the sex shop she worked in.) Instead of people, I loved dead kings and queens, which of course do not alone make a life, and now I am left with very little.

I took another gulp of the water, this time letting the liquid slosh from side to side in my mouth before letting it slip down, savouring the sensation of something that didn't sting to drink. Even by my standards, my thirst was curiously large. I glanced across at the decanter that sat invitingly in the opposite corner of the room and considered whether it was too early for a stronger flavour, but quickly decided against it. That would have involved getting up again, which seemed like too much of an effort. If only I could be kept in a comfy chair ten yards from alcohol for the rest of my life I might never touch a drink again. Perhaps I would share that thought with Henry. What time would it be in Jerusalem?

This time Henry picked up quickly, and I could clearly hear him munching on something and slurping a drink on the other end of the line, the buzz of a crowd in the background.

'Henry Ford?' he answered.

'Good morning. Are you busy?'

'Not at all. Sorry about yesterday, you know how it is . . . or maybe you don't. Anyway, trouble?'

Down the phone I could hear the clatter of a busy city in the morning, horns beeping, traffic rumbling past, people shouting at each other. Henry was almost inaudible amidst the din. I watched the sun lazily rise as we talked.

'Where are you?'

'Little independent café just off Ben Yehuda Street in the middle of town,' he shouted. 'You might have heard of it. McDonald's. I'm eating something they call a Big Mac out here, a sort of double beef patty and salad in a bun. Interesting. Tastes a bit like chicken.'

'They say everything does,' I smiled, waggling my toes and stretching out on the couch, stifling a yawn. 'Well, you've got to soak up the culture . . .'

'Oh yeah, soak up the culture. I'm a cultural fuckin' sponge.'

Henry took another bite of his burger.

'What are you doing in Jerusalem anyway? You hate it.'

'That's true, Henry, but duty calls, duty calls. I'll be in and out of here in under twenty-four hours, and glad of it, too. I'm flying back out this afternoon straight after this meeting. The papers say six people died yesterday morning in Gaza – three on each side – four the day before and two the day before that. So it's even more tense than normal, and there's bound to be retaliation tonight. City of bloody nutters, Henry, city of bloody nutters. It's just revenge after revenge after revenge. Is it so hard to work out there's no point in it all? I could be the fuckin' prime minister out here, bound and gagged, and do a better job than this guy, no question.'

Another bite and slurp. I could hear Henry draining the last dregs of liquid from the container. 'You should see some of the religious types round here. They stop you in the street and try and get you to say prayers. In the middle of the street! Wow. Can you imagine wearing all that black in this weather?'

'Are you safe? How are you getting around?'

'Taxis, my friend, taxis everywhere. Fear not. Won't go a hundred yards on a bus. Won't even stand near a bus stop; not worth it. Any form of transport that needs soldiers patrolling and checking under the seats for bombs at every other stop is not the form of transport for me. I can't believe they run at all. I hope the drivers get danger money.'

'Are taxis OK then?'

'Oh yeah. When did you last see a suicide bomber blow himself up in a cab? You can't fit enough people in one to do any serious damage; you'd be a bit of a crap martyr, wouldn't you? Much more likely a bus full of schoolchildren than an English guy in a taxi. I can just see the headline: *'Attractive English businessman turned to ash. Hamas disappointed. Corpse handsome, considering.'* Let the kids get it, I say, I'm just passing through. Nah, you're safe in a cab.'

Henry had made himself laugh, his familiar guffaw echoing through the mobile and into the hushed conservatory directly under Nathan and Arabella's room.

'It must be exciting going back there though. At least people care about *something*.'

'Nowhere's a big deal to me these days, Henry. The world's not big enough to still hold surprises any more – once you've seen the Sahara at sunset everything else seems a little dull. But you should visit. See what a mess your people have made of the country we gave them. It's your history, kid. Be smart, know about it.'

The sound of Henry picking something out of his teeth came down the line.

'What time is it at home? Can't be later than six o'clock. Is something wrong?'

'Well, things are a little strange, but it's OK. I'm just sitting up, watching the garden. I heard 'Rock Around the Clock' yesterday. It got me thinking.'

'Oh yeah?' Henry went straight into action. *'One, two, three o'clock, four o'clock rock, five, six, seven o'clock, eight o'clock rock . . .'*

More guffawing.

'Ha! What were we thinking? I prefer real music these days – Mahler, Chopin, Tchaikovsky – the kind of thing you imagine God would listen to, if he had a CD player.'

'Hey, that *was* real music! Those records were the best ever made. Those *days* were the best. We'll never get that back. Remember "Peggy Sue?"'

114

'"Peggy Bloody Sue"? That was shit as well!'

'Well, what *was* good – Cliff Richard?'

'*Little* Richard.'

'Richie Valence?'

'Muddy Waters, Chuck Berry.'

'Adam Faith?'

'Johnny Cash, you *idiot*.'

Suddenly he became exasperated.

'I don't know why I bother with you. You missed the point completely.'

'There *was* no point was there?'

'Exactly. You thought it was all about *you*. There was a revolution going on! Anyway, there's no use thinking about it now. It's long gone. Life is much better now.'

'For you, perhaps. Money, a big family, good health . . .'

'That was pretend life back then. Forget it.' Henry made satisfied noises. 'What are you doing at the moment anyway? You never mention it any more.'

'The usual, that's why I don't mention it. I've got another appointment with the doctor this week, but it'll just be the same as always. They hardly even do any tests any more. They just take one look at me and sign . . . Actually, I've been thinking about giving up the teaching altogether.'

'You're always saying that.'

'Well, this time I mean it. I'm bored. I want to do something else.'

'You get bored of everything. And anyway, how can you be bored of teaching? You've not taught a lesson since Christmas!'

'I'm serious, Henry . . . I'm starting another job.'

'Excellent! Good on you. What is it?'

'Well, it's not teaching, that's for certain. This is more . . . research.'

'I'm glad you're doing something different, Henry. You need to.'

'I wish you wouldn't call me Henry, Henry. It's so confusing.'

115

Henry thought for a moment and then, as if it was the first time it had occurred to him, said:

'You know what else you should do, Henry? Find yourself a good woman. And do it right this time. You must learn to do things properly. Find a good woman and settle down. Get a finger, put a ring on it, that's what I say. You're always letting the good ones go. Remember what happened in '89 with that little brunette from Greece? Or was it Turkey? The one that walked a bit like a goose. She *really* loved you.'

'You say the stupidest things.'

'Once the ring is on though, that's when the hard work starts. You need to make her feel special, attractive, loved, needed, show her you respect her – don't fuck around. Treat her good and she'll never leave you.'

'This is irrelevant. I still owe the last one enough to keep me in debt till the end of my life . . . and the one before nearly bankrupted me in the courts for cheating . . . Marriage has been my downfall. How can you say I should jump into another one? . . . And anyway, there isn't anyone.'

'There will be, there always is. And when she comes along, you'll remember what I said. Look at my Beryl . . .'

Henry always returned to the topic of my love life and, eventually, Beryl, whatever the original conversation. His enthusiasm for her was tireless.

'Look at my Beryl. There's a fine woman! Rich, intelligent, good cook, marvellous lover, plenty of meat on the bones, what more could a man ask for? *That's* what you want. The local paper has a "Looking for Love" section. Get yours in, mix it with the young folk.'

I remembered Nathan and Rachel upstairs, and Arabella, and shuddered.

'Henry, it's too early in the morning to be thinking about that. And I'm too old to go "Looking for Love". What is there left to advertise?'

'You always have a reason not to act. Fuck you.'

The echo of Henry's 'Fuck you' resonated in the receiver

for a second and I was left listening to the sounds of early morning Jerusalem once again while he chewed, waiting for an apology. Our conversations were often punctuated by these lengthy silences, telephone face-offs, where each waited for the other to speak first. Several seconds passed. The tiredness was returning. Rachel might well still be upstairs riding Nathan again; I imagined she liked it in the morning, all sleepy.

'I'm starting to have senior moments,' I said.

'No such thing, Henry. You just need to exercise your brain more. Think of Verdi!'

'Verdi? Look . . . Evelyn's been sending me letters.'

'How do you mean?'

'Since she died. Letters have been arriving. In the post. Every morning. I'm scared another one's going to come in a few hours.'

His tone changed immediately.

'Hmm, I see. Well, my plane gets into Manchester about seven tonight. If everything's on time, I'll be round for nineish. Don't do anything stupid.'

And then he was gone, without a goodbye, as if he suddenly had to be elsewhere. As Henry put the phone down and the noise of the hustle and bustle of early morning Jerusalem disappeared, I noticed the sun was almost up, just a small crescent still hiding below the hedge in the back garden, bright rays shining through it. Wife Number Two said I had no appreciation of nature; at the time she was right, but that's changing. I'm seeing more, sometimes. I looked idly at the phone for a few seconds as if my old friend were still on it. Henry never gave up on me, or never gave up on trying to change me. As I thought this, Lucille's tiny frame appeared shyly round the door, hair fuzzy, eyes half closed. She was not pleased.

'Why are you up? You woke me.'

'I couldn't sleep, so I phoned Henry.'

'You were being very noisy. Are you going back to bed?'

'Not yet. It's pretty in the garden at this time in the morning, don't you think? The willows seem sadder every year.'

Lucille had little interest in the willows, sharing Evelyn's view that they were a mistake that it was too late to correct. Oak trees would have been better. She scanned the view dismissively, pale face contorted in disapproval, thin lips pursed.

'I don't think much of it round here. I'd rather have been born in Ancient Greece or Egypt. That would have been cool.'

She rubbed her eyes.

'What were you talking to Uncle Henry about?'

'Nothing. Why?'

'He does some bad things, you know. We were talking about his business after you'd gone yesterday. I told him I didn't think it was right.'

'Oh yes? And how did he respond to that?'

'You know Uncle Henry. He didn't care.'

Lucille was more awake now. She bounced onto the other chair, crossed her thin legs and pulled her nightie down over her knees.

'Can I sit with you?'

'Always.'

'Granny Evelyn says hello.'

'That's interesting. Anything else?'

'She just said to say "Hi", and not to worry. She mainly talks about herself these days, or the government. She's not very happy.'

'That doesn't surprise me. Send her my love.'

'But she's changing, for the better I think. She's even being nicer about you. She wondered if you had any message for her.'

I tried to remain calm and make the letters seem as unimportant as possible.

'Well, she's been leaving me letters,' I said, trying to make it sound fun. 'There was one left out in her room the other day, and now there have been two through the post. You could ask her why she's doing that, if you like. I'd love to know.'

Lucille didn't seem surprised by this revelation.

'Well, of course I don't know,' she said, 'but I'm happy to ask her anything you like . . . We talk a lot.'

'Thanks.'

Lucille's accomplished adult behaviour was unsettling. Despite her games, in conversation she no longer seemed to be a girl speaking in adult language but a small adult, sharper than most, unafraid of confrontation. Things had changed even since Sunday's service, like she had realised something that could not be unrealised and could not go back. There was a brief gap while my eyes returned to the swaying willows Evelyn had planted half a century ago, which now spread wide over the garden. Lucille considered my last remark. She was not like a fourteen-year-old at all, but then she had never really been treated like one.

'What are you doing in the morning?' I asked her.

'Nothing, stupid. I can't go to school, remember?'

'Well then. I'll take you for a drink and you can tell me what you think, decode the letters for yourself.'

She nodded her head firmly.

'I like a challenge.'

'Great. I'll get you up at normal school time then. Does Dad know what happened yet?'

'No.'

'Let's keep it that way. We can get another couple of hours sleep if we go to bed now.'

She rubbed her eyes again, harder this time, exactly like Nathan used to when he was her age. We had all neglected Lucille for so long.

'Arabella called to speak to you yesterday,' I lied, as we climbed the stairs. 'She says she'll be home soon and not to worry.'

'Arabella would never say that.'

I thought quickly.

'Well then, she must be changing too. Because that's what she said.'

119

Once back in my bed, I reached for the same book I had translated for Lucille on Sunday night and read for a few minutes, not really taking anything in, just enjoying letting my eyes drift in patterns across the page. I enjoyed taking in the German, a brief passage about Hitler dancing like a small child after hearing about the capitulation of France, and wondered what it might be like to live in dramatic times. We take our cues from smaller things these days. Henry complains there are no real tests any more, of friendship, character, strength, to determine the good men from the bad, the worthy from the worthless. I envied the hunted German aristocrats of this world and lay awake for a long time romanticising their lives before finally falling heavily asleep. Instead of me waking Lucille, it was the other way round.

'Post!' she said. 'I got a postcard from Arabella, the rest is for you.'

She dropped a package and four letters on my lap: a reminder from the doctor about my hospital appointment for Friday morning, another, sterner demand for my signature from Wife Number Three's solicitors, a fourth letter from Evelyn, and a final reminder from one of the debt-collection companies urging me to call them about four months' worth of outstanding payments. Inside the package was my wallet and a note from Lenny:

Dear Abe,
    Found this after you left tonight, so we thought we'd drop it round. See you Thursday! The service starts at seven-thirty. Directions are in your wallet, if you need them.
    Best wishes,
    Lenny

I sat up, drowsy. Checking all the compartments, I saw that nothing had been stolen, but somehow felt cheated into going to something I hadn't really agreed to. Or had I? Surely the Jews would be fine without me. They'd survived thousands of years of persecution, multiplied to greater numbers than ever before, defied Hitler – more, they'd even learnt to persecute others! They certainly didn't need me to go to synagogue so early on a Thursday morning to listen to a boy pretend to turn into a man. Besides, I had other things to attend to. I dismissed Lucille from the room, dressed grumpily and stomped downstairs, where Rachel and my son were enjoying a continental breakfast in Nathan and Arabella's matching dressing gowns, seemingly unashamed.

'Dad,' said Nathan, 'this is Rachel.'

We shook hands, Rachel's sitting limply in mine before withdrawing as soon as it was polite. She was holding her red and swollen ankle softly with one hand and pressing an ice pack to the other side of it.

'Rachel's a colleague, from Child Psychology. she's going to be staying for a few days. In Granny's room.'

'Are you all right?' I asked.

'I'm fine,' she said curtly, wincing at the pain. 'I tripped on my way out of the bathroom.'

'Well, it's been nice to meet you. I'm just taking Lucille to school, so we'll see you both later.'

I snatched Lucille's hand, picked up her schoolbag on the way out and dragged her outside, Nathan's voice cheerful in the distance.

''Bye, sweetheart! Have a good day!'

16

Emporium

Lucille and I walked to the car, a tired old thing Wife Number Three had left on the drive when she moved out but was now trying to claw back from me, along with everything else I ever called mine. We got in, belted up quickly and sped away in the direction of Lucille's old school, cutting through a couple of side streets once we were out of sight and heading for a café close by once it was safe. Lucille was sulking, but the sight of Rachel at my kitchen table massaging her swollen foot had left me strangely chipper. I wound down my window and popped in a tape, *I Love 1957*, my favourite, and tapped along to 'All Shook Up' on the steering wheel, shaking my legs like Elvis on the accelerator and clutch, making the car jolt a little.

'Who was that woman?' asked Lucille.

'She works with your dad.'

She pursed her lips, unimpressed.

'Dad doesn't *go* to work any more. *Nobody* works in our family. Arabella will be home soon. She can't stay.'

I nodded weakly.

In time Lucille settled a little. She started singing along to the music and wound her window down too, resting her elbows on the ledge. She enjoyed watching all we went past on the roads, taking everything in; like a computer mathematically processing information, her brain was always whirring. Watching people fascinated her – their movements, behaviour, interaction. She clocked it all and stored it. Despite all that conspired to dismantle her, and some strangely childish habits – the teddies, the prayers, the bedtime stories – she was somehow becoming a remarkable young woman: principled, admirable, apparently unaffected by the dismal example set by the adults around her. We stopped at a set of traffic lights. All four of Evelyn's notes sat in my back pocket awaiting examination. Lucille, who was playing with her new mobile, broke into a mischievous grin and, without looking up, said:

'I put a brick outside the bathroom door this morning. That'll teach her.'

The lights changed to green and we moved off.

Soon we pulled over outside our destination, wheels groaning at the abrupt halt, and Lucille dashed eagerly off to the toilet to get out of her uniform while I parked the car, which still smelt of the menthol cigarettes Wife Number Three chain-smoked while driving; smoking, she had said, was her slow revenge on my lungs. She really hated me. In all my years dealing with women I had learnt nothing, it seemed, about keeping them happy.

I slotted the car neatly into a small space, locked up and crossed the road, keys jangling in my pocket and the smell of freshly brewed morning coffee wafting onto the doorstep welcoming me in. Emporium was quiet, the young people behind the counter still yawning their way bleary-eyed into the day, twisting and clanking the coffee machine on autopilot.

'Good morning,' I said cheerily to the young man at the counter. 'Heavy night? You don't seem to need as much sleep at my age . . .'

He looked at me disapprovingly; I smiled.

'Though I do sometimes nap in the afternoons. And every so often I have a small one early evening as well. Two coffees please, and a slice of fruit cake.'

The cost rang up on the till. He shook his head in amazement.

I put the coins into his cupped hands and waited for our drinks, hands in pockets, watching people going past on the street outside through Emporium's large windows. Everyone seemed to be in such a rush, desperately trying to cram everything they needed to do into the short day. But days were long for me; only four had passed since the service for Evelyn. Easter decorations were appearing everywhere now, the windows of shops stacked high with chocolate eggs and pictures of bunny rabbits. From where I stood the display in the charity shop across the road was clearly visible, Gilda on her knees sticking something to the glass. I collected the order, found a small booth by a window and sat down. Behind me, the counter assistant seemed to be waking up. He turned to a colleague and laughed.

'Did you hear what that crazy old guy just said? When I get like that, I hope they shoot me.'

'Like what?'

'I don't know. Just . . . *desperate* looking.'

'You're desperate looking *now*.'

They laughed.

'You're such a loser,' one said.

I took out my mother's letters and laid them out on the table.

When Lucille returned she scanned the room before sitting down, searching amongst the morning's coffee drinkers for undercover agents who might be spying on our meeting and taking in every last facet of the people around us. She loved the detail. A businesswoman reading the paper, a young man writing on a laptop, a mother and two young children, one in a pram, one's legs swinging from the high seat. All very suspicious. I don't notice much. It eats up all my concentration to focus on one thing, but with Lucille it's often a struggle to get her to keep looking at me when we're together; too much else is interesting.

'Here you go.' She took out a glitter-soaked notebook and pink pen from out of her bag. 'You can take notes.'

As she summoned me to attention, tapping a teaspoon on the side of my coffee cup like a miniature version of Henry, I wondered how normal fourteen-year-olds behaved; where her friends were, if she had any; if she had a boyfriend yet, or even wanted one. What *are* fourteen-year-olds like? I tried to remember how Nathan used to be. Sporty, popular, normal. Hardly ever at home. I wanted to kick Lucille onto a pitch somewhere, throw a ball after her. She moved the coffee cups to one side of the table to make writing space for me, placing the tiny pink mobile Henry had bought her carefully down next to the drinks. I'd left my new brick at home.

'Don't you want your coffee?' I asked. 'It's going cold.'

Lucille shrugged.

'Cake?'

She gave another dismissive spasm of the shoulders, dragged her hair back with both hands in a business-like fashion and tied the loose strands together in a ponytail. I pulled the cake over to my side.

'Now, down to business,' she said. 'Tell me about these let-ters.'

'Well, at first they just warned there was more to come, telling me to do something with my life and saying every-thing was about to be explained. But she seems to be talking about herself, not me. The last letter said she was born in Berlin . . . I thought she was Israeli. How could she have hid-den that from me for so long? Is she lying now or was she lying before?'

It was easiest to keep things business-like, talk calmly, function as if this was all normal. If I lost control there was a fair chance I might not get it back. Lucille rubbed her chin, thumb and forefinger spread fanwise, preferring a question of her own to mine.

'What do you think these notes are leading to?'

'I hadn't really thought about that. I was waiting to be told.'

She gestured to the pad. I wrote down: 'WAIT TO BE TOLD.'

The little detective tutted several times under her breath.

'Do you think Granny Evelyn had many secrets like this?'

'Hundreds, I imagine. And if they're all that dramatic, I'm not sure if I want to hear them.'

'SECRETS,' I wrote, urged on by a pointing Lucille.

'Then there are going to be more clues,' she said, very definitely.

Lucille linked her hands together, tapping one finger on the table, deep in thought.

'Who do you think is sending them?' I said.

'Granny Evelyn, of course!'

'But Granny is dead.'

'EVELYN DEAD,' I wrote.

Lucille was now doing something with her phone while talking, tapping away rapidly on the keys. Children understand new technology so quickly.

'How else do you explain it?' she replied, eyes still fixed on the phone. 'Whose handwriting are they in?'

'Granny Evelyn's . . .'

'And who do they sound like?'

'Granny Evelyn . . .'

'And where did you find them?'

'The first one was in her room, but that doesn't mean . . .'

'Be like Sherlock Holmes, Grandpa. *Eliminate the impossible.*'

I wrote down: 'BE LIKE HOLMES. IMPOSSIBLE.'

Lucille continued to play absent-mindedly with the keys, while I took another sip of the coffee, cooler now, munching on cake while trying to think of an answer. There was none.

'Give them to me then,' she said bossily.

I handed over the first three envelopes but held back the unopened one.

'I've not seen this yet. Let me read it first.'

She was not upset: there was plenty to concentrate on without it. Before opening them she studied the envelopes carefully, checked the handwriting on the address close-up and even inspected the postmark. Locally posted, each time a day before arrival.

'Hmm, very interesting,' she said.

Lucille was often fascinated as she read the letters, but sometimes she could seem completely disinterested. She seemed to flip between the two responses. Neither was she shocked by things that left me reeling.

I tossed the newest letter from hand to hand a few times, rubbing the red wax seal a little, wondering whether there was anything left my mother could say to shock or upset me. I opened the letter, forcing through the fat paper of the envelope with the end of a teaspoon, sloppily removing the sheaf from its container. Evelyn's handwriting was definitely getting worse; her usually round, ultra-clear shapes now looked more like something from a doctor's scrawled prescription note. More like my handwriting, actually. Since dying, her high standards had dropped. Across the table, Lucille said, 'I see,' and 'Oh!' and 'Well, well, well.' I read the new letter, sinking further down into the seat with each sentence.

Hello, Avraham, are you still there? – Good.
You are doing well.
This is the story of my journey.
My parents were strangely, quietly respectful of my wishes to abandon them. They were, perhaps, too ashamed to admit to themselves what their daughter was becoming. Perhaps they didn't care or knew they could not stop me. What parent can prevent their child from running away if they really want to? I was twenty-three in 1933 when I started to regularly meet other young communists, some of whom were preparing to escape Germany. They showed me underground newspapers, which I devoured, and filled my head with politics. They made me really believe that you could make a difference in the world; it took me a lifetime to realise how untrue that really is. Sometimes I still forget. I listened in while others talked of great times to come, and though things actually seemed to be getting worse, the excitement of hoping was enough for me, at least for the time being. Some of these people were Jews, one or two were Zionists, and I thought that by following them all my problems would be solved.

127

Shortly before I left, my father was stripped of his job, but nobody tried to do anything about it. My family stayed at home waiting for the next disaster, and, unable to respect them, I stomped around sulkily, plotting my escape. The opposite of the nervous young Jews around me, I was avoided by many, cast out for not being ashamed. Some people I knew prayed for better times, some joined what resistance there was, but none of that was enough for me. I left in the middle of the night at the end of 1933 for Israel, leaving a note urging my parents to follow me as soon as possible, though I knew they never would; that would have involved packing a suitcase properly, which my mother would have taken until the end of the war to do. My boyfriend at the time offered to join me on my journey, but he was only a child himself, and I did not love him, so I refused. Instead, I let him accompany me to the border, from where I ran away to a kibbutz on the outskirts of Jerusalem with two others from Berlin. I grew up quickly; I had to, unlike you, hanging onto my money and good will for as long as possible. When I got there I was exhausted, confused and lonely. Sometimes I think that journey, across land and sea, running from my home and family to an unknown future, punctured me for life.

I looked up to see Lucille busily taking notes on the detail of the first three letters. Her help made it all a game. It was almost as if Evelyn wasn't really talking about us; I was reading about somebody else's life, about some poor soul who had to read a letter in a coffee shop just to find out who his dead mother really was, because she didn't know how to tell him while she was alive. Perhaps she'd thought he wouldn't believe her or would hate her for keeping so much hidden for so long. I read on, feeling sad for the man in the coffee shop, but with each new shock it delivered I recognised less of myself in him.

The kibbutz was on the outskirts of the city. When I arrived, new members were still welcomed enthusiastically and I was popular because I worked hard, questioned nothing and had no ties to the outside world. Also, few were jaded enough yet to resent the naivety of new arrivals. The place was truly international and still so when you were born (which is why so many people spoke English), and this excited me, as I had only met a few people from outside Berlin before. I thought I had won in life already. Why were people fighting each other when it was so easy to live in harmony? We shared everything: clothes, food, partners, living quarters, we ate in the dining room for every meal. It was a completely different life, one that has now failed so spectacularly it's odd to try and describe it at all to you now. It wasn't always Thai workers in toy factories making bears for American children, you know. I went to Israel to escape Germany, but I was also running towards something. I didn't want to be part of the next generation of dentists, lawyers, doctors and officials that the next generation of Nazis would want to eliminate all over again. I wanted to be part of something far more ambitious, a new world where Jews were strong, had a homeland and weren't just visitors in somebody else's country, dependent on their reluctant hospitality – a place where we could set an example to everyone else by showing them what Jews could do when given a chance. Idealism wasn't laughed at so much in those days. Now, it is dead. For me, kibbutz life was not about picking fruit, which I hated; it was about creating a little universe of equal people who chose something other than greed. That seems ridiculous now. I only realise how long I have lived and how much the world has changed when I think about how that last sentence might sound to Lucille.

And there Evelyn stopped suddenly, mid-flow, yet again.

She had splurged and was done, for now, dropping me into her mysterious world for three pages and then jolting me back out of it.

For a few seconds I sat perfectly still, eyes staring at my mother's letter. The longer I looked at it the more the words became fuzzy, the letters dancing round the page teasingly, not really letters or words at all any more. I tried to picture her in bed writing it, but couldn't. Some days she could hardly raise her head, too weak to even speak. Some days she didn't seem to move at all. When had she had the strength to do this? It must have been a while ago, when she was still writing letters, keeping the door locked so we couldn't disturb whatever it was she called her business correspondence. Never have I known a nonagenarian get so much post.

On Lucille's paper in front of me were the words: WAIT TO BE TOLD SECRETS EVELYN DEAD BE LIKE HOLMES IMPOSSIBLE. I read them a few times in the hope they would begin to mean something, perhaps rearrange in front of me and make sense, but of course they did not.

Lucille was standing by the entrance to Emporium, whispering to a boy in school uniform. He said something, and she giggled. He said something else. He held her hand; she pulled it away, looking round for me. I finished my coffee and cake, stuffed the letter into my jacket pocket and approached the two of them casually. It was the same boy from the hall on Monday. Why wasn't he at school? When he saw me he ran out of the shop and across the road without saying goodbye to Lucille, just as she had done last time.

'We have to go,' she said urgently, taking my hand and dragging me towards the door.

'Do you two always run away from each other so suddenly?'

'That's what he does.'

'Who is he?'

'Nobody.'

I put my arm round her and lead her over the road, but she wrestled free.

'So what did you make of the letters?'

Lucille frowned.

'Well, there are definitely clues, but it looks like Granny plans to explain everything anyway, in the end. She's just getting round to the point in her own way . . .'

On the way back to the car I was beginning to feel a little uneasy, but cold fresh air and Ventolin cleared up most of the temporary sickness I felt after reading about Evelyn's fantastic journey. How strange bodies are, how unpredictable. Sometimes I felt I could live for a hundred years. Sometimes it was more like minutes. It made me think about my own journey: where I wanted to be, if I wanted to make one at all. If I was going to, I should probably know why I was doing it.

As we walked Lucille and I discussed the school search. She told me there were a couple of places she was interested in that Uncle Henry was writing to this week on her behalf. She knew what was coming.

'It's time we told your dad about what happened at school,' I said, putting an arm back round her shoulder. 'Let's go home and do it now.'

'Fine,' she replied, 'but first I want to get changed back into school uniform. He'll be more annoyed if he thinks we've hidden it from him. We have to pretend it all happened today. Promise you will?'

'OK, I promise,' I said reluctantly, hand on heart. 'The events of Monday morning will be transported for ever to Wednesday, from this day forth.'

I felt like Henry. I unlocked my side and got in the car, my door still open, she waiting outside hers. Then, as I leant over to open her side, she said casually:

'Why don't you and Dad talk to each other?'

'We do. Don't be ridiculous.'

The door unlocked. She opened it and got in.

'Are you annoyed with him about something?'

'Of course not.'

'He doesn't talk much at all, does he? Why is that?'

'Be gentle with him. Things will be back to normal soon.'

'There's no such thing as normal,' said Lucille bitterly.

We belted up and drove back home in silence, Lucille back to worrying about telling her father about what had happened at school, and me wondering, as usual, not whether I had missed something, but how much I had missed.

17

No Questions

When we got home, Nathan and Rachel weren't there, so for now there was to be no confession. But Lucille wasn't thinking of that any more. She sped past me and went to check all the rooms, returning downcast, but it wasn't until she looked up at me sadly and said, 'Still not back,' with tears in her eyes, that I even realised what she was looking for. We hugged. I should have been praying for Arabella's return as much as she was; my selfishness took me by surprise.

'I'm sorry,' I said softly. 'Soon. Soon.'

As I spoke, I was surprised to find myself so angry, not just with me but with Arabella too, for leaving Lucille when she needed her so much; also with Nathan, for thinking of himself before his beautiful daughter and what all this would do to her; even with Rachel, for treading so clumsily over everything, for assuming it would all be fine, for moving from father to son without a thought. Lucille pulled away from me and went upstairs.

I looked around at the hallway, which was a mess; the kitchen too. Nathan and Rachel's breakfast plates were still on the table, their half-full glasses near discarded dressing gowns, both lying on the floor. Even a few coffee cups and sandwich plates left over from the service still lingered, unwanted. Nothing had been done, and this annoyed me even more. I pulled open the fridge door looking for something to drink but found nothing – just some butter, half a pint of out-of-date milk, one last, lonely sausage and some shrivelled vegetables Arabella had bought last week. Someone would have to go shopping. I wished I hadn't wasted yesterday's breakfast, which now lay splattered over the insides of the bin. We were never out of whisky though. I poured a small one, opened the conservatory doors and stepped outside, trying to calm myself and think of other things, anything but the rapid, almost comical collapse of my family.

Though it was still only April, you could already smell the promise of summer coming in the newly born spring leaves. I circled the sad and overgrown garden, pushing the drooping willow branches left and right, peeping through the old gap in the hedge that looked out onto the road. Perhaps I could do a little work in the garden with this new-found time off. Wife Number One often tried to usher me into hobbies – gardening, cycling, football – and I always ignored her. I quite fancy all of those things now. There was probably a bike out the back somewhere, perhaps in the shed, rusting. Maybe I would go and get it later. At the top of the sloping garden I sat on a bench with a moat-like rock garden surrounding it that Wife Number One had put in herself, the tiny stones so smooth, light in colour and so tightly packed together that from a distance they looked like water. Again I saw the gap in the hedge and thought with fondness of the first time I saw her walk past. She never said much to anyone but had a naive happiness about her, even then, that I found fascinating. Trotting along at the back of the family queue in her ill-fitting, stuffy Shabbat clothes, she seemed utterly unaware of anything, and I liked this. That's how I felt sometimes too. And besides, even then I enjoyed watching girls doing nothing much.

I sipped my drink, the blocks of ice now tiny clear blobs in the black, and stretched my legs and arms, feeling strangely weak again. My body seemed sapped of all strength, my chest reluctant to breathe deeply or easily. Getting up seemed impossible. One day I would die in this house. The old metallic-dial radio sat beside me and Gilda's Bible was still in my inside pocket. As the radio was slightly out of reach I took out the Bible instead, randomly picking a page. It fell open at 1 Corinthians 7, Paul's first letter: 'Questions about Marriage'.

7:8 Now to the unmarried and to the widows I say that it would be better for you to live alone as I do.

I arched an eyebrow.

7:9 But if you cannot restrain your desires, go ahead and marry – it is better to marry than to burn with passion.

I put it back in my pocket and leant over stiffly towards the radio instead, flipping on the old rusty switch. A harp plucked softly and sweetly. A choir sang.

In death's dark vale I fear no ill
With thee the Lord beside me . . .

I changed the station.

'– It was long after proving my parents innocent in the High Court that I became a lawyer. I went into the circus as a trapeze artist first – that had always been my dream. Now I spend most of my time with the family or in the farmhouse I built on our land.

'– That must be very satisfying . . .

'– Oh, it is, it is.'

And again.

'. . . the War on Terror is going into a new phase. The search for weapons of mass distraction, sorry destruction will be stepped up, and . . .'

Listening was exhausting. I fell asleep with one hand on the dial and the other around my glass, the kettle whistling in the background.

It was funny how easy it had become just to fall out of consciousness these days. I dreamt about Shmuel, finding me tattered and torn on the side of the road, picking me up and taking me home for repair on his bike. That dream then descended into an eerily powerful fantasy in which all my wives featured: each one was taken away from me at the moment I was about to reach out for them by a smiling Shmuel, who was riding his bike away from me and into the sky, the wife in question dangling off the back of his baker's cycle. I see all my wives in my sleep. My nightmares are cluttered with images of them – the ways I cheated on them all, how they left me, what they have left behind. They are a constant, endless source of guilt.

When I woke, Rachel was turning the radio off and gently taking my hand off the dial, smiling sweetly in a pair of Arabella's old jeans and one of Nathan's woolly jumpers. I growled at first but couldn't pretend to be angry at her. Somehow, I wasn't. She sat down on the bench between me and the radio and linked her arm through mine, her slender fingers wrapping themselves round my forearm, warming it.

'Where's Nathan?' I asked.

'He's just got in the shower.'

We sat awkwardly for a few seconds. Rachel tried to catch my eye.

'The garden is beautiful here, Abe. The willows are a cred-it to you.'

She shuffled round to face me. No answer.

'I'm learning to appreciate nature more now. It's that pub. It makes you really need the fresh air more.'

I waited, watched for a moment, and then asked coldly:

'Do you always respond to being stood up like that?'

But Rachel was not riled. She was calm, unruffled, polite.

'You sound very offended, Abe, but you changed history yourself by not turning up. It was you, not me, in the wrong.'

She stopped, lowered her tone, and only now was apolo-getic.

'This is going to make life complicated for you, Abe, and I'm sorry, but I have fallen in love with Nathan.'

'How sure can you be after one day?' I asked dully.

'Oh, very sure. Very sure indeed.'

'I see,' I replied, without seeing.

Suddenly Rachel seemed a lot more dignified. Something about her that before had struck me as shallowness now seemed to be a kind of depth, just one I didn't understand. She sat upright, proud and sincere, the setting sun shining dimly behind her shoulders, as if her love for Nathan were the most natural, honourable development imaginable. And so I tried to accept it.

'How did it happen?'

'He opened the door – that's all.'

'He didn't ask who you were here to see? Why you were dressed for an evening in the country? Why your overnight bag was already sitting in the hall?'

'I think he just thought his prayers had been answered. He didn't want to know all that. You don't mind, do you? You didn't plan to marry me?'

'What if I said I did?'

Rachel laughed uncertainly.

'Then I'd know you were a liar,' she said finally. 'You don't want to get married again. It's obvious.'

Her scent, which I had found potent so recently, was strong, the smell drifting slowly over towards me in the cool late-afternoon air and lingering there. She too had recently showered; hair still wet, skin damp. She wanted to talk about Nathan, but I still wanted to talk about myself.

'Why does an attractive young woman like you spend her break from work in the back of a car with a sixty-one-year-old man?'

'Sometimes women just want to have sex, Abe. They don't necessarily feel bad about it afterwards, and that doesn't make them whores or weak or dirty. Can you understand that?'

'Yes, but why with an old man like me?'

'Stop talking about your age. You aren't that old. It's pathetic.'

'I know, it's just . . . I've been a young man all my life. It's hard to get used to something else.'

I paused, feeling stupid.

'What about the morning after? Why did you come round like that?'

'I was horny. And you'd left your wallet behind. Then, I was a single person who needed a place to stay that was better than the couch at The King's Arms. Single people can do as they please . . . within reason. Can't they?'

She smiled cheekily.

'That was it?'

'That was it.'

'Most people would find that hard to believe. I'm always losing that wallet, though. Thanks.'

'It's OK. You've already thanked me.'

There was another, more natural pause in the conversation while we looked at each other. The sun showed up freckles on her nose I'd not noticed before, her cheeks a vibrant ruby red. I wished we had spent more time looking, but then remembered abruptly that we didn't know each other at all, it only felt like it.

'What about you?' she said. 'Do you always pick up barmaids like that?'

'Not usually so easily.'

'I'd be interested to know what you go for.'

Wives and mistresses flashed through my mind. Nathan's mother stood out far above the rest; in a way, the garden still belonged to her, though I had driven her from it.

'I always liked women to be different from each other. It was the different *smells*, the *feel* of women, that's what did it for me. Different *flavours*. It has been my downfall.'

'And is that still how it is?'

'No. Now, I give up. I'm going to try God or Jesus instead. They say once you're hooked, you never want to change flavour.'

Rachel laughed and stood up, ready to leave.

'That's very profound,' she said, and smiled. I grabbed her arm.

'I disagree. Look, if you want money, there isn't any, it's all gone. All my mother left behind went to Lucille, apart from the house, and nobody can touch that unless I agree. You'd be a lot happier if you left and never came back. Nathan is . . . not well. He just acts as if he is. And then there's Arabella . . . you won't know about her.'

'He's told me.'

'He told you everything? In a single night?'

'Sometimes remarkable things happen.'

'They're still hard to understand.'

Rachel bent down, kissed me on the cheek and then on the lips.

'You need to be looked after, Abe. You know that?'

I shook my head, looking idly into the glass I was still holding to avoid her gaze.

'You are very wrong.'

'I mean it,' she said, now stroking my head.

I looked back up.

'You should meet my friend Henry. You two would get on.'

'It's going to be OK, Abe, I promise.'

'What is?'

Rachel kissed me again warmly and I found myself kissing back. Her mouth was dry from the cold, but soft too. She had thin lips, like all my wives; it was always the mistresses that had full lips. We stopped kissing but were still almost touching.

'What brought you here?' I whispered.

'My husband left me for a younger woman with three children; you walked into the pub, face crying, "Rescue me." You were late so I met Nathan. And here I am, pulling pints and destroying other people's families.'

We smiled sadly. Her voice was so quiet it was almost silent.

'That's all there is to it. Sometimes things really are simple.'

'Not that simple. Child psychology? What about that?'

'Oh . . . yes, that was weak. Nathan needs a little coaching.'

At this she cheered slightly. I began to feel dizzy and had to lean away, trying to laugh it off but holding her arm to steady me.

'I'm just tired,' I lied, lines from Evelyn's letters dancing in front of me and her voice in my ear. 'It's nothing.'

Rachel looked on, concerned, like a vet inspecting a sick dog. She stroked my head some more, and with each stroke my eyelids became heavier. I enjoyed the hand being there, so soothing. It was hard to imagine anything but the touch of a woman being as comforting.

'Sleep now. When you wake up, we'll eat.'

'Hmm,' I said, 'steak would be nice,' and passed out again.

I woke briefly as she and Nathan were putting me into bed, but quickly passed out once more. This time a giant Shmuel was carrying me in his big arms, high up above the clouds, over the seas to Jerusalem, and laying me down on a kibbutz doorstep. Everything made sense. There were no questions.

18

Occupying a Sleeping Mind

When I came round properly I was in old man's pyjamas, Nathan and Lucille standing round the bed looking concerned. Rachel was gently dabbing my nose, which had been bleeding again. Looking down it at her, for a moment she looked a little like an older Arabella. Everyone was turning into everyone else.

'Do you think he'll eat?' Rachel was saying to Nathan.

'Maybe tomorrow. Not now.'

'Arabella, I'm OK,' I said quietly. 'I'll eat.'

Rachel smiled; I realised my mistake.

'We ate a while ago,' she said gently, 'but there's plenty left downstairs.'

She left to get my dinner.

'Isn't it nice of *Rachel* to look after you, Dad? You remember *Rachel*, right?'

'Mmm,' I said quietly, still dizzy, unaware. 'Too good to be true. I don't trust her.'

Nathan turned to Lucille for support.

'Isn't it nice? Isn't it lovely?'

But Lucille didn't feel like she had to reply. Even I could see how much it was all hurting her. A wave of rage visited me briefly but was, as usual, gone before it had even really made itself known. Lucille winked at me but left the room without saying anything to her father. He and I were alone.

There was something different about Nathan, who stood by the door, looking down at me with his arms crossed. His eyes were surer than I'd come to know them recently, his manner more patronising. He was more confident again, and, I was conscious enough to be able to wonder whether Nathan's meditation sessions had gone the same way as the doubt. Arabella, who left him in his hour of need, had been cast aside like a gooey tissue and had, so easily, so quickly, been replaced. If she'd have arrived back only a few days after her departure, as we hoped she might, she would most probably have found her husband and Rachel curled up by the fire with a video and a curry, as if it was what they had done every weekend for a decade. If she was coming back she would get quite a shock. But why would she? Evelyn would have been proud of her grand, ambiguous departure. We were entitled to no clues. I beckoned Nathan over to the bed and, as he sat down on the edge of it, pulled him towards me.

'I promised Arabella I'd see you got work,' I said, forcing each word out slowly. 'And help.'

But now my vow was as ridiculous as the mention of her name.

'I *have* a job,' said Nathan flippantly. 'I'm starting back at work; everything's going to be OK. There's going to be money again.'

A hand came to rest on mine. I'd started noticing that a lot recently.

'Really? You had the hearing? Good. We'll both be working boys then,' I said. 'I have a job now too, a new one. I start tomorrow.'

'Of course you do.'

I glanced down at my white, wavering hands and noticed there was no watch on them.

'What time is it?'

'Don't worry about that. You're not going anywhere.'

He patted my wrist. I wanted to smash him.

'Nathan, what's happening in my home?'

'Things are changing, Dad. You can't stop it, or go back.'

'But is change always right? What if things were good before? What if they don't need to change?'

'But they did, Dad. And they have. Things are better now.'

As Rachel arrived with dinner he stopped talking and tucked my sheets under the mattress. Rachel put the meal on my bedside table and they both left me to eat.

'My God,' I heard Nathan say on the way downstairs, 'not again.'

'It's OK,' said Rachel, 'I'm here.'

I called down the stairs:

'Rachel?'

'Yes?'

'Can you tell me the time, please?'

'The time? Sure, it's eight-thirty. Now *eat*.'

I touched my left nostril and found it was steadily dripping blood onto my pyjamas again, a dark red pool spreading slowly around the centre-left of my chest. I blocked it with tissue and ate. The food was good but I left most of it on the plate – the steak was too heavy for my delicate stomach, the potatoes too sweet and my appetite not quite what I'd thought. Somebody must have been shopping though. Perhaps the house had been tidied too. Certainly my room looked clean.

I rested a while longer in a state of half-sleep, a place where there was no Evelyn, notes or revelations, until the noise of someone knocking on the downstairs window woke me, the muffled hum of a curt exchange downstairs then filtering through the floorboards to my room. Nathan's voice was raised. This was replaced quickly by the sound of Henry bounding up the stairs. He burst in the door, put down his bag and embraced me tightly as I imagined he might if we were both about to die.

'Abe,' he said over and over, 'Abe, Abe, Abe – you're so white. What the hell's going on?'

My old friend rubbed my arms softly with his hands, and to my surprise I started shaking while he rocked me slowly, Henry's body so much bigger, broader and stronger than mine, clamped right round me like a warm vice.

'Lock the door. I don't want anyone coming in,' I said. 'They think I'm dead already, damn them.'

Henry got up, shut the door firmly and insisted I tell him everything, so I did – Rachel, Nathan, Arabella, Lucille,

143

Evelyn's notes, Gilda and Nas, Lenny and Ben, Rachel and Nathan together, and then finally Rachel again. Henry listened intently, occasionally stopping me when he could see me getting tired, sometimes insisting I drink some of the water Rachel had brought, shaking his head and nodding gravely. The only thing I didn't mention was the present Gilda had given me. For now, that was our secret.

An hour later Nathan knocked and demanded to be let in, but Henry told him no one was going in or out of that door until he said so, and that was the end of that. Nathan shuffled away without complaint.

When I was finally done I felt better, the fever subsiding a little. We sat for a while in peace. Then Henry reached into his bag and with a smile took out his marble chess set from the early seventies, which only came out on special occasions: a Hollywood special edition that to my knowledge had never left his house – Marilyn Monroe the Queen and Elvis the King, naturally. I smiled. He took out the pieces and put them on the board, which balanced perfectly on the old plastic desk on wheels I thought I'd broken in my drunken rage the other night. Perhaps we had two, or maybe I hadn't broken it at all and it had been moved from Evelyn's room to mine. Henry sat on the lower part of the bed; I sat up and moved my legs to one side so he had space to sit. We set up in silence as we had done a thousand times before and I prepared to be beaten, as always. For me, there was as much enjoyment in setting up and anticipating the game as there was in playing it; I never got any better. For him the joy was in winning. Henry's voice sounded unusually desperate as yet another hand rested on mine and squeezed.

'There is no doubt in my mind that next time you won't just pass out. You will perish. You are lonely and scared, I know. I'm afraid it may kill you.'

I wanted to say I didn't feel lonely or scared, and that I didn't know you could die from loneliness, but thought it best not to. Perhaps in the end that's what had finally killed

Evelyn off. Not the overdose, not the bitterness, but simple, awful loneliness.

'White or black?' I asked.

'Black, always black.'

We played at a leisurely pace, chatting easily between moves. I came closer than usual this time, but James Dean got me in checkmate. Only afterwards did I realise I could have avoided it by making a different penultimate move. I toppled a marble Elvis and we shook hands: it was getting late and I needed to sleep.

'I'll call again tomorrow morning,' he said as we happily packed away the pieces. 'For God's sake don't do anything stupid between now and then.'

'I'll try.'

'Don't just try, *promise* me you won't. I don't trust you.'

I sighed and smiled.

'I promise I won't do anything stupid.'

The last of the pieces was put away.

'Abe . . . I'm sorry I wasn't there when you needed me.'

'I should really be looking after myself. And you can't always be around.'

'I know, I know . . . Listen, ignore those letters. Don't let her ruin you like this. God only knows what's to come, but what good can it do? Think of that before you open any more.'

Henry patted my hand, smiled sadly and then made to leave. No joke, no quip. I wasn't used to it.

'Henry?' I asked, stopping him.

'Yes?'

He closed the open door and waited.

'How was Jerusalem? You never said.'

'How do you mean?'

'The place. The people. The atmosphere. Tell me, what's it like? I want to know.'

My friend indulged me, closing the door and coming back towards the bed.

'Still full of nutters, I'm afraid. The Holy City of God-Knows-Why, that's what it is. I've changed my mind; you shouldn't go – don't even waste your thoughts on it.'

'Oh, I see. And the meeting . . . did you get what you wanted from it?'

'Abe, I *always* get what I want – now shut up and get some rest. Nathan's right, you need to sleep.'

As soon as he was gone I set an alarm for the morning just in case I felt well enough to go to synagogue to see Lenny's son get called up. A good talk with Henry always made me want to get up and live, no matter what he said, and who knows how I might feel in a few hours time. From bed I heard a noise and struggled out of bed to see what it was: Henry was slipping a piece of paper under the door.

'Death is not the end for those Jesus has set free.'

I went to sleep undecided about synagogue and Jesus, but sure I would know the right thing to do when morning came. Maybe I wouldn't need to choose between them at all.

19

A Chazan Please God

Shortly before I awoke, Shmuel dropped me back home, put me into bed, tucked me in and kissed my forehead, leaving the house by the window and cycling away into the early morning. The further away he cycled the more anxious I became, reaching out for him in my mind as he turned into a full stop on the horizon. I opened my eyes, got up and staggered sleepily across the hall to the bathroom, where there was a sign waiting for me on the door:

'DAD – GO BACK TO BED.'

Even when Nathan was being caring he couldn't help being lazy. I removed the note, took off my blood-soaked pyjamas and got into a hot shower. Apart from a little light-headedness and slightly sore arms, everything seemed operational. I made a slight wave of my fingers and toes as a tester. Fine. I wasn't even tired. This was part of a familiar cycle. As soon as pain disappears, it always seems ridiculous that I or anyone else should have ever taken it so seriously. My body, if determined enough, can rapidly rid itself of whatever it pleases, and usually pleases immediately after a scare. Henry's concern and insistence on promises now seemed a needless over-reaction: the dizziness, weakness and confusion that I'd found so intoxicating last night were gone. Everyone else in the house was still in bed, the soft crash of wet stream on porcelain the only noise in the whole place. Would anyone notice if I left it? A pool of water made several large swirls around the plughole before disappearing down, only to be replaced by more.

I checked my arms, chest and legs for any damage that may have been done in the darkness, much of which is achieved in a state of aggravated half-sleep. It had been quite a good night. Evelyn had exhausted me so much I couldn't even hurt myself any more. Cuts were beginning to heal – the backs of my legs no longer so inflamed and bright red, my shins less discoloured than yesterday, the smell of cream mixed with blood less pungent, replaced now with my morning body odour, deeply musky. Even breathing was easier. I plucked the showerhead from its attachment and first slowly ran the hot water over each part of my body, holding it close to the skin, stroking the sparse and furry hairs, enjoying the prickly excitement as it moved up and down. It was perfect, and I was alone.

The instant I stepped out of the shower Evelyn's voice returned, right on cue.

'You never wash your feet when you shower. What kind of a man doesn't wash his feet in the shower? You think they're gonna clean themselves? Is that what you think? Or are they going to clean each other? Disconnect themselves from your legs, grab a bar of soap and go to work on the other one? Is that it?'

I reached for the towel and looked at myself naked in the steamed-up full-length mirror, patiently studying my body, occasionally strong, despite everything. Evelyn left me to it. I flexed my arm muscles, satisfied at the small outward bulge that appeared at my command, and wondered at the magic of the human body. Today I seemed younger than yesterday. Balding, yes, wrinkled, maybe, and certainly no longer the biker Teddy Boy that won over Wife Number One all those years ago, but still hanging in there, still going . . . and that was something. All I needed was some clean air; the short walk to the synagogue would be refreshing. I dressed in my only suit, which was still lying where it had been dumped on Sunday night, and sneaked out of the house, this time through the front door, picking up the Bible on the way out. Another piece of paper was stuck to the door handle. This time the letters were larger and more insistent:

'I SAID, GET BACK INTO BED!'

I tore it off, smirked and put it in my pocket. Nathan had completely lost it if he thought I was going to take orders from a man who had wept openly so recently about bank gremlins. Pulling the door towards me slowly and quietly on my way out, the smoky smell of The King's Arms wafted from the suit up to my nostrils, intermingling with Sunday's stale sweat and the lingering hot aroma of Rachel's perfume. Evelyn's voice might have been briefly drowned out by the stink but was certainly making up for it now, whispering in my ear as I walked, even disagreeing with me about the quickest way to get there. '*Left* out of the house? Are you insane?' As I turned left out of the driveway and onto the pavement in front of the house (I would not be persuaded otherwise), the blinds in the house opposite twitched again. Is that where she was hiding? I walked on.

I hadn't stepped inside a synagogue in the thirty years since I'd given up on Judaism, and the time I'd been a regular came rushing back to me as I arrived at the old place. When Wife Number One died I avoided Jewish people and Jewish women like I avoided anyone who had the same hairstyle as her or a similar voice, or people who worked for the same company she did. Soon that all became a distant memory, an embarrassing, failed experiment difficult to believe I had been involved in. Of course, the way she died didn't help.

'Where was her God when the number twenty-four came hurtling round the corner, eh?' Evelyn said over dinner one night, stabbing a fork at her vegetables. 'I bet that made you rethink the Almighty!'

And, of course, she was right. Wife Number One had been finally leaving me to return to her parents' house, but never got to the car on the other side of the road. As well as her head, the suitcase she had packed so hurriedly packed split on impact, scattering clothes all over the road. It's something I still see. Praying, learning Hebrew, talking about Israel almost to the complete exclusion of other topics – after that, all these things became absurd almost instantly. I did consider going to a Reform synagogue for a bar mitzvah for Nathan, but it was just too soon, and the time for it passed. Besides, Evelyn disapproved strongly. She called the Reform division of Judaism pretend Jews, and this had never left me.

'Judaism without the pain and sacrifice? What on earth is the point?'

It was one thing we agreed on.

I wheezed lightly as I approached the synagogue, weaving slowly through the few cars parked on the drive and searching my pockets in vain for an inhaler. I had none of the required accoutrements but entered anyway in hope, stepping anxiously into the decorative hallway and looking through the small window to the main room, taking in the smell as I looked around. Strangely, it drew me in. Resisting it was like resisting the inevitable. The hall was nearly empty, no more than twenty or so people in the whole building, but like at Sunday's service I noticed that most of those taking part were at least my age. This time though, I felt more comfortable in their company.

'You're plasticine,' said Evelyn.

Behind the bars of the separate gallery three women sat, one with a restless child on her knee who was disturbing the relative quiet with questions and demands. Everyone else seemed to accept this noise; nobody asked them to be quiet.

Lenny, Benjamin and family stood beaming on the front row, the tiny boy who was the centre of attention for the morning dwarfed by the adults around him, standing in a large white shawl that went down to his knees, reading solemnly from the prayer book along with everyone else. Lenny put an arm protectively around him and squeezed; a younger boy whispered something and laughed. An elderly man standing by the door smiled at me as I hovered, peering through the door.

'Are you Jewish?' he whispered.

I nodded.

'Are you bar mitzvah'ed?'

'Many, many years ago.'

'Well then, come this way. I know you – you're Evelyn Stone's son, right? I heard your sad news – they say your mother was a very special lady. I wish you long life.'

He grasped my hand with both of his.

'But that's not why I'm here. I mean . . . I'm not in mourn-ing . . . I mean . . . I am, but . . .'

'It's OK, you're here for the call-up. Lenny said you might be here. I'll get you some things.'

As he patted my shoulder something licked my free palm, leaving it cold and sticky. A large yellow Labrador appeared as if from nowhere, lapping enthusiastically at my fingers, nuzzling at my crotch and gawking at me.

'Don't mind Dispensable, she's harmless.'

'You call your dog Dispensable?'

'It's the Rabbi's little joke. She's not mine.'

'Don't you let guide dogs inside?'

'Oh my, of course! But this one is long retired. A dog on wheels would be more use, I'm afraid. Brian just keeps her for company now. She can't see a thing either, bless her. They're like a pair of lost puppies, the two of them.'

He slapped the dog's back warmly, ruffling her coat, then slapping some more. He stooped down to her level and kissed her.

'Good girl, good girl. You're gorgeous, aren't you? Yes, you are, yes, you *are* . . .'

The labrador happily wobbled its from head side to side, trying to find a hand or body. We left it chained to the coat stand, contentedly rubbing at the coats.

The man started talking to me again while leading me towards the entrance, but I could only hear Evelyn, who had begun to talk over him, almost crowding him out completely. Listening to the mesh of their voices but looking at this little person I instantly liked him: everything about him gave off the scent of peace. He was wrinkled like a prune and almost as small as the bar mitzvah boy, though more hunched, his brown, bald head hidden almost entirely by an ornate multi-coloured head covering; seeing me looking at it he smiled, the loose skin on his cheeks gathering unexpectedly in folds by his ears.

'You like my kippah? My son made it,' he grinned, taking it off to show me.

'Your son must be a very talented boy.'

'Oh yes! But not so much of a boy any more, I'm afraid. Ben is a thirty-three-year-old orthodontist now.'

Another thought came to him.

'But you know, they're never too old to borrow money!'

He reached into a glass cupboard, took out a tallis and tefillin and handed me a yellowing kippah, which read on the inside: 'On the occasion of Ben's bar mitzvah, 14 April 1982.' He chuckled. I followed him back the way we had come, through the entrance hallway and into the main room. As the door swung open I shivered.

The man ushered me around the outside of the raised plat-form, which sat in the centre of the room, past the worship-pers and towards a row of empty seats at the back. The old men gathered round it were rocking back and forth, mutter-ing under their breath, some clinging onto the wooden row in front of them, some swaying freely, lost in God. I glanced around the synagogue, trying to seem casual while taking it all in: the perfect low-ceilinged red brick rectangle was exact-ly as I remembered from my visits so long ago, the same red carpet matching the design on the walls. I felt a hundred years old. Wife Number One once said she liked that design, though it's more worn-looking now.

The tiny windows were evenly spread over the four walls, modestly decorated with pictures of the twelve Jewish tribes on coloured stained glass. That was unfamiliar. They were almost like small church windows, nothing like the grand ones Henry had told me he'd seen in Europe, where he said synagogues were either palaces or bunkers. In between two of these was an unattractive set of unkempt velvet curtains, which I assumed still contained the Torah, a tired gold-coloured pulley rope hanging limply from the side, and above all this a small decoration relating to the Passover festival, which must have still been going on. The platform at the back for the Rabbi to stand on was low and so was the other main one, where the lead singer was standing, delivering a prayer: it looked like the architects wanted to keep the news that people were praying quiet, just like the Jews Evelyn described in Berlin. She was happier when the ceilings were high, whereas I had always been a low-ceiling Jew, if one at all. We were still walking when a white-haired man on the platform pulled the cord to reveal the five Torah scrolls behind the curtain; they were so much smaller than I remembered. When I first saw a Torah, not long before my first wedding, I laughed. It no longer seemed so ridiculous.

The service was all being conducted in Hebrew. I hardly recognised any of it, though the tune they were singing as I was being showed to a seat was vaguely familiar, perhaps from my visits all those years ago, or from Sunday. Were the same prayers said in celebration and in mourning? As I watched the tiny movement of those rubber, geriatric mouths of the old men praying, I wondered if they were actually saying any words at all or just keeping up appearances in the hope no one would notice they didn't know what they were doing. Meanwhile, my guide indicated a particular seat at the end of a row, handed over a slightly damaged blue hardback prayer book and set about hanging the leather on me, as if he knew I had forgotten how to do it for myself, which I had. The little black box rested in the middle of my forehead and the rest of the cord wrapped tight around my arm, spiralling downwards until there was none left, from my puny arm muscle to my hand. The man put the remainder of the cord into my palm, and I gripped it, shaking. He covered my shoulders with the shawl like a jacket as I nodded to another wrinkly face that turned around to see what was going on, and this man too smiled at me; instinctively I copied his mouth when he said, 'Amen.' One of the friendly prune faces whispered something to the Rabbi, who nodded sagely in my direction as if he had been waiting for my arrival, then turned to a different section in the Siddur. There was a great deal more whispering and some shuffling, many turning round to look me up and down. Lenny saw me and waved. I was pleased he was happy to have me there.

I wanted to linger over the pictures on the windows some more, to see and remember rather than take part – it's so tempting to wallow in memories – but was too aware of being watched, so I rocked when they rocked and muttered when they muttered, expecting at any moment to be exposed as an imposter and hauled out of the building. I even watched for pages being turned, flipping onwards when others did, though most of the Hebrew was still just rows of shapes and dots to me. Some words in the mesh were becoming clear – I could even translate a few of them – but most of it was still nonsense. Strange how you choose to remember some things but forget others. Though I mastered German with little problem, these peculiar symbols had to be learned and relearned again and again, though I had spent the first years of my life in Israel surrounded by them. Strange also that later, when I was learning German at school in England, Evelyn had never been persuaded to confess she spoke it too. I would have liked to have asked her about that when she was still alive. Maybe Lucille could still do it for me. Hopefully she would get up and pretend to go to school on her own today.

Little Lenny was very good. His still unbroken voice was already strong and distinct, not at all the whine I had been expecting, and though he had little to do, he opened his mouth wide and sang proudly when called upon. When he walked back to his seat, unable to contain a beaming smile, the congregation broke into spontaneous congratulations. A low rumble of voices echoed their way around the hall as he sat back down next to Lenny and the rest of the family. The entire front row oozed with pride. It could have been propaganda for Judaism, but though I was jealous of Lenny it still felt like someone else's religion, not mine. How could it be that something could feel so inevitable but also so alien? Was it possible to return to this funny little religion? Was it bound to happen?

When the service finished I headed straight for the exit, but was stopped in the hallway by a familiar face standing in my way.

'Rabbi! I'm so sorry about the other night, it's just, your card . . . I shouldn't have . . .'

'Oh, don't worry about that! I hope I was some help, that's all. I don't always make complete sense at that time in the morning.'

'Well, neither do I. But you know that now.'

'I just wanted to thank you for coming. Hashem is always ready to welcome back his people, after all. I hear Lenny invited you. You're friends then?'

'We met recently, at the pub. He was drinking orange juice; I wish I could say the same.'

'Lenny is the secretary here, you know.'

'Well, he does a lot of good PR for you too. He was very persuasive.'

I was surprised to be happy talking to the Rabbi again. It seemed a long time since Monday night and I thought I'd feel like I used to after bumping into someone I'd had a one-night stand with – uneasy, afraid, desperate to get away.

'Yes, he's very involved,' said the Rabbi. 'We are a small community these days – you have to double up on some duties – but as long as we have people like Lenny around, we can continue our work. He is overseeing the construction of the Memorial Hall as well. Did you know that?'

'We haven't known each other long. He never said.'

'Well, you can be sure Evelyn's legacy is safe in his hands. Anyway, so tell me . . . how does it feel coming back to the old place? It must feel strange, no?'

'It's certainly been a long time. My first wife used to like it here and said I would one day. She was right about most things.'

The Rabbi looked to the skies wistfully.

'Ah, Abe, the things we resist most strongly in the rashness of youth can be our greatest comforts in old age, don't you think? Not that you're old, of course! A mere babe in this building!'

'Yes, I noticed.'

I put on my coat and scratched my ankle with the tip of the other shoe, getting a little itchy. The Rabbi's manner was particularly chirpy.

'I hope you enjoyed the service this morning,' he said. 'You don't get much of a turnout for these things – there's more interest in the big celebration on Shabbat than this symbolic gathering – but it's still an important occasion, and I'm glad you could see it. Will you be here for the bar mitzvah on Saturday? Lenny's son has a fine voice, does he not? And he's a lovely boy too, a source of great nachas for his parents. Maybe even a Chazan he'll be one day please God!'

'He certainly sings well. But things are difficult, as you know . . .'

'Maybe we could find something for you to do. Pull back the Torah curtain perhaps.'

'Really, Rabbi, I'm not sure I could . . .'

'Oh, nonsense. How hard can it be? It's a mitzvah! And we'll all look forward to it; it'll make you feel better. I'll show you the Memorial Hall afterwards. It's so nearly finished. Your mother was very pleased with it, you know. Of course, she never saw the work-in-progress in person, she was too ill for that, but once she knew it was going to be in her name I sent her some photographs and she seemed very impressed by its development.'

'Mm,' I croaked, 'I'm sure. She was very good at keeping secrets . . . I wish I'd known about it then.'

'I'm sorry,' said the Rabbi, suddenly apologetic. 'It's too soon. Forgive me. It must be very hard for you.'

Other people began to appear, some going straight past to their cars, others waiting for a word with the Rabbi. The clutter, even of so few people, made me nervous. Sensing the intrusion he took me to one side, big brown arm slipping around my shoulder and sheltering me from the other bodies around, and again I was overcome with a rare honesty. I almost felt on auto-pilot, that any sudden movement could jolt me out of it and back into myself again. I was sure to be still just in case it disappeared.

'How are you? Really?' whispered the Rabbi. 'How are you finding your journey?'

'It's tough. She left a lot of questions unanswered. I can't get her out of my head, but can't seem to act either. *None* of it makes sense, Rabbi. And there are so many shocks, one after the other. If I could just understand *why* . . . I would feel so much better.'

'I know, Abe, I know. But as long as you remember it is your journey that matters now I'm certain you will be fine.'

'Yes, she's been talking about journeys . . .'

'Well then . . . You know, your mother told me a great deal before she died – some of it lies, some truth, most fantasy. If you allow yourself to become preoccupied with it you will never be able to move on. And that is important, especially at this time. Do you understand?'

His large body, standing like a fortress between me and the rest of the crowd made me feel safe but also afraid. I nodded, unable to speak.

'We'll talk again,' he continued, 'but be sure to come on Saturday. Let Hashem guide you through, like he did your namesake, our forefather. The Lord does not let down those who come to him in good faith. Remember that when Hashem asked Abraham to sacrifice his only son he prepared to do it without question. And because of this, Isaac was allowed to live.'

He patted me once as I imagined he might pat Brian's blind guide dog, and immediately the warmth was gone. Whoever it was that reached out to me, it seemed they always managed to spoil it somehow.

The Rabbi was pulled aside by Lenny, but before he could recognise me I left, keeping my back towards him until I was outside. I turned and fled, going as fast as I could down the road in the direction of the town, trying to block out the sound of Evelyn chattering away nonsensically, now challenged by the Rabbi too, until after a few hundred yards I had to sit down on a bench to rest. It was twenty minutes before I was able to walk again, and my whole body shook with confusion and fear and anger and resentment. I would not be controlled any more, by anything – apart from, perhaps, my own body.

My shift at the shop didn't start until midday, so after leaving the synagogue I went home, hoping no one would stop me from going back out. I don't know if anyone was there at all; I just picked up Evelyn's letter and turned around to leave. She was more relaxed now, starting to enjoy it all a lot more. This time, below 'KNOW THYSELF,' it said '5A'.

Good morning, Avraham –
This is just the first half of today's challenge. I am sending you on a trip. Get yourself a strong drink – you're going to Schiller's.

20

Schiller's

I remembered Schiller's being a filthy, dimly lit building that sold old books, relics and tacky memorabilia. Evelyn used to take me there when I was a child. I disliked it for many reasons back then. Things were always just strewn about the place, apparently thrown rather than carefully placed around the shop, and this lack of order offended me. It smelt of paint stripper and was eerily silent. Old black-and-white postcards that had already been written and sent decades ago, tired old tables groaning with the weight of boxes of ancient novelty LPs nobody wanted, antique badges stuck to the walls with Blu-tack, ugly ceramics – these were the kind of things you could buy in Schiller's. A broken gramophone lay camped in one corner for years; I never saw anyone buy that or anything else. The dusty atmosphere made me scratch, but every Saturday Evelyn dragged me there regardless so she could catch up with Mr Schiller Snr, one of her few close friends, whose family had owned the shop for as long as anyone could remember. She said he was one of the world's few remaining true gentlemen. If I complained about going she beat me, and if I scratched too much while we were there she whacked me and told me I was disgusting. Old Schiller, a grumpy man with stringy, slicked back grey hair, never addressed me directly, though he did allow his son to play with me whenever I was around. Old Schiller died a year before Evelyn did, and his son – a rosy-cheeked, tubby manic-depressive, who still harboured long-suppressed dreams of interior design – took it over and changed the formula. I still saw him intermittently but hadn't been in the shop since the reopening and expected to receive a telling off when we arrived.

I knocked just as Schiller Jr was opening up, turning the key gracelessly in the lock and trying to light a cigarette at the same time.

'Good morning,' he said through the smoke. 'So finally you've arrived. Well, you'd better come in then . . .'

I walked in the door. The familiar gentle bell I remembered tinkled happily above me, but apart from that the shop had changed beyond recognition. Schiller Jr had introduced a shiny yellow and green colour scheme – brash, sickly yellow stripes divided the wall into four lime-green squares. Just like in the town centre, everything seemed so much brighter than I remembered. Where in the past there had been the piles of old artefacts and unwanted bits and bobs around to trip you up, now those old things were gone and shiny brass shelves had been erected in their place, stacked neatly with new books, leaving plenty of space to walk about. The dust was gone.

'Come in, come in, stop hovering . . .'

Schiller Jr was a different creature to the jolly idiot I remembered, giving off a pungent air of gloom. Even his hair, knotted and unruly, and clothes, now so unkempt – a dirty shirt partly untucked from stained grey trousers – made him almost unrecognizable next to the smart, well-kept gentleman that used to potter around in his father's wake. He pushed me inside and grumpily put me into a seat across from his desk as if I had disturbed something important but he felt it his duty to entertain me, and then shuffled away to make tea without asking if I wanted one. He was back quickly with it – too much milk and sugar, tea bag still popping up intermittently over the top of the whiteness. It was briefly like being in the old Schiller's again, the hushed morning atmosphere akin to the barrenness that used to dominate the place so totally, and the tension was thick in the air. We sat awkwardly across from each other, clutching our mugs tightly, and I tried not to think about what Evelyn could have brought me to Schiller's for. I didn't know if I could take any more surprises. Finally Schiller Jr spoke, almost deadpan in tone.

'You like what I've done, right? You like the yellow?'

'Yes, lovely,' I said politely.

He looked round the shop, unable to hide his satisfaction.

'My father, may he rest in peace, would have approved of the colour scheme,' he continued, sipping at his tea. 'He always loved limes, you see. And lemons. He would have done the makeover himself if his poor bones had been up to it . . .'

'Mmm, yes. Actually, I'm here for something in particular I hope you can help me with. My mother has asked me to . . .'

'Oh, say no more, say no more!'

Schiller Jr banged a fist on the table in irritation to stop me finishing.

'Let us not turn this nonsense into a charade. I have been given instructions; your mother posted them to me and they arrived this morning. I'm not awake yet; give me a chance to do that first, will you? How is your mother anyway?'

'How is she? Are you *joking*?'

'Yes, of course. A stupid question – there's nothing fun about being trapped in one room day and night. Sorry, I shouldn't have asked. Anyway, there's plenty of time for all that later, I suppose. Stay and drink your tea first. Nobody comes in here before twelve anyway and I get lonely. God knows we all get lonely.'

He thought of something and perked up slightly.

'Postcards, you want any postcards? There are some good ones of Blackpool at the turn of the century, written on, of course. The waterfront looked so different then. Need a record player? A couple of cupboards?'

'No, thank you, I have enough cupboards for now.'

Schiller reached for a couple of old trinkets on the sideboard, stroked them and put them back again.

'I'm getting rid of a lot of stuff, you know. I'm going on holiday tomorrow and don't want it all rotting while I'm gone.'

It was hard to imagine some of the things he was talking about looking any worse than they already did, and besides, surely he could still enjoy them on his return. I just wanted to get the letter and leave with as little fuss as possible. Where was it? Schiller looked hard and deep into my eyes, almost challenging me to ask him why he was selling his treasures, the reel of smoke unwinding from his cigarette and wafting unhurriedly over his desk and directly into my eyes. I rubbed them softly, trying to suppress a cough.

'Going anywhere nice then?'

'Poland.'

'Great.'

'I don't expect so. It's a convention for collectors. I'm not looking forward to it. It will be hellish.'

'You'll have a good time, I'm sure.'

'Not at all, Abe, not at all. It will be horrid and uncomfortable and impossibly depressing. I wouldn't wish it on anybody. I can hardly bring myself to pack. The suitcase has been open and empty for days.'

'Then why are you going?'

'Why? For a break, I suppose: I've hardly had a day off since I took over here. And to meet people.'

'What's wrong then? Why so unhappy?'

'Because I don't want to *advertise* myself to strangers. What have I got to offer? I just want to *have* friends. I want people to know me already. But this shop is all I have now, and what comfort can you get from four walls?'

He sighed deeply.

'But I have to try – we are all responsible for our own journey, after all. My family is long gone, and old friends don't seem to be replaced with new ones any more, do they? That's one of the disadvantages of getting older. You're inclined to make intimate contacts with fewer people.'

His gaze was unflinching, his stare frightening. The deep creased web at the corners of his eyes spread out unforgivingly to the edges of his face, like a harsher, colder version of the gentle prune-faced man in the synagogue. They were both somehow instantly recognizable as Jews, but in starkly different ways. I just wanted to get up and demand the letter.

'I'm sure you have friends.'

'Used to. Most are gone, though. The smart ones left for more exotic places – some made Aliyah – and would you believe I'm nearly sixty now? Will I still be meeting new people in ten years' time?'

'Come on now, you're not old! People live a lot longer these days, you know. I certainly plan to.'

I laughed nervously, imagining myself reaching over, grabbing Schiller Jr and shaking him until he gave me what I wanted. Instead, I said:

'It's no big deal to be sixty any more. Ninety, yes! But what with medical advances you and I can quite properly expect to live until we're at least . . .'

'Oh, do stop prattling, Abe. It's the quality of life that matters, not the life itself, you idiot! I *am* getting old. And so are you!'

He reconsidered.

'You're on your way, anyway.'

More thinking.

'You look pretty good, actually, for your age.'

I smiled inwardly. Accidentally, Schiller Jr had sprayed spit across the table as he said 'actually'.

'Thanks,' I replied.

A drop of spittle settled on the end of my nose. He screwed his face up like he used to years ago as a child throwing a tantrum in his father's shop, and I waited for the tears, but none came.

'We lie to each other and ourselves so much we don't even notice ourselves doing it any more. Do you ever think about that? My poor father, may he rest in peace, used to say that all the time. The man was a pillar of truth. Like your own mother. They were made for each other, really.'

He looked away, embarrassed, and I wiped my nose quickly with my hand before he could spot me doing it. Schiller Jr lingered for a moment and then sat, drank down the rest of his tea in one and gestured I should do the same, though it was still too hot for me to drink. I sipped at it, burning my tongue. He was now pacing the shop floor, brow furrowed.

'Well,' I said, 'I'm sure it won't be that bad. I hope you enjoy yourself.'

'I know I shall worry about the shop. I can't help it. Your mother was always telling us not to though, whenever she was in here. "The shop won't warm your grave," she used to say. "Nothing will." And she was right. Graves are very cold. A very clever woman, your mother.'

I nodded.

'Yes, very,' I said meekly.

I was getting used to fielding compliments about Evelyn. Suddenly Schiller Jr became angry, returning to the table and stamping a fist down on it, rattling the till in front of me.

'Damn right she is! A bloody genius, I say! And a complex woman too, Abe, more complex than you know. A woman of *wants* and *needs* and *desires*! Something that's properly understood within these walls!'

Some toy soldiers on the desk fell over. He sat them back up again, one by one.

'Now come on, there are things to be done. You ask for a drink and then won't sup it! This shop will be full to bursting come midday. It always is.'

He clapped his hands twice and took my unfinished cup from my hand, pushing me out of my seat.

'Right, let's go.'

Schiller Jr lead me to the back of the shop, through a door that said PRIVATE, through a large room that seemed to have been transported in time from Schiller's half a century before (with all the postcards in it), and finally to a small windowless box room piled high on all sides with books.

'Now, I've got a lot to do today,' he said impatiently. 'So I'm just going to leave you to it. As I'm sure Evelyn has told you, everything in this room is yours now. Regrettably, she has decided not to keep her valuables here any more, though

God knows I tried to persuade her otherwise. They've been safe here all these years – why change?'

He didn't wait for an answer.

'Anyway, it's her decision, and obviously she is in no state of health to come and get them herself. Oh, the box you want is just on the table there. As for transporting all this stuff . . . well, that's up to you. I'll be out the front if you need me.'

And, suddenly, I was alone, and it was all mine.

Evelyn's things were all around me, stacked sideways on the shelves, right up to the ceiling, waiting to be pored over. Prayer books, novels with Hebrew writing on the spine, a collection with 'Haggadah' written on the front in gold block shapes, piles of bound letters, photographs, diaries – even framed paintings of places in Israel packed together neatly by the door. This all seemed remarkably narcissistic, even for my mother; but here I was, doing her bidding, as usual. I picked out the Haggadah and turned to the first page, where in writing similar but different to Evelyn's a message was written in German:

Dearest Evy, Happy Pesach,
    May you find a lifetime's joy and comfort in these
pages, lots of love Mummy and Daddy, April 1923.

I closed it again and picked up some photographs, grey hands shaking more than ever, but was flipping through them all so fast, trying to devour them all, that I took almost nothing in, especially in the dim light of Schiller Jr's back room. The mass of black-and-white smiling faces meant nothing and everything at the same time. One was of a young Evelyn holding a baby, me perhaps. That picture was blurred. Others were of groups of men and women working or posing, arms around each other, and one where Evelyn was smiling at a man close by. Who were they? Did Evelyn miss them? Were any of the surrounding letters from these people? If they met me today on the street, would any of them recognise me as Evelyn Stone's little boy? On the back of some photographs Evelyn had written messages in German: 'Outside the eating-house, 1941', 'Working the fields, 1943', 'Celebrating, 1948', 'Leaving, 1953'. Already I was struggling to breathe, even the sight of blank countryside in the background behind all these strangers making me want to climb into the photos and kiss the ground.

I put everything back for inspection later and opened the box Schiller Jr had pointed to, a small wooden chest that looked like it was made for pirates to hold gold coins in, not for dead mothers to put letters; E.S. was engraved on the front and a tiny key was in the lock, ready to be turned. Inside was an envelope numbered '5B'. Evelyn's voice was still just as I remembered it, just the same as the one following me around. As I read it felt like she was in the room with me, sitting on one of the shelves, swinging her legs and reading over my shoulder.

Hello again, Avraham –

The things of greatest worth are always where you least expect, are they not? Did you think last week that you would be here, searching for parts of me amongst the dust? Of course not. You thought you would be rid of me. But still you don't know what to do with all this time Almighty God has given you on earth, and so I cannot leave you yet. I brought you to this room so you could understand what I left behind, what it means to me. And, of course, to pick up my things.

On the kibbutz, a hierarchy began to creep up on us, the work was backbreaking, relationships broke down completely. You fall into comfortable old ways. Some of the rules we'd imposed on ourselves – sharing partners, particularly, and living separately from our children – stopped being liberating and became impositions to many. Many of us were from countries where life was very different, and after a few years rebellion, many yearned for the past.

After I fell pregnant with you, not sure who your father was, I realised I too couldn't follow the rules of the kibbutz any more. By the time you were three I had retreated from the main group completely and removed you from the children's house, apart from when I was working. We moved into a small bungalow on the edge of the grounds with a good man I grew to depend on, one of several who may have been your father. I still don't know who that is, and I suppose you never will, but that man gave us everything we could ever need. He came back to us every night after a punishing day's work and didn't want anyone else. He made me feel special, and you too. I wanted to believe he was. You liked him, Abe, and would do still if he was alive. He was loyal, proud, determined to make the kibbutz work, his way. I still think of him sometimes.

There had been an initial rush of excitement when the state was founded, but by the early 1950s people were already leaving for other cities or countries. Some went back to where they had come from. Children of the founders of the kibbutz grew up, left and didn't come back. Nobody was there to replace them. Some of those who stayed became lazy, and those who wanted to stick to the original dream became marginalised. I was once again in the majority. 1953 was the year of the Doctor's Plot, and many of us felt that even those who liberated us from Auschwitz hated us Jews. Also, Palestinians needed a homeland too and I couldn't understand the obstinate attitudes of everyone around me. We deserved a home but they didn't, apparently. Then came the raid.

One night two men broke into the kibbutz, crept through the window of the hut we were staying in and shot the man I loved – once in the chest and once in the head, just to be sure. Noise carries in that atmosphere, and many of the living quarters were in close proximity to each other, so nearly everyone was woken and within minutes half of the kibbutz population were crowded in or around the flat, weeping and wailing as the murderers escaped, the body lying bleeding all over the sheets below. (We were short of sheets. I remember thinking it was a shame he couldn't have bled on the floor.) I was bathing at the time of the shooting; had they come a few minutes later, I would surely have been killed too. You were sleeping in the next room. Others were confused by my response. I wasn't angry with the killers, and I didn't mourn for the man I had made mine. Instead, I was angry at Israel – for its borders, its allies, its very existence. Once again, I prepared to leave.

When I arrived in Jerusalem I owned nothing, and when I left with you twenty years later we owned nothing together. The kibbutz kept every shekel I earned: you were supposed to be there for life. I thought we would be. I felt so let down – by other Jews, communists, Palestinians, the British, the Russians – everybody. Even by human nature. Avraham, for many years I have been ashamed to have spent so much of my life on something that, for a long time, thought it was something else. But now, near death, when I think of whether I have seen anything better since, the answer simply has to be no.

Around you at this moment, on these shelves, is my entire history – all my books from home, the things that kept me company when I had nothing, not even a man to help steady me. Mr Schiller Sr came closest to fulfilling that role during my life in England, and so for many years I entrusted my portable history to him and his family, in order to keep it from mine. The Rabbi has now shown me I don't need to hide any more – from God, my family, my instincts – not even from death. I am going to make things right. Look around: I give you all this because it is yours.

I wept silently, head in the box, to the sound of Schiller Jr giving a little old lady the hard sell over some crockery. For how long, I don't know. Eventually I dried my eyes and began to sort through the rest of the things. Each time I thought I was about to get some control, Evelyn wrestled it back off me, each time more dramatically than the last. The image of my faceless, nameless father bleeding all over the bed sheets made me feel so ill I was frightened to move.

Schiller Jr returned; obviously the shop wasn't as full as he'd hoped. He leaned in the doorway, eating an apple, now more awake and a little friendlier, though everything he said was still delivered sharply. I made sure to put the letter in my back pocket while he wasn't looking. I didn't want to discuss what Evelyn was doing.

'How's that granddaughter of yours?' he said, chewing loudly.

'Lucille? Fine. Why?'

'Very clever girl that. A bid sad looking, a bit shy, but you can still shake it out of them at that age if you put your mind to it. Looking for work, is she?'

'She's a bit young for that, I think . . .'

'Rubbish – you're never too young to make use of yourself. I was near running this place by her age. Tell her there's a job here for her – lifting and shifting, nothing glamorous – but it'll put a bit of muscle on that skinny frame and give her some valuable pocket money. Good experience. You've got to learn about money early in life, and you can tell a lot about a kid from what they spend their pocket money on. Very interesting topic, that is.'

'I suppose so.'

'Suppose nothing, Abraham! You've got to keep a keen eye out for your kids! God knows that one doesn't have much of a father, and no mother, of course, God rest her soul. Someone's got to look after her! It's the least I can do for Evelyn, after all she's done for us. Tell Lucille she can start a week Saturday on my return, and to be here for nine on the dot. How's she doing at school anyway?'

'Oh, fine, just fine . . .'

'End of year exams coming up, are they?'

'In a few weeks, yes. She always does well. Nothing to worry about.'

'Glad to hear it. It's a first-rate institution, Nayborough Grammar. Your mother is very proud of her going there. Excellent pass rates, the best in the north, she always says. No riff-raff in those corridors.'

You could almost hear Evelyn saying it, propped up on one side by her walking stick and her other hand on the table we had just been sitting at.

'Very true, very true. Anyway, I really must be going. I have an appointment at twelve. Thank you again. I'll be back to get the stuff soon and will tell Lucille about the job.'

Schiller Jr was not pleased I was going but came to the door anyway, waving his chamois at me as I walked away, asking me between bites of his apple to send his good wishes on to Evelyn.

The gushing nosebleed started as I turned the corner. Big red drops splattered all over my white shirt and the paving stones on the high street. It was more blood than I'd ever seen come out of me at one time. The bleeding seemed to go on for ever and I panicked; I had no tissues and there was no pub close enough to go and ask for some apart from The King's Arms, and I didn't want to see Rachel, who might be on duty. I struggled on. I would have to go home again and change. At one point, because of the heat inside me, I had to stop and scratch my arms until I forgot completely why I'd started, leaking from my nose all the while.

21

A Day's Work

When I arrived at the shop I was fifteen minutes late. Gilda
and Nas were sitting behind the counter in deckchairs, playing cards like two old pensioners on the waterfront, whispering conspiratorially. On seeing me they both smiled but
quickly returned to their conversation. The shop's Easter decorations were completed now, every corner of the place covered with pictures of chocolate eggs and bunny rabbits, the
noticeboard full of children's new drawings, this month's
theme 'The Miracles of Jesus'. I stopped at the board to buy
myself a few seconds to get my breath back. The whispering
stopped.

'The whole dying-on-the-cross thing isn't very popular
with the children,' said Gilda dryly. 'We try and stay away
from it. Grab a chair and sit down. This is Nas.'

She gestured vaguely towards a serious, intelligent looking
young man in stylish glasses, the same one that was wearing
the T-shirt the other day. Nas nodded serenely. I bowed.

Nas was only about eighteen or nineteen, with babyish
features and soft puffy cheeks contrasting with a close-
shaven Afro on his scalp. There was nothing immature
about his manner though. Actually, I was a little afraid.

'Sorry I'm late. Nice to meet you,' I said, very slowly.

Nas smiled.

'If anyone comes, the code for the till is twenty-five twelve,
like Christmas. Sit down.'

'Isn't there anything you want me to do?'

He shook his head, pointing to a couple of blue-and-white
striped chairs propped up against a wall, one of which I
unfolded and put down next to him.

I didn't know what to do next. It had been months since I'd

had a job of any kind, and even longer since I'd worked behind a counter. But these two didn't seem to be doing anything; it was a long time until five o'clock. We sat underneath a large poster, which almost covered the whole of the back wall and said:

'Then Jesus said to the disciples, "And so I tell you not to worry." (Matt 12.22).'

A pencil sketch of a bearded man ponderously looking towards the sky loomed large over the three of us.

'I'm taking that down. It's taken out of context,' said Gilda, irritably, seeing my eyes drawn to it.

I was slightly taken aback by her tone. Nas seemed so too.

'There'll be none left soon,' he said sternly. 'Why are you taking everything down? Maureen will only put it back up again when she gets back.'

'Maureen's a dinosaur.'

The two of them scowled at each other playfully. The pencil drawing seemed to be smiling at me.

'Well, I think it's nice anyway,' I said.

But Gilda was ready for that.

'You wouldn't think so if you knew the book of Matthew. The disciples have no clothes, no food and little faith. The next six verses go on to give you plenty of reason to worry. Look, half of these posters are just there to give false hope to people who can't be bothered to actually open the Bible. Don't pay attention to them. Read it instead. You know what I'd like to see? A quote up there from something really obscure, something boring. "The Lord Condemns Insincere Fasting"; "Sinful Deeds in the Valley of Himmon". Then we'd all get a laugh. But that doesn't bring in the crowds, of course.'

Nas laughed confidently.

'Actually, *nothing* brings in the crowds. Ignore her.'

Gilda folded her arms in objection.

'If I had my way the Church would be very different.'

'Yeah, everyone else would be kicked out.'

They shared a private look.

'Where do you get all these posters from anyway?' I asked. Gilda shrugged.

'Oh, they just arrive in the post. We get sent all kinds of things, mostly from American Bible corporations that want us to shut up, do as we're told and contribute to the Republican Party.'

More laughing.

'I'm going to start doing my own soon. They can't stop us writing in felt tip, can they? *We know our rights!*'

Nas cut in.

'Like I said: ignore her. Today she's a rebel, tomorrow she's a mouse.'

'And you're a *real* rebel, are you?'

'More than you'll ever be.'

Gilda turned to me and whispered as if letting me in on an exciting secret, her voice laced thick with sarcasm, one hand patting Nas mockingly on the thigh.

'Nas thinks we're all idiots. He could run Britain himself . . .'

They laughed again, looking fondly at each other and then at me. I couldn't see what was so funny.

'Sorry,' said Nas. 'We have this argument all the time.'

He took a deep breath and became more serious.

'I only came here to go to university and can't wait to get back – I'm doing Shipping, you know, which there is a great demand for in Uganda –' Gilda rolled her eyes at this –' . . . and the attitude of the other students baffles me. They have no real interest in shipping. Many of the people in the English Church are like that as well, actually.'

'What, no interest in shipping?'

'They're lazy. They're not doing it for the right reasons.'

He paused, embarrassed.

'I'm told I repeat myself a lot . . . but I really feel people don't appreciate what they have here. My country has been ravaged by corruption and war for decades. Education is a privilege few can afford. Here, people can have whatever they want, and they choose nothing – a shallow, drunken, Godless nothing. They stand outside clubs at three in the morning kissing people they don't know and being sick on pavements. It's crazy. Don't you agree?'

All this skipping between joking and seriousness left me unsure how to respond.

'Hmm, yes,' I said in a voice somewhere between the two.

This seemed to satisfy him. Just then, Gilda spotted a bloodstain on the front of my shirt. I looked down to see Daffy Duck poking out through my fly, just below the stain, and blushed scarlet.

'What happened?'

'Oh! Just a nosebleed, it's nothing. I've not been well . . . but I'm OK now.'

'What exactly is wrong with you?' Gilda asked seriously.

I sighed, tucking my Daffy boxer shorts back in and zipping up.

'Oh, you know. Nothing quite big enough to warrant immediate action, nothing small enough to ignore.'

'Well, take it slowly today. You're no good to Jesus in the grave. You should have told me, though. *Bad* boy.'

She smacked my hand playfully, and I felt very, very old.

'Don't tease him,' said Nas. 'It's not fair.'

I watched Gilda for a moment as she and Nas retreated into a conversation of their own. Her necklace was a chunky silver cross which seemed to dangle comically in front of me as she moved – left, right, left, right – like a hypnotist's watch, endlessly swinging. I imagined a tiny pained Jesus hanging there, struggling with the nails through his hands, and winced – but could I believe in this, or anything, if I really tried? It happens all the time, Henry says, to all kinds of people. Accountants get out of bed one day and just change their lives for Jesus: one day it all makes sense. Businessmen pack it all in for God. It even happens to Jews! The imaginary Jesus winked. The last remnants of the nosebleed resurfaced on my tongue and then slid back down my throat, gloopy and warm.

'You should come to church on Sunday,' said Gilda, turning to me. 'We were just talking about it.'

'Shh – no,' Nas hissed.

'Why not?'

'It's just . . .' he nudged Gilda in the ribs, 'it's not a good time.'

Nas gripped Gilda's hand tightly and took control.

'We'd love you to get involved. It's just that . . . there might be no one to lead the service. The vicar's on holiday, you see.'

Gilda snorted, folding her arms.

'Sabbatical, more like!'

'It might be better to wait until he gets back.'

'*If* he ever gets back.'

'I'm not sure I follow you.'

After a few furtively exchanged looks, Nas gave up the pretence. He looked at me very gravely and spoke quietly, first checking that no one was in earshot. The shop was almost empty. I leaned in close.

'The vicar has been suspended,' he whispered. 'There's been an investigation . . . we're not supposed to be talking about it . . .'

' . . . But everybody knows what's happened.'

Gilda's voice was much louder. Nas nudged her again, but she was far too excited to be quietened.

'Ow!' she said, too loudly.

A browser turned round to see what was going on.

'We don't really know anything. We have to wait for . . .'

Gilda was talking fast and excitedly now.

'They say he was caught after the service on Sunday having it off with one of the women in the choir, Mrs Davis . . . in the pulpit! She's left her husband, who says he's going to get the vicar struck off. There might not even be a service on Sunday at all, and it's Easter. He's chosen a bad week to be suspended . . .'

I was starting to feel like an intruder and wished I was back in The King's Arms with Henry and a drink someone else was paying for. My gaze went back and forth between my two hosts.

'. . . I heard he worked his way through the whole choir and she was the last one.'

'That's ridiculous.'

'Why? You'd hardly pick her first, would you?'

'Gilda, stop it . . .'

'. . . *The whole choir*, that's what I heard, including the two *men*.'

'Don't be stupid. The vicar isn't homosexual . . .'

'No, you're right. He's just *sexual*.'

Gilda collapsed into a fit of giggles.

'You can't say that!'

'Oh, rubbish. I heard he did the same in his last parish – somewhere in Hampshire – and that he was in trouble for fiddling the books too, but they hushed it up and just moved him here.'

'*Allegedly*,' butted in Nas.

'Perhaps I won't go on Sunday then,' I said. 'It's all a bit too soon anyway . . .'

My voice trailed off, but they weren't even listening to me any more; instead, they were quietly making up. Gilda's hand covered Nas's and touched the wooden chair arm under it with both her thumb and little finger. They shared another look of love. My being there made no difference to them at all.

For the next couple of hours I sat between Gilda and Nas while they talked. On the rare occasions they asked about my life, I lied about it. My mother was still alive and well, I said. We got on great. I had recently retired from a job as head of the History department at a school out in the country, about ten miles away. Nas was self-assured, calm, interesting, relaxed. He knew a lot about royal history, more than me actually, which was annoying.

176

Customers did appear sometimes, but it was almost like they weren't really customers at all. Most addressed Gilda and Nas by their first names, some stopped by for a chat or even a cup of tea. Nearly everyone had something to say: people talked about the weather, their plans for the Easter weekend; some wanted to discuss the news. Three children and a pregnant woman had been killed in the West Bank mid-morning; another suicide bomb had gone off, this time in the centre of Jerusalem near the McDonald's. What can you do, they said. I spent much of the time going to and from the kettle, being introduced to the regulars, listening to Evelyn's interruptions in my head. She didn't approve of my new career. I went through to the back room to put the kettle on for the fourth or fifth time since my arrival, and while I picked through the fruit-flavoured tea and Fair Trade coffee, she screamed:

'Jesus? *Christians? FRUIT TEA?* Have you finally lost your mind?'

I replied calmly, under my breath, that it was possible.

During this period I learnt how to use the till and got up several times to serve customers; and I made a lot of tea. Initially this had been enjoyable and I had wondered whether I might happily be able to do it for the rest of my life – Wife Number Two used to talk about the joy of work after a good, hard day at the council offices – but after a few tries at the till I was bored and hoped Gilda or Nas would get up next time someone needed seeing to, which sometimes they did. Lethargy punctured me. The original thrill of working in a new place, of new hope, was soon replaced by something far more mundane, and I thought of the bloody damp patch on my shirt sucking out all my energy and ability to move, fantasising about getting a rare killer blood disease that I could not be blamed for contracting. Gilda's hand stayed on top of Nas's. My eyes slowly shut. Then, quite out of the blue, there was a noise and I was brought out of my daydream.

'Abe! What's wrong?'

'What? What?'

I started awake.

'Your face is pale, you're sweating, your hands are shaking.'

'Really? I . . .'

I rose to my feet and tried to pull my hand from her grip but quickly became unsteady and sat down again, almost missing the space between the two chair arms.

'Don't fuss, please,' I laughed desperately, holding onto the chair. 'I have a . . . it comes and goes . . . Funny how one minute you're fine and . . .'

I stuttered to a halt. For a second my mouth moved without making sound.

'You shouldn't have come here today,' said Gilda calmly.

I gasped for breath, reaching for my inhaler and taking a puff. Nas ran to the sink to get water and returned with a glass, which he put to my lips, forcing me to drink from it; all I wanted was for him not to be annoyed at me. Muscle spasms shot into the ends of each of my limbs. I shuddered. Everything became impossible.

'I'll be fine in a minute,' I wheezed quietly.

They took me to the office and Gilda knelt by me, softly rubbing my back as she had done Nas's hand earlier. He cleared the shop of browsers and closed it. My throat relaxed, the shaking subsided a little and some colour came back to my cheeks.

'I know how it must look,' I said eventually, sitting up. 'I'm sorry . . .'

'Shh, don't talk,' said Gilda.

She laid me back down on the floor and propped my head up with cushions. After a few minutes sipping water I persuaded them there was no need for alarm, and they let me sit by the front desk again, but I had shocked them and now there were no more games. Debate was abandoned. They took turns to watch me while the other busied themself on the shop floor, stacking and restacking. The shop was reopened.

Nas put on some music, nothing I recognised. It was nearly five o'clock.

Gilda sat with me at the desk, chatting in-between what were now more regular intervals between customers. Some religious books were sold but mainly people bought second-hand crime thrillers. (Crime was what kept the Christian bookshops open, Nas informed me.) A lonely looking old man took one of the 'Acceptance' booklets I had picked up the other day. Bags of clothes arrived. Two uneven piles built up behind Gilda, who began to sort them. I noticed while watching her watching me that she was doing so with pity and realised she was not the first since Sunday to do so. Her hand caressed my back again, warming it, like Rachel's had, and Wife Number Three's had done in the hallway last Christmas when I'd had my first funny turn, and my first two wives, and even Evelyn had once done when I was a child. Many women had cared for me through various minor illnesses and things like this – year upon year of little health hiccups that turned out to be nothing, often exaggerated: lots of rubbed backs and sympathetic smiles, some earned, some milked, some both. The women I had loved the most had helped me by not helping me at all when I wanted looking after. That was something Evelyn always understood; that given the chance I would soak up every last sympathy without a thought for doing something myself. Now I was embarrassed to be accepting gentleness at all, though I finally needed it.

'Tell me about your family,' said Gilda softly, putting the bag of clothes to one side and coming closer. 'Maybe that will help you relax.'

'I have a son . . .'

'Oh?'

'Nathan is a psychiatrist, or was. He got ill.'

'Oh . . .'

'. . . But he seems to be getting better now. Then there's his wife, who's away at the moment, and Lucille, my grand-daughter. They all live with me . . .'

'You must have quite a houseful!'

'I suppose so, yes.'

'I wish I had a big family like yours. It must be very satis-fying. You know, to look around and know you've really achieved something. What's it like in your house? I can't real-ly see you ordering everyone around.'

'I did insist on something once, thinking my family wanted me to. But even then they expected me to do it in a particular way, and I chose another. They were bitterly disappointed and I haven't really done it since. I do love them, but I think it's time to make some decisions on my own. I just wish they would let me.'

'That sounds like me and Nas. You know, you can save yourself a lot of trouble by just admitting you can't please everybody. Our parents won't leave us alone; they think we're always trying to have sex. We're just getting on with our lives.'

'And are you?'

'Are we what?'

'Always trying to have sex.'

Sex. The word itself was without suggestion for me now. There was no shiver inside me as I watched Gilda's blouse fall open a little.

'I'm old enough to do what I want, aren't I? And we're not *always* trying anyway. Besides, I love Nas. But that's some Christian parents for you . . . don't know much about the teachings of Jesus but can somehow tell you plenty about right and wrong. Usually, how wrong sex is. Especially with a black man from Uganda.'

She laughed lightly.

'Jesus is my guide in this life; that's good enough for me. I was going to take a purity pledge at one time . . .'

'Pardon?'

'It's when you sign a contract to say you won't have sex before you get married . . .'

'Really? That kind of thing goes on?'

'Oh yes! You look shocked . . .'

'Well, I am . . .'

'Anyway, I was going to do it, and my parents were very keen – you get a ring for your wedding finger and everything, they take it very seriously – but in the end I decided not to. I asked Jesus what he wanted me to do and he told me that sharing something so beautiful with Nas couldn't possibly affect my walk with him. You have to find your own way. My parents just had to accept that. In the end, you've got to stop listening to your parents, don't you think? Respect them, yes, but stop listening.'

A calm silence passed between us, and Gilda removed her hand from my back. Something about the atmosphere between us, her touch, her intense, searching blue eyes, seemed to make it OK to say anything. Nas was at the other side of the shop. I wanted to keep talking.

'You keep thinking someone is going to appear and make you understand everything and turn your life around completely,' I started, unsure why. 'They don't, but somehow it doesn't stop you looking for them. I miss that person, whoever they are.'

'That's who Jesus is in my life.'

'I think it may be too late for me. I can't hear him. Or my Jewish God. I can't hear anything. I get these rushes of determination and belief . . . and then . . . they disappear.'

'It's never too late, Abe.'

A pause.

'I'm sorry,' I said quietly.

'What for?'

'I don't know.'

It was finally beginning to hit me that my body and mind could not be trusted any more. At this point Nas appeared with more water for me and said:

'We'll show you the way, Abe. You can rely on us. Give yourself up to God, and anything is possible.'

They both smiled tenderly, but with all that came with that

sentence I desperately wanted to be elsewhere. I was just starting to wonder whether coming to the shop that morning had been unwise when the lights went out on me for the third time in four days.

22

Hospital

This time I woke up in a hospital bed. It was Friday. Seeing Henry talking seriously with a man in white above me, I closed my eyes again. The antiseptic smell of the ward hit my nostrils for the first time, pulsing deep into my lungs. My empty stomach groaned.

'He has been lucky,' said the doctor, 'but may not be so again. I fear it is not illness itself but the refusal to heed simple instructions that will kill him. If a patient does not take the medication they are supposed to, there is not a lot we can do.'

Somewhere above my face, the previously humid, dead air was disturbed. The doctor must have been close.

'Abe has had a lot of bad medical advice,' replied Henry's voice icily. 'It can be difficult to know which misdiagnosis to follow. There are so many.'

'He has also undoubtedly ignored a lot of good advice. Stubbornness is a killer, Henry, as is stupidity. If you have any influence on your friend at all, I advise you put this to him bluntly and see if you can arouse any panic. It may turn out to be the only thing that will save him; he is a nervous patient and may only respond to a sharp shock.'

Henry grunted seriously and took a seat near me, rustling a newspaper. I remained perfectly still, eyes closed, willing the itch in my nose and the doctor to go away while my mind jumped back and forth between the hospital and other things I could not see: Lucille kneeling at her altar, Rachel kneeling at Nathan, Gilda and Nas at church.

'You still haven't said what was wrong with him,' said Henry to the doctor.

'Yesterday I could not have told you,' he replied, finally opening the door to leave, 'but now I suppose it's obvious.'

He shrugged.

'That's medicine for you. Be gentle with him if you can.'

Once I was sure the doctor had gone I reopened my eyes and sat up in bed, dimly noticing tubes coming out of machines by the bedside and into my body. I felt a little dazed but was otherwise in quite a surprisingly bright state: I am quickly learning that extreme states of health can follow each other quite comfortably. Henry was on a nearby chair reading the *Telegraph*; I was not alone then, at least. I wriggled a little, trying to make myself comfortable in the bed, getting used to my new home.

It was a single room off a busy corridor, with doctors and nurses passing through often. The view outside through the small window was unknown to me, but we were definitely high up. Actually, the hospital was new to me too. Fruit lay by my bedside, partly obscured by a pile of things that had defined my week so far: the book I'd read to Lucille, the Good News Bible, the 'Acceptance' leaflet, Evelyn's letters and some post.

Henry hadn't noticed me awaken so I did a quick inspection, as much as was possible in the circumstances. The cheeks of my backside were frozen stiff from inactivity, my arms covered in something alarmingly like blue crêpe paper, a horrible plastic hospital body sheet that crackled at every small movement, and there was a nappy-like softness around me that had somehow replaced my Daffy Duck boxer shorts. I had been tampered with, and I briefly wondered whether to feel violated. The nappy was quite snug though; no complaints there. Henry glanced up from his paper, looked me over, saw me awake and almost immediately returned to the business section of the paper.

'What happened to me?' I said meekly. 'The doctor was a little harsh, don't you think?'

Henry continued reading.

'What happened?' I repeated.

'You were an idiot, many times over,' he said finally.

'That's what happened. And eventually you had a mild heart attack because of it. But, miraculously, you seem to be OK. You'll be out of here in a few days. Now go back to sleep. You must rest.'

'He *was* cruel though, right?'

'Ryan was completely correct.'

'Ryan?'

'I spoke up for you out of habit, Abe, not conviction.'

'But you said . . .'

'Just because others have been wrong in the past, doesn't mean that you haven't been negligent too. You won't help yourself: you have no one else to blame. I warned you this would happen, and you laughed.'

'You sound like my mother.'

'Your mother wasn't always wrong,' he snapped, still from behind the headlines.

I waited for my friend to start laughing, or put his paper down to reveal a mischievous grin, but the paper remained stubbornly between us. I wanted to rip it from his hands.

'What ward are we in, Henry? What hospital?'

'The coronary ward, at St Mary's.'

'St Mary's?'

'I could push you home from here in ten minutes.'

'Oh. Is this the private place then?'

Henry had never paid for my treatment before. I wanted to say thank you, but just then had a marvellous idea and was overtaken with enthusiasm for it, forgetting everything else completely.

'Let's go on holiday,' I blurted.

Henry answered sarcastically, gesturing towards the tubed attachments coming out of my arms and face.

'Do you want to bring the hospital with you?'

'When I'm better, I mean. Really, Henry, it's just what we need. Vienna! Barcelona! Prague! Oh, *Prague*. We could hire a yacht. I've always wanted to sail . . .'

Finally the paper came down.

'It's a little late for a mid-life crisis now you're lying here, don't you think? I've seen the world. Go by yourself. Though you'll find no sea for sailing on in central Europe.'

A sharp rush of energy shot through my system. No amount of scorn could crush my new-found purpose.

'I've been trying to persuade you to change for decades and you've always refused to listen to me,' he continued. 'Now all of a sudden you want to have a breakdown! You haven't the money to travel any more, and anyway, movement is never the answer. Surely even you know that.'

'I know no such thing!'

He sighed, but my idea made complete sense. I cried out joyously:

'It is, it is! Moving *is* the answer. I understand now! Let's *go*, Henry . . . to *Jerusalem*!'

The wires and tubes in me suddenly seemed so horribly unnecessary, holding me back when I needed so much to strike out. I yanked at one but it held firm. Henry put a hand on mine to stop me and spoke now even more as if he were talking to a naughty child.

'Try to relax. Forget about this for now. You need your strength for getting well.'

His tone changed into something lighter and the hand came off.

'But now that you're open to ideas, I recommend Jesus, I really do. You don't need to go anywhere to find salvation.'

'Hmm, so they say, so they say,' I replied thoughtfully, calming slightly. 'That's what my friends at work think, too. Gilda and Nas. Lovely couple. Doing a lot of good work.'

Was Henry a Christian? I couldn't remember. The urge returned and I had to make him understand. Now I held Henry's hand tightly and said anxiously:

'Evelyn is trying to tell me to go to Israel. I think that's what's coming, in the letters. You always said I should go, before . . .'

My voice became nothing again, and as I looked pleading-

186

ly at him my friend's face seemed different somehow, almost unrecognisable. He was rarely completely serious; perhaps that was all. I had always believed Henry, about everything. It didn't seem right to disagree. His whole manner was more superior than I ever remembered it being before.

'That was prior to this, Abe. Things have changed now. You need to live differently. Besides, you've not left Britain in fifty years. You hate travelling, you have a pathological fear of planes and boats, you dislike foreign cultures, you're afraid of things you don't know or understand, you appreciate nothing about politics, you won't touch spicy foods, you despise being even slightly unsafe and you don't recognise beauty when it is right in front of you. Trust me, if you go to Israel you'll loathe every minute of it, and you won't find any answers there either; only questions that cannot be answered.'

'Those aren't good reasons!' I protested, folding my arms in disgust. 'You won't change my mind. I am determined.'

'It doesn't matter what you are,' Henry replied in a resigned tone. 'You can't go. Look at you! And anyway, since when did you want to do anything your mother told you to?'

The paper came back up again, like a drawbridge shutting me out. But Henry couldn't stop me; nobody could. All that was needed was enough money for a plane ticket, and any adult can easily get a loan of a few hundred pounds these days, usually with immediate effect, if you're prepared to look a little. I could probably get one over the phone, even on a weekend. Maybe I could work out there, like the kids you hear about. I wasn't too old to get my hands dirty. Work on a kibbutz like Evelyn did, earn my meals, toil in the fields – even settle there if they liked me. My whole life could change for the better. Who knows, maybe I might even meet someone special.

'Lucille will go with me,' I snapped.

'Lucille wouldn't go across the road with you right now.'

'Why?'

'You promised her you would look after yourself. I told her you went to work in that shop yesterday and that's why you collapsed. She thought you had died there.'

'But I'm not dead! Look! I'm still here!'

I grabbed wildly at myself.

'That's true, you aren't. Not yet anyway. But yesterday it wasn't so certain . . .'

Lucille would be sympathetic; she always understood in the end. I just had to be patient. I could even show her Evelyn's photographs and letters, show her she had a family, a past, a future – if I could get out of this hospital and back to Schiller's to pick everything up. We would go to Jerusalem together, as soon as I got out of hospital. She'd be proud of me. A wish to relive those moments with her headmaster and once again see that admiring look on her face swelled within me, until soon I felt fit to burst quite gladly all over the walls of the hospital.

'God knows what Evelyn is telling her about all this,' I said to no one.

Henry returned to his reading, or pretended to. The front page of his paper showed a picture of a street turned to rubble by an army, the back page a smiling footballer celebrating scoring a goal, his shirt lifted high to reveal a vest with the imprint 'JESUS LOVES ME'. The army, the caption said, was Israeli, and in the corner of the photo were the remains of a child's bedroom. The footballer had suffered a heart attack after last night's game and died. Several wordless minutes passed. I thought hard for something to talk about. Finally, I said:

'Any good-looking nurses around this place?'

Despite himself, Henry cheered slightly.

'One or two . . .'

'Oh? And did any express an interest?'

'*Got a phone number for the dribbler in bed 6 in case he wakes up?* Is that what you want me to say? There was *one* who came by asking after you though . . .'

'Really?'

'Yeah, a blonde. Tits and hips type, you know the kind. Beautiful big blue eyes, rosy cheeks, about thirty-five. Just your sort. Similar to that one you met at Butlins in '79, the Turkish girl. Or was she Greek? The one who walked a bit like a goose . . .'

'You say they all walk like geese . . .'

I did perk up at this –'79 was a good year – but strangely I felt like I was pretending to be interested rather than actually being so. Still, I continued.

'There must be something appealing about your snore,' said Henry. 'She came by about an hour ago to check your pulse.'

'And what happened?'

'You still had one.'

'No, not that. *And?*'

'And what?'

'And what did she ask?'

'Oh, you know, the usual . . . asked how we knew each other, what kind of person you were, that kind of thing. She would have asked you herself, but you were out cold. It was difficult.'

'So what did you tell her? How did you describe me?'

'Selfish, but charming. No, *charmingly selfish*, actually. I think that's fair, don't you?'

'More than fair.'

'She responded pretty well, considering. She said that's what her ex-husband was like – a bastard – and then she went away.'

'Oh . . . well, what do you know anyhow?'

'I know you can't leave that bed for a good few days, and that you should go back to sleep. You're safer with your eyes closed.'

Henry returned to his paper again.

'You're lying. She didn't say anything, did she?'

'Of course I'm lying, you daft old sod! Now settle down, get some sleep.'

Those days were over. I should have known. Almost

instantly I obeyed Henry's order, letting heavy eyelids fall over my eyes.

I should have thanked him for paying for my treatment, but before any more words could come I fell asleep. The next time my eyes opened he was gone and I was alone in the big white room once again, waiting for somebody to come by. It felt like a long time had passed. The pile of letters and books called out to me, and I wished whoever had brought them had left them at home. What I really wanted were Evelyn's valuables, but no one had brought them. I shoved the letters in a drawer in protest, took a handful of grapes and closed my eyes once more to work it all out for myself. Was she really telling me I had to go back to Israel? If so, then why didn't she just say? Like the Rabbi had said, it wasn't her style to be coy. Shmuel cycled by the hospital window and up into the clouds, while Evelyn's voice drummed loudly in my ears, driving all other sounds into the background.

'What is happening to you, Avraham? Bicycles in the sky, now? Bibles? Running away like a depressed teenager? You've finally joined the ranks of the mentally irretrievable. *I surrender! I surrender! I raised an idiot! Are you even listening to what I am trying to tell you?*'

I opened my eyes and saw Lucille, her back to me, turning the volume up on a set in my private room and settling herself in front of a piece on the effects of war in Afghanistan, popping grapes playfully into her mouth as she watched.

23

A Plan Hatched

A needle taped onto my forearm stung deep and wooziness washed over me. Its hot sting shot round my body, up and down the pierced arm like a pinball, hard and fast, unremittingly, as it had done a hundred times since I had last been able to sleep. And then it was gone again. In the empty aftermath of the pain I tried to focus on watching Lucille, considering what best to say. It was not the first time in my life I had needed to appeal for forgiveness, but I wasn't quite sure what to say sorry for and this always made apology more difficult. My discussions with Henry seemed a long time ago and I couldn't remember much he said; only that I had done wrong and should make right. Whatever it was, nothing could be worse than having to suffer Lucille's disapproval; Rachel would know that by now. Also, I wanted her to accompany me on my great adventure. While studying her legs swinging from the chair I repeated a clumsy first line several times under my breath but could not get it out.

Lucille was still watching the TV, completely unaware, now seemingly enthralled by a dry news report by a scientist on how middle-aged women could best protect themselves from cancer. (Stressful careers were to be avoided.) The subject didn't matter though. The information could be regurgitated and told joyfully as fact: that was what was important. Lucille was just like an angel. I drifted happily off into dreams of the fantastic adventures we would have together, me showing her all the places and things in the Holy Land that Evelyn had turned her back on so forcibly (at least until the last moment); and her finally enjoying herself, free of the fear of whatever she was afraid of that made her pray to cushions every night and enjoy stabbing bullies with penknives and hide away reading books under the duvet instead of playing with children her own age. I was still dreaming when she turned around and said defiantly:

'You don't look well. I hope they're looking after you properly.'

Without waiting for an answer she began inspecting my attachments from her chair – three pads attached to my top half leading to a heart monitor at the bedside, a needle going into my left arm, one coming out of both sides of my nose and a couple of other tubes whose purpose I didn't understand. She pulled her chair round to face me, sat on it, put her pink mobile phone down on the bed in front of her and continued:

'Perhaps now you will learn to do as you're told,' she said sternly. 'I'm very annoyed with you.'

After a short silence she went on:

'According to this programme, five out of ten women over fifty don't go and get their breasts checked regularly enough. Amazing, isn't it? That's thousands of people that might get sick every year just because they can't be bothered to go to the doctor.'

An answer planted itself in my head and I felt wise, as if my propped-up mattress were a throne and the hospital room my palace courtroom. I replied in my gravelliest voice, slowly and assuredly like an old, experienced king.

'That's a terrible shame for those women who aren't being treated when they should be,' I said, sitting up a little, 'but have you considered that perhaps they don't want to know if they have the disease?'

'Why wouldn't they?'

I let out a low kingly rumble. They say Jesus solved disputes with mere gestures.

'Because once you know, everything changes and cannot go back to being how it was before. Some people will do anything to prevent that.'

'Well, I think they're idiots. How can you sort out a problem if you don't know you have one?'

The king in me was gone.

'Er . . . I suppose you can't . . . right.'

Lucille came closer to the bed. Her face screwed up in deep concentration.

'Are you OK then? What's *wrong* with you exactly? What are all these tubes for?'

'They say I had a heart attack. Just a mild one. But I'm going to be just fine.'

'Yes, but why?'

'Why what?'

'Why did you have it? Something must have brought it on. Did you go to the doctor's?'

'Yes, I did. All the time.'

'Good.'

'Not really.'

'What?'

'I said not really.'

'How do you mean?'

I reorganised myself in the bed, sitting up more to see her better. Lucille did the same in her seat. The King was making a nervous reappearance.

'Well, I went to the doctor's once or twice a month for more than twenty years. They took blood from me regularly, sent me for tests, looked into my mouth, up my nose, in my ears, put me on all sorts of drugs, all in the name of trying to make me better . . . and here I am lying in hospital anyway. I'm only sixty-one and have no history of heart failure in the family at all. Your great-granny, on the other hand, hardly set foot in a hospital or doctor's surgery in her life – didn't trust the smell, she said – and she lived to ninety-three with barely a day's illness in all her first eight decades of life. How about that, eh? What does that mean?'

Lucille processed this patiently, which pleased me, but seemed uninterested in offering any answer.

'Why have you got a Christian's Bible by your bed?' she said finally, noticing the bright red book by my bedside. 'And

what were you doing working in that shop? As you keep saying, we're Jewish.'

I laughed.

'Well . . . sometimes in life, when someone you love dies,
you start to wonder about your own life. You look around,
perhaps to God, for a bit of comfort. I was just doing a bit of
looking around, that's all.'

'But you don't even know which God you believe in yet!'

'I was still deciding on my God when this happened. I'm
not even sure if I want one at all.'

'Surely you either do believe or you don't.'

'Maybe. I worry though. Perhaps sometimes the belief
itself might need a little help.'

'Auntie Beryl says you'll worry yourself into an early
grave.'

'I almost did.'

And we were back to talking about the heart attack.

'You said you'd be careful, but you sneaked out of the
house when you were ill. Dad even put a note on the door as
a reminder. You promised to protect me. I had to pretend to
walk to school on Thursday because you'd left the house and
not told me what you were doing. That woman wanted to
take me in the car, and I had to make sure she didn't. I nearly
cried.'

Some of Lucille's words were lost to the atmosphere, so
pleased was I to be finally acquiring some gravitas to my
voice, albeit fleeting – surely it was only a matter of time
before true wisdom followed – but I did notice that at the
mention of the word 'cried' her confidence started to evaporate. Tears began to appear, her small face reddening quickly.
Her breathing became erratic. She hadn't cried for a long
time, longer than I could remember, and I looked on with
interest at the emergence of this other, new side to her. She
was such a remarkable little thing. Her speech became faster
as she struggled to contain heavy sobs. It all spilled out. But
though I wanted to, I was chained to the machines and could

not console her apart from stupidly repeating, 'Shh, it's OK,' over and over. Lucille stayed in her seat.

'Arabella's been away for ages now, and we don't know when she's coming home, and I miss her . . . and now that woman is in the house, and Dad didn't even ask me if it was OK if she came to stay and I think that's very rude because I live there too and so do you, and especially because they're always kissing and how can he be so selfish, and why does nobody think about me, everybody wants me to do things for them and keep secrets and I don't know if I can and . . . and . . . and . . .'

At the final 'and' her little body gave up, caving in to the overwhelming sadness within, and her alarmingly quiet sobbing, more like a constant, barely audible whine, took over completely. What kind of treatment had taught her to cry so quietly?

'Grandpa, when's Arabella coming home? Is she coming home? Her postcard made it sound like she might not come back for ages . . .'

And then she gave in to more tears, floods of them.

'Come on, it's going to be all right,' I whispered.

'No, it isn't, it isn't, it *isn't* . . .'

'It is . . .'

'How can you be sure? You're always saying things are going to get better . . .'

I thought quickly, and my mind took another one of its dangerous leaps into the unknown. Before my mistake could be realised, I said:

'Because we're going to escape from it all, just like Arabella. We're going to *Israel*, you and me. It's what Granny Evelyn has been trying to tell us in her letters. She hasn't said it exactly, but I know, I just know. I have it all planned out already.'

'But you can't . . . not yet . . .'

Almost instantly the tears stopped, but the little frown stayed.

'They wouldn't let you go anywhere. You have to stay in hospital . . .'

I pointed grandly to the skies, pleading my case with a smile.

'Now you listen to me, little one. This is a free country. I know my rights, and I know I can discharge myself from hospital whenever I like. It's in the *Geneva Convention*!'

'You're ill though. Seriously ill, Dad says.'

'Aren't I the same person you remember from yesterday? Can't I talk, and touch my nose with my tongue?'

To prove the point I touched my nose with the tip of my tongue. Lucille ignored this.

'You've been here two days now – but I suppose you don't seem any different . . . apart from all those, of course . . .'

She pointed to my attachments.

'Right then!' I said. 'Sorry, I should have looked after myself better.'

'Hmm,' replied Lucille. 'I'm sorry for crying. Friends?'

'Friends. But you don't need to say sorry for crying.'

The last of the tears were wiped purposefully away.

'Look, Grandpa, I've been thinking about these letters, and as you know I've been talking to Granny a lot. I think she wants you to wait.'

'What for?'

'Well . . . I don't know, but I'm sure she doesn't want you to leave hospital before you're ready. Didn't she say she'd make it all OK if you listened to her?'

'You leave the big decisions to me. Who knows what's best for me better than me? Nobody, right? Granny Evelyn's been telling me I'd be all right if only I'd listen to her for as long as I can remember. I've done a lot of listening, and things are still a mess.'

Lucille looked to the ground, distracted, annoyed. I tried again.

'Look, I'm going to get out of here tomorrow morning, and then you and I can get away from all this. I'll book us flights straight away – whatever they cost – and we'll just *go*. Remember all those places you were saying Granny told you about? Jerusalem, the kibbutz, her old house? We'll see all of those. Don't you want to?'

'I put laxatives in that woman Rachel's tea this morning,' interrupted Lucille. 'She's spent half the day in the toilet.'

'Lucille, be nice.'

'If we're leaving I won't have to, will I?' she snapped. 'At least not for a while. So . . . what's the big plan then?'

'Well, I can book us tickets for tomorrow from here, with my credit card. There's a phone by the bed here, and I'm certain there'll be no trouble getting them. Israel's hardly the most popular holiday destination right now, is it? . . . I'll discharge myself in the morning and get a taxi, say to Emporium, and we'll go from there to the airport . . .'

'What about Dad?'

I nudged her chummily.

'You'll have to sneak out, but if I can do it, you can, right? You said it yourself, he doesn't notice much at the moment. We'll call him from the airport, of course – we don't want to worry him – but he'd only stop us . . .'

I was so excited it was almost as if Lucille wasn't there. She looked at me uncertainly.

'It'll be fine, I promise, *an adventure*. Don't you want to go on an adventure?'

She nodded meekly.

'Of course you do. So, once I've booked the flights I'll call you on your mobile and we'll make arrangements for tomorrow. OK?'

At this point our preparations were interrupted by Nathan and Rachel arriving. I was sweating now but was unsure whether I was hot with anticipation or with the knowledge of having just made a catastrophic mistake.

'Hello! And how's the invalid?' said Nathan.

Immediately the atmosphere cooled. His manner befitted more the visit of a polite distant cousin after a mild anaes-

197

thetic rather than a son after a heart attack, but I played along, distracted by my plans. I thanked them, and we all kissed. They had brought yet more grapes. It was all very friendly, but Nathan and Rachel behaved like amorous teenagers in front of a clearly pained Lucille, who withdrew increasingly as the conversation wore on, retreating towards the TV and finally distancing herself from us altogether. It was hard to believe no one else had noticed this, though I get less surprised at Nathan's neglect of her as time goes on. The only mention of her silence was from Rachel.

'You're not very talkative are you? What's wrong, sweetheart?'

In the face of no reply from Lucille herself, she turned to me, saying, 'You must be very proud,' as if that was the end of the matter.

Nathan and Rachel saved most of their attention for each other, sharing in-jokes, laughing at unspoken things, leaving us to guess. Soon they began to talk only to each other, as if we were not even there, discussing my treatment, my medication, my recovery and what the doctors had said and what was the best thing to do with me once I got home.

'Do you think he might be more comfortable in Evelyn's room?' asked Rachel. 'After all, it's already set up for the sick . . .'

'God, no! It's too soon, *far* too soon. What a thing to say . . .'

'Sorry . . . I just thought it made sense . . .'

Neither of them once mentioned the actual heart attack itself, as if I had done something dirty not to be discussed openly. Instead, we were all to pretend.

If you ignored the fact that Lucille hated her, Rachel had fitted into Arabella's old role remarkably well and she seemed to be making Nathan extremely happy, at least for now. I watched her carefully. She was no longer a sex object to me, but neither was she repulsive because of what she had so easily succeeded in doing to my family. It was almost as if

Rachel had studied Arabella from afar before we all met, taken notes and devised a thorough strategy for after her departure. That was how good she was. The result was astonishing: complete and instant success. Her effect on him was almost magical. As they discussed which brand of shampoo to buy that night, I tried one final time to remember any details of our fumblings either in the house on Monday or in Rachel's car on Sunday night – to summon up the odour of her sweaty body as she dropped to her knees in the front seat, recall the feel of her skin as she touched my back, bewildered at how quickly things were happening – but the memory of it was almost completely gone. Perhaps the experience had not been with Rachel after all but with a different barmaid of a similar shape. I had enjoyed the sluttishness of what that woman was doing, whoever she was, but when I looked at Rachel holding hands so softly with Nathan I saw only a caring, mature woman helping my son through a difficult time; something I was not doing. She seemed to care more about me than my son did and more about him than me. But for Lucille's rejection, it really was as if she had been in our family all along and things really were getting back to a kind of routine. The future was bright at least; Nathan's wage was a handsome one, enough to support woman and child if needed, with plenty left over to clear their debts, given time. Anyway, Rachel had business plans of her own. She had no intention of being a housewife. My brain buzzed with possible futures: perhaps when they moved out I could rent out the rooms to help clear my own debts.

The conversation continued without me. Nathan and Rachel discussed what the coming months might hold in store for them; their bedroom needed redecorating, they said, a holiday would be nice too, perhaps at the end of the summer: they deserved one. There was no mention of anyone moving out of my home any time soon. On the contrary. Rachel said she had changed the locks on the house (problems with the front door, apparently) and a new key had been brought for me for when I came home, which Rachel put in the pile by the bedside amongst the books and post.

'It looks like you're going to need us now,' she said sympathetically, planting a kiss lightly on my forehead and turning back to Nathan. 'He's lucky really, isn't he? All of us here to look after him.'

'Dad needs to rest. We're probably tiring him out.'

'No, son, it's fine . . .'

Nathan made for the door and beckoned Rachel to do the same.

'Come on, Lucille. Say goodbye to Grandpa. You'll see him soon.'

But Lucille stubbornly refused, holding on tight to the rail on the side of my bed. She gravitated towards the headboard of the bed for cover from her father.

'I don't *want* to come with you . . . I'm staying at Uncle Henry and Auntie Beryl's tonight.'

Nathan snapped.

'You will *DO AS I SAY!*'

Lucille appeared visibly to shrink waiting for her father to speak, but though he threatened to burst with rage, it was a threat never carried out. Instead, the only sound was that of Nathan trying to bring his breathing under control.

'Come on, let her stay there,' said Rachel. 'She deserves to. And Henry's still out in the corridor. He's been here an hour waiting for her.'

Nathan nodded in reluctant assent as Rachel led him into the corridor, waving at me on her way, and soon they were gone.

'Good thinking,' I whispered to Lucille. 'Now you don't need to sneak out in the morning.'

'Yes, I do,' she replied angrily. 'Uncle Henry and Auntie Beryl won't let me come any more than Dad will. I just don't want to be with them. Listen, another letter came for you this morning. I thought you might like to see it.'

'Come on, don't be angry. I'll phone you later, shall I?'

'I don't think you're well enough to go away.'

'Lucille, trust me. This is really important, and it's what your Granny wanted, I'm sure.'

'But if Granny wanted us to go to Israel, she would say, wouldn't she? Read that letter and see what it says first.'

'When did it come?'

'Yesterday.'

'So there *was* a letter on Friday then . . . anything in the post today?'

'I've not checked yet. But I will. Please do what this one says though.'

'Thanks, but whatever this letter says we have to go tomorrow. I don't know how long I've got. Are you with me? Please?'

Lucille nodded solemnly, kissed me on the cheek, dropped the letter in my lap and was gone, taking Henry's hand in the corridor. Perhaps it was only family visiting hours or something. Henry would have come in if he could.

24

Confirmation

As soon as Lucille was gone I opened the letter, hardly thinking of what might be inside. Instead, I wondered if I would have time to get to Schiller's before going to the airport. Perhaps all that stuff could be shipped over later.

Hello again, Avraham –

This is the last part of my story. Then, we shall get onto yours.

By 1953 Berlin was a city divided, caught up in an uprising against the Communists. My family was scattered or dead, and I had abandoned them too long ago to go back anyway, and so, through chance and circumstance, you and I ended up in this funny little country that doesn't know what it is any more than you do. A close friend on the kibbutz had given me an address for her father, who lived near here, and helped me set up on my own when we arrived, even renting us a cheap room until we could afford something better.

When we got to England the country was obsessed by the coronation. I was so disappointed with the place that I almost got straight on the next boat back, but by then I was too tired and ashamed to do so. Instead, I started to rebuild our lives, without money or knowledge of the country. You adapted better than me. It was as if you'd been on holiday for all that time and were glad finally to be coming home. I have never felt this is home, though I have been here fifty years.

You won't remember this – you remember so little – but we were in that room together for over two years, saving, planning, starting again. I taught you to play chess in that

202

room; you read *Animal Farm* for the first time in the bed by the window. I taught you about the Greek and Roman gods, told you stories, played you Mahler and Bach; you could even quote a few lines from Freud, Marx and Einstein – do you remember, Avraham? Was this you or some other curious, intelligent child I bore, who smiled so much and always wanted to know more? I was so dedicated to your development; sometimes I think about that time and wish for it, but become too annoyed thinking about what followed.

In the year we moved into 174, I left the toy factory, and the father of my friend and I went into business together: we began turning our idea into the success it became many years later. It was satisfying to succeed, and of that I can be proud, but I had no passion for it. The products we made were not important to me. I missed home, both my homes: Berlin and Jerusalem – Jerusalem the most. I felt increasingly that I had wasted my life on something worthless because I had decided to run from something else imperfect but more valuable. But what else could I have done? When you have put all your belief and energy for so long into something that you thought turned out to be a lie? You must turn your back on it completely. I had no choice. And so I chose something that was the political opposite of the kibbutz, of communism, of equality: I became the boss, buying out my friend's father on his retirement and throwing myself completely into making money, and lots of it. It was the only thing left.

Britain has changed me in ways I do not like. My speech has changed, my instincts, my opinions. I have even begun to think in English, and I hate myself for leaving Jerusalem. Seeing you grow up and love it here, become it so completely, only makes it harder. For years now I have fantasised about returning to Israel but have pretended to myself and everyone else that the place meant nothing to me, hoarding my most precious things at Schiller's. There

203

is still much I dislike about Israel, of course, and the government there is still full of parasites, but I am alone and have been for so long now that I often lie here longing for that community spirit we had in the early days, the hope, the purity of it all, even for scraps of it. Israel has often seemed an inevitable thing, always there, silently pulling me back towards it, but now I cannot return. Instead of admitting my mistake and going back when I was still able, I hid from life, much like you do.

I do not need to tell you what has happened between us, Avraham, but try to understand what it is like for a mother to see a change in her son and be powerless to stop it. You did not want to listen to me any more. You got older but did not grow up. We had nothing in common. And, because I had not given you anything to grow into or rebel against apart from me, I lost you. It was my fault. Don't ask me about the void between your youth and now, because I don't know about all that. Your string of marriages, your career that never was – the rank distraction of royal history that you have made your life's obsession – to me all of those things were just a succession of wrong turns, mistakes, false hopes, and they have left nothing behind that has endured. Before is everything. When my God asks me about my life, England will not even be a footnote.

Far from the panic that I expected to set in after reading Evelyn's latest letter, a new peace came over me, one more complete than the shiver of recognition experienced in the synagogue listening to little Lenny's beautiful voice and more satisfying than the one that came and went in my shift at the shop. Those things had been distractions disguised as solutions; I had stumbled on my true path and could not now veer from it. It all made sense now. And so, the calm that comes with true understanding seeped right through me. I knew what I had to do; Lucille would be so pleased to hear of it. I didn't need Evelyn to tell me my part of the story: I could work it out for myself.

Cheerily, I put her letter down and opened the rest of the post that had been brought for me. The first thing in the pile was a further demand for action from Wife Number Three's solicitor, this time more threatening, the second a letter from a company I had never had dealings with before, whose address was on our road, the third a solicitor's reminder to pay a debt-collection company that would take me to court if I didn't pay up, and the fourth an invitation to church on Sunday. They were welcoming new members, apparently, for Easter. There was no mention of the vicar. Perhaps they had prepared an understudy, just in case. Also, a small package containing my wallet was in the pile, complete with the remainder of Henry's money roll, which I had left in there two days ago.

In a quiet moment during the afternoon I lifted the phone by the bed to find out the number of a flight operator who could get me two tickets to Jerusalem for the following morning. When the airline rejected my card I used the emergency one Henry had given me in case I was ever in trouble and couldn't get out of it. If this wasn't an emergency, then what was?

For the next few hours I ate the meals brought to me, spoke politely to doctors and nurses, let them do all the tests they wanted to and pretended nothing was going on. But I knew. Smiling, I snuggled under the duvet like a small child and settled with the covers over me, strangely happy. It was almost a shame to have to leave the hospital so soon; I was just getting to enjoy my illness. Apart from the pains that came and went, the stiffness, the rawness and the discolour on parts of my skin, the experience was mainly pleasant. Perhaps there would be another meal coming round soon.

25

The Rabbi Visits

The Rabbi arrived just as I was beginning to read the New Testament, its big bright red title standing out boldly from the hospital room's whiteness all around. I couldn't get out of bed, and none of the magazines in the ward looked good anyway – I am not interested in what celebrities are doing to each other – so I'd selected something brought from my bedside at home instead. The Bible seemed lighter reading than the other options before me, so I picked it up and this time started from the very beginning. I wondered while flicking through the lengthy introduction whether Jesus had ever had a mild heart attack, and if so, how he might have dealt with it. I should really try to start acting with a little more dignity. Flirtations with the lunchtime nurse had been weak and unappreciated, and my attempts to squeeze sympathy from the doctors had so far failed miserably. I started as the Rabbi approached.

'Matthew 1:1: This is the list of the ancestors of Jesus Christ, a descendant of David, who was a descendant of Abraham.'

'Anything good in there?' he asked kindly.

I heard the Rabbi before I saw him, letting out a frantic high-pitched squeal in response, almost dropping the book right into his lap. My visitor, seemingly unperturbed, opened his long black coat, thrust it out to the sides and took the seat by my bed, heaving a great sigh of relief as his backside hit the plastic. He was clearly struggling, beads of sweat collecting around his face.

'It says I'm Jesus's grandfather,' I said, petrified.

'Really? Now *there's* a claim to fame.'

The Rabbi smiled, picking the book off the sheets, placing it carefully on the bedside table and then patting his brow with a handkerchief.

'It's OK, I'm not here on business.'

He panted heavily.

'Sorry, you'll have to excuse me for a moment; the lift was broken and those stairs are no fun at all.'

Surely there was a law against Jews reading the New Testament unsupervised; I was lucky to have stumbled across a liberal. I forced a weak smile in return but was unable to speak again just yet, struggling for a few seconds until somehow finally managing to say:

'Actually, it's not what I hoped it might be. The Bible, I mean. I've had a bit of an epiphany of my own, you see. What floor are we on?'

'The ninth,' came the reply. 'Some do say the New Testament's not all it might be. But few things are what the adverts lead you to believe, is that not true?'

He was beginning to regain his composure.

'The New Testament is no exception, but there's a lot of good in there. Plenty of action; more consistent than the Torah really, in places at least. That's full of *so-and-so begat so-and-so*, what people ate, death rituals, sacrifice – long sections of dry detail punctuated by dazzling splashes. I prefer the Torah in Hebrew; it brings out the true beauty that way. It's musical. What you've got there is more direct. That version, at least.'

'I thought you would disapprove.'

'Oh, on the contrary. I did a more general degree before qualifying as a Rabbi, covering all the most popular religions, and the lessons of the New Testament are useful in my day-to-day work even now. Persevere with it, if you can.' He tapped his nose conspiratorially with a finger. 'There's a lot of crossover. They say Jesus was *a Jew*.'

I laughed nervously as he came closer and put a hand softly on my shoulder.

'It's OK, *relax*,' he whispered. 'Listen: I brought you something.'

He handed over a small book, a collection of Yiddish tales

with a beautiful hand-woven cover, which felt almost weightless in my hand.

'For when you finish the New Testament, perhaps. I hope you like it.'

'Thank you. You didn't have to . . .'

'I know.'

I ran my eyes down the contents page.

'Anything good in here?'

'Oh, plenty.'

'Tell me a story, then.'

'What, now?'

I nodded.

'OK, which one?'

'Anything. Pick something you like.'

'All right then, how about this? Something short.'

The Rabbi took the book back off me, resettled himself in the chair and slipped into a lower, more thoughtful tone of voice, turning to a page in the middle of the book and holding it up so I couldn't see the page. The longer he talked the more I regretted asking him to start at all.

'Once, there was a man who studied the Torah and Talmud intensely every day, from early in the morning until late at night. Deep in his quest, he hardly spoke to a soul, instead locking himself away in his home searching for meaning in the word of Hashem. In time, he became the most learned man in his village, the district, some said in the whole country, but he was unsettled. He craved something more. One day, the Lord of Darkness came to him in a dream, saying, "What is all this you do? What can you gain from it? You sit down here all day trawling the books, you are more learned than anyone else for miles around, yet you are not recognised. Where are your honours? What do the Jews do for you? Nothing! You hardly have enough food for you and your family." "So what should I do?" says the man. "Well," replies the Lord of Darkness, "the *Christians* – now there's a religion that knows how to treat its servants. With your knowledge, in a year you could be a priest, even the Pope eventually. Riches await you, praise and glory. All you have to do is make the switch. They love a Jew who has turned. It's easy. Think of the money . . . "'

The Rabbi looked up to smile for a second and then returned to the book, flipping the page. He hardly seemed to be reading at all but telling the story from memory.

'"But what about my people?" asks the man. "How can I abandon them?" "You already have," says the Lord of Darkness. The man had no answer. And so, the following morning, he got up, put away all his books, broke the news to his wife and began his reinvention. Satan was right. He was a success in the world of the Gentiles. It took a while, but in time he was given his own church, then region, then country and many years later, after the death of the last Pope, who had been hugely popular and ruled for three decades, he took up the position himself. He was worshipped all over the world and became rich beyond his wildest dreams, but the man was still not happy. The rituals of Christianity did not satisfy him, the teachings did not speak to him in the same way. Secretly, he began returning to his old Jewish books, and eventually he could take no more. Tearing himself up inside with the guilt of what he had done, the man abandoned the Church to return to the religion of his forefathers, running away in shame, deeply regretting the decision he had made. But when he tried to return to Judaism the Lord of Darkness reappeared to remind him that by Jewish law no Jew who converts to Christianity may return. The man was devastated; in all the books he had read, in all the learning he had done, he had not come across this law. But it was true. "It seems you cannot know everything," he said to himself. The man became a beggar on the steps of the cathedral, awaiting his fate until the day the Lord of Darkness came for him.'

I interrupted the ending, unable to take any more.

'Why are you telling me this? Are you trying to frighten me? I thought you said it was *never* too late to come back.'

'You asked me to tell you a story.'

'Well, thanks.'

There was a moody silence. I sulked. The Rabbi tried again, putting the book back down on the table.

'Look, is there anything you need? Food? Drink? Perhaps you might like a newspaper . . .'

But his attempts to reassure only made me more nervous. I preferred working things out for myself; this imposition was most unwelcome. A nervous twitch under my eye started up in immediate response, flapping away uncontrollably, and sweat began pouring from my forehead. The nappy and crêpe paper became clammy on my skin, and suddenly I began to feel like a cheat. Perhaps Evelyn had been right when she was alive; I would never act, never change, never become anything properly. Perhaps the Rabbi was there to expose me as a fake.

'What's wrong? You've gone terribly pale.'

'Rabbi,' I stammered, 'you should go.'

'Pardon?'

'If you're trying to rescue me, I mean . . .'

He raised an unconvinced eyebrow in wry amusement as I stumbled on, but I needed to come clean.

'Look, Rabbi, I'm all talk. I haven't changed a bit. I'm a repeated adulterer, I've ordered the bacon and eggs for breakfast, I hadn't set foot in a synagogue for three decades before Thursday, I've basically given myself this heart attack through gross negligence, I'm not even a member of a Shule any more – if I die tomorrow they will bury me amongst the non-Jews. Why on earth are you here?'

'Shh, shh,' the Rabbi said soothingly, his hand now resting between my collarbone and shoulder. 'I have plenty of reason. I was in your home only last week, was I not? You were in synagogue two days ago. You called me at four in the morning on Tuesday. I knew your mother well, and she *was* fully paid up, despite what she may have told you. Actually, according to my records, she has also been paying your fees for nineteen years, so you are a member and will be buried along with the rest of us whether you like it or not. Is that not enough reason? Of course, I can leave if you prefer . . .'

Briefly my whole system seemed to shut down, and it took all my energy to crank it back into life again. I was confused, dizzy, unsteady. My visitor looked at me benignly as I struggled to get the words out.

'No, don't go. I'm glad you're here. I need to talk to someone.'

Just saying it cloaked me in shame.

'Let's start again then, shall we?'

'No, wait. How did you know where to find me?'

'The grapevine is not restricted to the secular, you know. How are you? That's the main thing.'

Finally I gave in to the undiluted truth. It sounded strange to hear it.

'I don't know,' I said. 'Changeable. Sometimes I'm in a lot of pain, other times none. Right now I feel able to do anything, but half an hour ago I was ready for death, and an hour before that I was giddily happy, laughing away in my bed like a madman for no reason. I feel like an idiot. I wish everyone would go away and rescue me all at the same time. I really think I might have hit upon an idea, something to do when I get out of here . . . but the slightest things send me right back to the beginning of the process.'

'From what I remember, that sounds perfectly normal in this situation; it's probably the shock. Don't be too concerned. It will pass.'

'Remember from what?'

'I used to be a doctor.'

'Oh, really?'

He smiled, embarrassed.

'Yes, in a past life. There have been several.'

'You've certainly lived, Rabbi.'

'I like to think so.'

He laughed, and tugged tenderly at his whiskers. It was a

nervous tugging. Perhaps he wanted to get away. There was a quiet sadness in amongst the Rabbi's humour.

'There was no beard in those days though,' he continued, seeing me glancing at his tangle of whiskers. 'Nobody wants hair in their kidneys. It tends to get in the way of surgery, you know? No tsit-tsit, no kippah either.'

I tried to imagine this man in a white coat instead of a black one.

'Were you a good doctor?' I asked.

'I think so. I *hope* so.'

'Then why did you give it up?'

'Simple: because Hashem told me to. And how can you turn down the Almighty? You can't, right? The King of the Universe asks you to make a career change, you don't ask questions. So I went back to university, and here I am. I was lucky. Not everyone gets such a clear sign. Excuse me a moment.'

He got up and left in the direction of the toilets. Evelyn cut in.

'They survive on gold alone. They demand, unthinkingly; they're like rats that way. You're nothing but money in the pot. Remember that when you're saying your prayers, when they're giving you presents, asking you how you are, how business is, telling you little fables.'

But that didn't make sense any more. That was the old Evelyn, not the new one. How could I know who to listen to? Who could I trust? To pay for his wars, on Woolsey's advice, Henry VIII's henchmen raided the Catholic monasteries and convents of England, raping the nuns and killing the priests, scavenging from the coffers until they were empty. But the Rabbi was no scavenger, at least as far as I could see. He didn't want anything, did he? He had been persuasive, but kind too. He'd helped Evelyn and was helping me. He was just a normal person who went to the toilet like everyone else. I was caught between deep admiration and a passionate jealousy, wanting to chase him into the Gents and tear off his hat and coat right there and then to see what was underneath, whether there was any ulterior motive. For the first time I felt like one of those vulnerable people you hear about on the news who bad people prey on. That would be hard to get used to.

'How do you know when God is talking?' I asked him on his return.

'When Hashem speaks to you, he makes it obvious,' he replied, dabbing his forehead with a tissue. 'If you're not sure, it's something else. A stomach ache, perhaps.'

He laughed lightly.

'Rabbi, do you think God spoke to my mother?'

'Oh yes, undoubtedly, although she would have never admitted it. That's why she changed so radically, so quickly. The alterations in her will, her attitude towards Israel, her sudden desire to learn about the Torah, the festivals, her heritage – the Almighty is there for us all if we want him.'

'But she always rejected God, and bid me do the same.'

'I know. She told me everything.'

'What did you discuss? Did she really regret her life? Why did she leave you her money? And how long had she been giving money to the synagogue? I'm beginning to think I didn't know her at all.'

'Don't feel bad, Abe. Evelyn felt misunderstood by everybody, me included. Only she knew what she really believed, and even then only sometimes. You have to remember how ill she was, in so many ways. You must mourn, but try to focus on the future too, on getting well again, living your own life. That is difficult enough.'

'But she won't leave me alone. I can still hear her, like you heard God, as loud and clear as if she was standing right behind me, but not always in the same voice. And she comes and goes . . . it's not constant. Sometimes she leaves me for a while, then comes back to remind me she's in charge.'

'Hmm. What has she been saying since we last spoke?'

'I think she wants me to go to Israel, back to the kibbutz where we lived. I think she wishes she'd stayed there.'

'I see. And do you want to go?'

'I'm starting to think doing anything else is just putting off the inevitable . . . though, as you can see, it hasn't stopped me exploring other avenues.'

I held up the Bible and smiled, embarrassed.

'Have you been to Israel?' I asked.

'Many times. It is beautiful. Every day I pray for peace there.'

'Evelyn used to say there would be none of that until the Israelis stopped treating the Palestinians like Hitler treated the Jews: like thieves on their patch. What's it really like?'

'It's the home of our people, what can I say? Magical, magical.'

'Then why don't you move there?'

'I often consider making Aliyah, and still might do it. But, for now, God wants me here. There is still much work to do in the diaspora.'

'What about me? Is my work over here too? How can I find out?'

'It's not for me to say. Just make sure you are running towards something, not away from something. That is most important.'

More truth poured out.

'I'd certainly like to run: to somewhere I didn't have to read the post every morning. Rabbi, did you and my mother ever discuss Pesach? She left me an old Haggadah, from her parents.'

'Pesach interested her a lot towards the end – like I said, the major festivals preoccupied her a great deal. She did say a few things to me about the wise son and the wicked son, but they were jumbled.'

'Think of them, please.'

The Rabbi was getting increasingly fidgety.

'I will, and shall return soon to tell you them, but not now. Now, I must go. Mrs Silverman in ward nine is expecting me before five o'clock. She gets very nervous if I'm late.'

'Of course. Thank you for coming.'

The Rabbi got up to leave, rebuttoning his coat as he rose.

'How is the Memorial Hall coming on?' I asked. 'I'm looking forward to the opening.'

For the first time the prospect of the hall being built made me happy, though I couldn't explain why. This feeling quickly evaporated as the Rabbi's expression change from a polite smile to one of dismay as he realised he would not get away from me today without mentioning it. He sat down again, steadied himself, looked at me sympathetically and said quietly, without drama:

'Abe, the hall burned down last night during the Shabbat service; we had to evacuate the building halfway through prayers. The police say the whole floor was smeared with petrol. We are lucky the old building is safe. I'm so sorry.'

'Who did it? Do they know?'

'We don't know for sure, but we have our suspicions. Graffiti left on the wall is similar to a symbol on a well-known anti-Semitic website.'

'Are there no police on the internet? I didn't think those things were allowed to exist!'

'Sadly, Abe, they are. There's all the usual talk . . . of Zionist conspiracies, atrocities, rich Jews and masons running the world, but what frightens me is how organised, how efficient, how intellectual some of these things seem. I looked up that website this morning and, frankly, I'm shocked. I didn't think I still could be.' The Rabbi laughed cynically. 'You know, I used to think there was not much anti-Semitism around here – too many Jews for that – but since the troubles started up again in Israel . . . well, things have got worse again. In Europe too. And not just for the Jews: Islamophobia is far more serious these days. Every time we think we are winning the battle against ignorance, it resurfaces somewhere.'

I almost felt like I should be consoling him.

'I was going to tell you when you were better,' he said.

'No, I needed to know. Thank you. So what happened to

Lenny's son's bar mitzvah? And how come you're doing the rounds in hospital the day after?'

'My duties are the same, Abe, hall or no hall. Besides, there is not much I can do standing in the rubble. The bar mitzvah is rescheduled for next week; of course, your invitation still stands, that's if you're well enough to attend.'

'Poor Lenny.'

'Yes, there has been great difficulty rebooking everybody. After all their careful preparations they may have to do without a live band, and there's no guarantee of a marquee in the garden any more. The whole family is devastated.'

The whole idea of the hall seemed an absurd ironic joke before, but not now. The one good thing Evelyn had made possible was lying wrecked, burnt out, hanging off the end of the surviving synagogue building. There was bitterness in my voice.

'You didn't seem very affected by this before. Why not?'

'Yesterday I was, believe me,' he replied. 'Since then I have felt many things. Anger, sadness, resentment, but now I have forgiven.'

'You recover quickly, Rabbi.'

'Sometimes, Abe, you have to.'

As he got up to leave, I realised how much I didn't want him to.

'Before you go, have you any advice for me?'

'Yes, if you would like it,' he answered. 'This.'

He took the New Testament and his present and put them together in my palms, giving them to me and clasping his hands around mine as if casting a spell.

'This is your choice.'

He shook my hands and the books lightly.

'Every man has the right to choose, but he must know he has to live with the consequences. Once he has decided to cross the disintegrating bridge, he cannot then expect to cross back safely should he decide he does not like the other side. Get well soon, and remember, if you don't want to read your post, you don't have to.'

He winked.

'You are the master of your letterbox.'

And with that he left me, passing Gilda, Nas and a flustered-looking vicar on the way out.

26

Gilda, Nas and the Vicar

My new visitors came armed with fruit: grapes, apples and mandarins cradled like babies in their arms as they shuffled through the door and crowded around my bed. (No matter how long I lived, I would never be short of grapes.) Each tip-toed about as if I might break at the slightest sound, and they were right to. Conversation with the Rabbi had left me exhausted and afraid to read more words that might only confuse me further. I had reached my limit for religion, of whatever shade, for the day, and certainly my limit for honesty.

'Come in, come in,' I said, hiding the book the Rabbi had given me. 'Don't be shy.'

'Hi there,' said Gilda quietly. 'We brought someone to see you.'

The vicar nodded. Gilda gathered the gifts and put them down in front of me, my bedside now overflowing with vita-mins and nourishing reading material.

'Was that man here to see you?' she asked.

'No, he was lost. Looking for Cardiology, apparently. Hello – thanks for coming. I don't know what happened the other day but thank you, for whatever you did. After chatting to you both in the shop, my mind is a blank. I'm so sorry.'

Gilda was embarrassed.

'It was nothing. Just a little mouth to mouth, that's all . . .'

'It was the ambulance crew who did most of the work,' interrupted Nas. 'But even after they'd arrived we were all pretty scared. I've never seen anything like that before.'

He became more serious now. Suddenly Nas seemed much younger.

'It reminded me how fragile life really is.'

He looked at me like I imagined he might look at a tattered old doll, and this made me reply harshly.

'Fragile? Don't be ridiculous – I could still live to a hundred and one! These things happen all the time.'

'I wish you were right, Abe, but you stopped breathing completely. Early on, your chances weren't good at all and as it was your first day at the shop we didn't have any contact details for you yet. It was only when Gilda went back there and found your wallet on the floor that we found a phone number for your son. Even then we had to leave a message for him to call the hospital, which he didn't reply to for another two hours.'

'That explains the wallet then.'

Nas was beginning to get irritating. He was too young to be reprimanding me.

'I don't think you understand how serious the situation really was. You can thank that wallet for your life. If we hadn't managed to get hold of Nathan and he hadn't told the doctors the medication you're allergic to just in time, you could have died. It's a miracle you're still alive . . .'

'Yes, a miracle!' piped up the vicar. 'You know, they won't say so but Gilda and Nas were quite the heroes. They were both very responsible: we're all terribly proud of them back at the parish. Everyone knows about you now! I'm Jim, nice to meet you. You must have had quite an ordeal.'

At the sympathetic mention of how difficult things were for me, I cheered up.

'Not really, Jim, I've known nothing about the whole business – your friends appear to have suffered much more than me. All the important stuff goes on when you're asleep around here! I have been treated marvellously by the nurses, fed well, and I don't feel I'm making it up any more, as everyone seems to be very worried about me. Last week, I thought I was going insane; now I feel vindicated. The only thing is the drugs – they seem to be affecting my moods. I'm Abe Stone, nice to meet you too.'

The vicar was a happy-looking, thin man of about my age, one unruly, bushy eyebrow framing his face and wispy grey hair spilling out in all directions, the physical opposite of the Rabbi. I tried to imagine him working his way through the choir like the stallion described to me the other day, doing all those filthy things to the saintly wives of the parish over the church organ, but couldn't. He simply didn't look capable. Indeed, he looked as if he would be horrified by the mere prospect.

'How are you feeling?' he asked. 'You must be in terrible pain.'

And then the image arrived, in glorious technicolour, dog collar and all. I tried to put it out of my mind.

'Oh, you know, a little better. They tell me I'll be fine.'

Gilda, Nas and the vicar noticed my bedside reading all at once, and a smile of pleased recognition went round the three of them. Because of the hefty introduction in my edition (which I had skipped), the place of the bookmark made it look like I'd read a lot more than I actually had.

'I see you have the best company of all already,' said the vicar. 'Gilda and Nas have been telling me all about your interest. Such keenness is most welcome! Tell me, how are you finding the Good Book? Quite a read, eh?'

'Oh, it is! It is!'

Gilda stopped and looked at the floor, a little ashamed at her outburst.

'I'm not getting through much at the moment, I'm afraid, Jim,' I replied. 'It's been quite a couple of days, really . . .'

'Mmm, of course . . . I understand completely.'

'You should know I really haven't looked into things very deeply yet . . . I am by no means sure I even want to . . .'

'Of course, of course, no pressure. There will be plenty of time for all that talk once you're back to full health. Faith is a great healer though, and there is no greater healer than Jesus.'

'That's what Gilda said.'

Gilda smiled, embarrassed but pleased.

'As it is said in the book of John, "*When I am lifted up from the earth I will draw everyone to me,*" and it is true. I am going through something of a difficult time myself at the moment, and you really discover who believes in you.'

Gilda's eyes still did not rise.

'Still, you must continue His work, whatever stands in your way. I don't know how I would have got through it all without the help of the Good Lord Jesus drawing me towards him.'

In my mind I saw the vicar and a middle-aged soprano bent naked over the stand in the pulpit, gurning, the entire congregation looking on in disbelief.

'Hmm,' said Nas.

'Hmm,' I echoed. 'What's been the problem?'

'Something too awful to say, simply too awful. But I am coping, that's what matters. And like I say, my walk with Jesus helps me through everything. You must find your path and follow it, Abe, and everything else will fall into place. No matter what life throws at you, you will come through.'

Gilda and Nas seemed different in the vicar's company and were dressed more soberly – Nas in a blue shirt, blue tie and black trousers, Gilda in a white blouse and long pleated skirt. I preferred them as mavericks.

'Actually,' said Gilda, changing the subject, 'as well as coming to see how you are, we wanted to talk to you about something in particular. We wouldn't mention it if you weren't in such good spirits, but you seem on the mend. We received this at the shop this morning. He seemed fine with us the other day . . . we don't understand . . .'

She looked at the other two for support, and, receiving nods of approval, unfolded a piece of paper and handed it over:

Dear Evangelists,

Leave my father alone. You should not be recruiting in this way. He is a vulnerable, confused person in mourn-

221

ing, in no state to be making decisions and not well enough to work for anybody, certainly not for you. We are lucky he is still with us, no thanks to your organisation, who obviously feel no duty to the health of your followers. If I find you have not obeyed this order, I will report you all to the police for intimidating an old man into a conversion he does not want or need. I know you people and will not be persuaded otherwise.

Nathan Stone.

p.s. Whatever he may have told you, he has no money. You are wasting your time – the pubs have it all.

Gilda sombrely retrieved the letter, folded it and returned it to her back pocket.

'We don't know why your son would want to allege something so serious. It sounds like he thinks we are part of some strange, immoral cult after your savings. I don't know where he got that idea from – we're only Church of England! And why does he say you are in mourning? Are you?'

I thought quickly, not quite understanding why I had lied in the first place.

'Nathan is deluded, I'm afraid. He's a recovering alcoholic and has a morbid fixation with religious cults. Nobody has died. Please excuse his behaviour. Part of his delusion is that he is convinced his grandmother – my mother – is dead. She isn't, of course. I got a letter from her only this morning – look.'

I grabbed Evelyn's latest letter and went straight to the bottom for the signature, then showing them the postmark on the envelope.

'There,' I said, 'this is dated Thursday morning. I'm so sorry about all this. Please ignore my son; he's insane.'

'That's such a relief,' said Gilda, realising her mistake almost instantly.

Nothing was said for a few seconds. The noisy pattering of doctors and nurses frantically running from place to place bled into the room, and briefly it was as if we were listening for some clue as to what to do next. Even Evelyn was quiet. In the emptiness, I almost missed her.

'We thought you had been lying to us,' Gilda said eventually. 'It's just that we would all really like you to stay involved, that's all. For your own good, of course. You know, Abe, within the church there is a very good support network of people in the community just like you. People of your own age. They visit each other, help look after each other, that sort of thing – we think you might really benefit from it. It could help your recovery, both physical and spiritual.'

Nas cut in again.

'We just want you to think about it. When we next visit we'll bring some literature just in case you decide you're interested. How about that?'

Gilda now.

'Of course, if you ever want to come back to the shop, you can do that too. Not for a while though, obviously.'

'We'll leave you alone now,' said Nas. 'Get well soon. And think about what we said. You'll be in our prayers.'

I was not on the team any more. Gilda touched my arm with her hand soothingly by way of goodbye, and the other two waved. Her skin was brown and healthy-looking, while mine was more and more like my mother's pale translucent film of her final days, more so even than in the pub only a few days earlier. The bite on my hand was going nowhere. The bruises were fading though, and that was something.

My three visitors shuffled out as they had shuffled in, and yet again the room was my own. I wondered whether it might be possible to disconnect myself from the tubes, if I had the guts, where to find something sharp to cut them. I would have to do it to get away. Just then, the hospital phone by the bed rang. Lucille was whispering:

'Hi, Grandpa, it's me. We shouldn't be doing this. I'm afraid, and I'm worried about you.'

'I'm fine, there's nothing to be afraid of. I've read Evelyn's

latest letter, and it almost *tells* us to do this. I promise, everything will be fine – I'll look after you.'

I enjoyed saying that. There was no noise from the other
end of the line.

'I was just going call you, actually. I've booked two tickets
to Tel Aviv for tomorrow morning; they don't fly to
Jerusalem. The only problem is, it's early, so you'll have to be
out of the house by six o'clock. I'll meet you in Emporium at
half past six.'

'It will be closed.'

'OK, outside then. I'll get the taxi to pull up.'

'Wait, wait . . .'

'I got a good deal. Don't worry. It's all taken care of.'

'One way or return?'

'One way, of course. We don't know how long we're going
to be gone, right? Got to go. Bye.'

The phone went dead. We were really doing it.

27

Escape

I awoke with a jolt in near darkness. The old day was finished, the new one not quite yet begun, and the soft light of the sun was only just beginning to surface behind the city skyline. The ward was spookily quiet, with very few lights and even fewer staff on duty, the only noises being the sound of two nurses talking at the opposite end of the corridor and the occasional snore or beep of technology seeping out of adjoining rooms, all sealed. I listened, remaining still in my bed. A woman's high-heeled footsteps passed my room, a dog barked somewhere in the night. The car alarm started up again. To my amazement, the wires were gone. I felt around frantically in the dark, almost wanting something there restricting me, but there was nothing. But when had I fallen asleep? Who had removed them? What had happened to the rest of Saturday? And how late was I? Would we catch the plane? I sat upright to be surer of reality, waiting for somebody to notice and tell me to lie down again, but the command didn't come. Even Evelyn was asleep; there was nobody to help or hinder me.

If I was going to get out without being noticed there would need to be a plan. Of course, I could try simply to check myself out, but I would be advised against it at the very least, if not forbidden by whoever I came across, and I was not a good liar or negotiator. No confrontation, no trouble, just get out. The Rabbi had said the lift was broken so it would have to be the stairs, but the chances of getting down nine flights without being seen were virtually nil, even at this time. There were too many variables. I was talking myself out of the whole thing before even moving; the only way was to get up and do it. So, without stopping to consider how long it had been since they were last used, I lifted my stiff legs, bent them, turned them round and lowered the soles of my bare feet to the cold floor. My arms, almost numb, fell to my sides and touched the mattress. I slowly stood and tottered to the door, my sweating fingers wrapped round the handle, waiting, waiting, waiting for somebody to catch me and stop me from doing anything this stupid now or ever again. But again, nothing. I glanced back into the plain room, so starkly decorated, so blank, and picked up my bag, with the clothes, wallet, books and letters hurriedly packed into it. I opened the door gradually, trying to silence the squeak it was making, and, taking a deep breath, crept out into the corridor. It was clear.

I tiptoed along like a criminal. Hearing someone coming – those high heels again – I instinctively dived into a nearby Gents. Peering out, I noticed a set of directions on the wall behind the woman – a sign, surely – and scanned the long list of instructions, grabbing the door knob ready to pull. But, as I prepared to leave, I caught a glimpse of myself in the mirror: hair stuck up on one side from sleeping on it for so long and red bags under each eye almost to my chin. I couldn't go out there like that. Pressing down stray tufts of brown and grey, checking the door in case anyone came in, I washed myself, heart pumping, and then stepped out of the toilet as calmly as I could, walking down three flights of stairs and into another toilet as if it was the most natural thing in the world. The floors were laid out the same, and so the toilets were too. How clever. In the toilet on the third floor (gone into with hardly a look to check it was the right room – instinct was kicking in now), I stopped for another quick look in the mirror. Much better, more alive. God, this was exciting. A pair of grey knickers peeped out from a cubicle opposite, and, realising my error, I smoothly slipped from the women's toilet to the men's next door without breaking sweat. An easy mistake, easily corrected. Not even an architect's sly trick could stop me now. I was soon on the ground floor, keeping close to the walls, darting from corner to corner of the hospital unnoticed.

The signs directed me towards the way out but I decided to take the back way as there was too much chance of being seen out the front. Soon I was standing right by an alleyway exit, ready to leave for ever. But not yet.

Two doctors appeared in my line of vision heading right for the door as I was beginning to step into the outside world. Patience, patience – mustn't blow it. Having to think quickly, I pulled the door towards me and hid from the doctors as they approached. They didn't see me and walked up to the doorway, stopping close to where I stood, leaning on the outer wall of the hospital and flicking ash onto the pavement while I held my breath on the other side of the door. The two doctors began talking about it being Easter Sunday and what time they were going to get off. One, called Ryan, was finishing at nine. The other was on duty all day. I had no option but to listen to their grumbles. They both complained about having to work on a holiday. Ryan was on his way up to see a patient on the ninth floor, a friend of a friend whom he had just collected some test results for – bad news – while the other doctor was taking a quick lunch break, if you can call it that at six o'clock in the morning. Though thwarted by the doctors, I felt alive. While they sympathised with each other's situations, I took a moment to consider my own. A great idea came to me, and immediately I began to put it into action, fumbling for paper and pen from my jacket pocket (edging my hand slowly in so they wouldn't notice) and writing a short note to the hospital receptionist on the back of an old off-licence receipt. Perfect. The staff were reasonable people: they would understand a reasonable request. The door proved sturdy enough for writing up against; my fingers were still a little stiff and my breathing was a little irregular, but otherwise I felt strangely fine. I was ready for the trip of a lifetime. I had allowed for us being slightly late and was certain we would still make it:

'*Dear Hospital Receptionist,*' I wrote frantically,

You may soon notice I am no longer in my room on the ninth floor. This is because I have gone to meet my granddaughter; we have a flight to catch in an hour or two and must get to the airport. Let me take this opportunity to thank your company for looking after me so marvellously over the last few days and say that my early departure has nothing to do with the way I have been treated. It is purely a family matter.

Yours sincerely,
Abraham Stone.

P.S. Please do not call the police; I have not been kidnapped or anything. As you can see, I know what I'm doing. If my son Nathan calls, tell him I will be in touch and not to worry. He panics terribly and may cause a fuss.

P.P.S. Your steak casserole truly was something to behold. Please pass on my compliments to the chef.

The result was so pleasing that I almost ruined the whole escape, letting out a quiet, unmanly whelp of excitement while writing the final full stop.

'Did you hear something?' said one of the doctors.

'What?'

I could hear their feet shuffling on the other side of the door as if they were my own.

'I don't know. Forget it, it's probably nothing.'

It was safe again, the conversation turning quickly back to medical matters. They took an age to finish their cigarettes.

I tried to stop getting carried away with excitement over the glory of what had not yet been achieved. Visualising celebrating with Lucille at the airport, running to get the plane together, giggling during the journey about the moment one of the doctors thought they'd heard something and I almost ruined the whole thing, how we almost missed the plane but got there just in time – it was all so mouth-watering that I hardly had the patience left in me to do what was necessary to succeed. Even as the two doctors finished their cigarettes and began walking back up the corridor I wanted to stop the game and collapse into fits of childish laughter. If only Lucille could see me. She soon would. Another shot of discomfort passed through my system. A surge of impatience infected me and the soldier in me, secret agent, detective or escaping prisoner, I didn't know which, was no longer prepared to wait. I instigated an immediate change of plan, risking everything all at once. In seconds it was done. Puffing loudly and swinging my arms I ran through the main hallway of the hospital like a madman chasing his own sanity, right past the two doctors I had been hiding from, throwing down my note at reception and dashing out of the front door before anyone could do anything about it. Once outside, a black cab arrived right on cue and in seconds I was inside, watching the hospital getting smaller and smaller in the distance.

'Emporium, please, then the airport,' I said gleefully, gasping for breath. 'And quick!'

The taxi driver grunted in reluctant assent, shifting the machine clumsily through the gears. When Charles II was escaping from England, he revelled in the danger of walking amongst his enemies, often in scant disguise. He and I were the same.

The taxi was stuck in traffic. An accident on the main road had slowed all the vehicles to a crawl, so even the short journey to Emporium seemed to take for ever. As time went on I became more agitated – I couldn't even call Lucille, my mobile was at home – so I had to just stare out of the window and try to remain calm. I looked out at the familiar streets where I had accidentally spent my life, at people and things as we crept through the town centre; the places that last week seemed to have changed so much. The pavements were still pretty quiet though; you have to have a good reason to be up so early, but like the sleepy people passing me in cars, buses and on foot, off on another day of their important lives, I could now finally claim to be doing the same. Easter decorations covered every shop window we passed on the high street; crude adverts screaming about This-Week-Only offers and Easter specials – a cartoon rabbit pinned to a cross in the window of the butcher's shop grinned at us as we drove past – but the only reference to Easter's origin on the whole high street apart from the charity shop was the reminder outside the church itself, the same one I'd been passing all week in Gilda and Nas's parish not far from my home: 'THIS EASTER, REMEMBER JESUS. WORSHIP HIM HERE,' it said, on a backdrop of a burst of bright light and two outstretched arms. People need to be reminded of such blindingly obvious things. As the taxi shifted back into gear and slowly passed through the high street I thought of Gilda and Nas, of the vicar, of the career I could have had in the shop, and felt a light twinge in my back. It was a shame we couldn't take them with us, but Lucille and I had to do this alone.

The Rabbi said it was magical in Israel, and I knew it would be for Lucille and I. Together, off on our great adventure, away from Nathan and Rachel and letters and solicitors and hospitals and everything else that got in the way of life. What could be better? As the taxi pulled up outside Emporium I realised Lucille was not alone, and my heart sank so hard and heavy that it seemed to fall right out of my body and through the floor of the taxi, as if spattering onto the concrete below. I stared at the point it might have dropped through in disbelief.

'Here we are,' said the taxi driver, pulling up next to a frantically waving Lucille, who was already running to the taxi, dragging a bemused-looking young boy behind her. 'Are we picking these two up?'

'Mmm,' I replied, unable to offer any more.

I was too confused to answer. My mind was a pale, dead space.

Meanwhile, Lucille had got into the seat opposite, kissing me on the cheek, and she and the boy had dumped their small suitcases between us.

'This is my friend,' said Lucille brightly. 'He's coming with us. We bought him a ticket.'

'Sorry I'm late,' I replied. 'The alarm . . . I don't know what happened . . .'

'It's all right. We were late too. It was more difficult getting out of the house than we thought it would be.'

The boy was a scrawny ginger-coloured thing, pale-skinned and even thinner than Lucille, something I hadn't noticed when I had seen him outside the headmaster's office or outside Emporium the other day. His blazer and oversized trousers disguised a frame hardly sufficient to hold a body; now, in jeans and T-shirt as if dressed for an Own Clothes Day at school, his pasty arms and neck were dangerously exposed to the elements. One small hand held Lucille's tenderly. He smiled.

'What's your name?' I asked him.

There was no answer.

'Your name? What is it?'

Still nothing. Now sterner:

'If you're going to be coming with us I'm going to have to know what your name is, aren't I?'

'He has a rare disease,' chipped in Lucille cheerfully. 'He's afraid to answer questions. You kind of just have to wait for him to talk when he's ready.'

It took several seconds of spluttering before I could reply.

'How can that be? There's no such disease . . . that's ridiculous.'

The boy looked pleadingly at me.

'Yes, there is. He told me. And he never tells lies. Never. That's the thing about him.'

'How did you find this out if you couldn't ask?'

'He just came out with it one day.'

Lucille's companion blushed scarlet and looked intently at the floor.

'I see,' I said, suspiciously.

'He's called Johnny,' said Lucille proudly. 'He thinks you're very brave.'

We had stopped again.

'Thank you,' I said to the top of Johnny's head.

The taxi started back into life once again and we continued on to the airport – slowly past the shop where I had lasted only one shift, The King's Arms and the synagogue, all part of the same one street where years had quietly passed, unnoticed. Soon I would have left these things behind for ever. I tried to coax Johnny out of himself by asking about his parents, if they knew where he was and how to get in contact with them, but found Lucille, frustratingly, to be right. A flood of questions went unanswered.

'You're wasting your time, Grandpa,' she insisted. 'If he wants to tell you anything, he will. Until then, you have to wait.'

I brought my face closer to his until our noses almost touched, testing, testing, trying to beat him, but Johnny just looked vacantly right through me. I seethed. For a moment I longed to be back in the warm hospital bed clutching a hot-water bottle, picking at grapes and idly flicking through the Bible with no intention of taking it seriously. They would be bringing breakfast and the morning papers about now; Henry was supposed to be coming to visit. Perhaps if we did miss the plane I could just get back in the taxi, go back to the hospital, sneak back into bed and wait for him.

28

Departure

I was the last out of the taxi, Lucille insisting on taking my bag for me, helping me out of the car and guiding me through the mass of people, one tender hand slipped through my arm.

'Don't rush,' she said. 'Take all the time you need. Your health is more important.'

But it wasn't. Nothing was more important. It was precisely *because* of my health that we had no time.

'Please,' I whispered, trying to disguise my breathlessness, 'let's just get there.'

'You don't look well, Grandpa. Maybe I can stop the taxi driver before he goes . . .'

She turned to Johnny.

'He doesn't look well, does he?'

Johnny shook his head.

'See? Johnny thinks so too.'

So he could answer when he wanted to. How convenient.

'No, Lucille. Come on. We can still make this flight.'

I rubbed my neck, which had gone into spasm. I wasn't going to turn back now.

We had been straining up at the vast departures board for a minute or two, frantically trying to find our flight, when Johnny finally spoke for the first time:

'Check-in desk number 21,' he said drearily, as it flashed up on the screen. 'It's boarding now, last call.'

'How can that be?' I screamed. 'We can't be that late!'

But we were. And so we hobbled across the airport entrance lounge, one panting pensioner, one reluctant teenager and another with new-found voice, past the chain shops flogging the last of their Easter bounty and towards check-in desk 21. It wasn't how I'd imagined it. Johnny and I stood awkwardly together as Lucille reached for the reference number I had given her for safe keeping in the taxi. How was I going to get rid of this boy? I stared at Johnny, hoping he might go away. I wanted to be sick. Airport officials strode around purposefully, the attendants at the desk shuffling papers and laughing, finishing another shift. Time was running out. Lucille was still looking for the number.

'Can't we just go up and explain?' I asked. 'Surely they'll understand?'

'It doesn't work like that, Grandpa. There are strict rules. And anyway, the reference number is in with the passports. I'll find them in a minute.'

As I tried to control my panicked breathing, unable to watch the smiling automatons in bright coats and make-up at the counter, I looked, with pity, back to Johnny, a pale, ginger clutter of bones and mere slither of skin, hardly the type I imagined for my granddaughter, and just for a moment I forgot about how urgent the situation was. He was calm like the Buddhists Nathan had seen on TV and had the same unhurried aura. Johnny seemed to be somewhere else entirely, not merely unconnected to this world any more but actively in another one far more exciting, one he could see in his mind's eye, apparently somewhere near the fruit machines. I too felt that jangle of excitement – at the age of sixty-one I was finally in an airport ready to go abroad – but, freckled mute in tow, that excitement was dampened by fear.

'CHECK-IN DESK 21 FOR THE EIGHT HUNDRED HOURS FLIGHT TO TEL AVIV NOW CLOSING. WOULD ALL REMAINING PASSENGERS PLEASE MAKE THEIR WAY TO THE CHECK-IN DESK IMMEDIATELY.'

'Come on. *Come on.*'

'It's in here somewhere, I know it,' said Lucille.

Just then I realised that as soon as we passed through the gate I would become a criminal for the first time in my life, surely charged with kidnap, and I hesitated. What if something happened to Johnny while he was in my care? Perhaps this was a bad idea after all. He looked like he might simply snap at any moment, and I would surely be blamed, whatever happened to him. That's how the law works. They might even charge me with child abuse for snapping at him – God only knows what a crafty lawyer might dream up. I thought of the vicar, fighting for his innocence under a mountain of circumstantial evidence, and shuddered.

'I am going to the toilet,' announced Johnny, 'for a wee.'

'Now?' I snapped. 'You can't go NOW! *We're going to miss the flight!*'

'I am going to the toilet,' he repeated more firmly.

Johnny looked at me quizzically for a second before trundling happily off in the direction of the Gents. The situation pleased him, at least. I pleaded with Lucille, desperate, with one eye on the girls at the desk.

'Can't you stop him? Doesn't he understand what's happening?'

But Lucille didn't seem to be in a hurry either. Why did no one want me to make this flight?

'Johnny cannot be bargained with,' she said calmly. 'We will have to wait, whatever the consequences.'

She held up a piece of paper.

'Here's the reference number! And the passports – good.'

There could be no drama before we got on the plane or we would risk capture, and given the choice of kidnap or failure, I'd happily choose kidnap. The boy was nowhere to be seen though. I cast a quick glance around for any potential rapists and kidnappers, seeing nothing. Where was he? I could almost smell the tarmac of the runway outside from where we were standing, but the sickening feeling that accompanied the excitement was beginning to take over, smashing everything else. Visions of Johnny mutilated, murdered, chopped into little ginger pieces and dropped inside my suitcase along with a note explaining why I did it forced their way to the front of my mind. Innocent people get framed every day; Henry talked of little else after he came back from Thailand.

There were probably drugs in my bag, too.

Time inched by and nothing happened. I would have to go and check on Johnny, bring him back from the toilet – disturbing his record-breaking piss if necessary – and protect that boy with my life. Getting him on the plane first, of course. If I was kind to him there was less chance he'd turn me in to the police.

'He-he's been a long time, hasn't he?' I stuttered, afraid to leave the bags to find Johnny in case they closed the desk, afraid to ask the staff to hold the flight, afraid I might find him and something awful would have happened. 'You stay here with the bags; I'll go and get him. I refuse to miss that flight.'

'Grandpa, we won't make it now.'

I kissed her head and left without speaking.

'Be careful!' she shouted after me. 'Please!'

The walk to the toilet on the other side of the terminal took for ever, though it could have been no further than a couple of hundred yards. I tried to jog but couldn't, and so had to walk as fast as I could, like a wheezing Olympic walker at the back of the pack. With each lumbering step my reservations grew, with each breath my doubts became more oppressive, but I was determined to do this one thing properly no matter what: go and get Johnny, get us on that plane in time, get away for ever or at least for a while. No spotty fourteen-year-old mute with a weak bladder could be allowed to prevent that. Why had I let him go? Whether my rapid, drum-like heartbeat was caused by fear of getting caught and dragged back to hospital, or of something horrible happening to Johnny, or of Lucille insisting on going back home to Nathan I wasn't sure, but the beat drove me on, on, on to the big yellow sign in the distance: *Gents*. I finally arrived and felt something had been achieved already, reaching for the inhaler in my back pocket by way of reward and leaning on the door in blessed relief. I realise now how typical that is of me, to celebrate before the game is won. When I entered to find Johnny

lying on the toilet floor, unmoving, it took me several seconds
to register the new problem and react. I crouched down in
total panic. Evelyn used to play this game to toy with us,
sometimes holding her breath for up to thirty seconds as we
stood around her bed discussing whether she was dead or
alive. I waited nearly a minute in the deserted toilet before
pulling away.

Somehow, Johnny looked at peace. There had been something behind the void before, perhaps a sense that he knew
what was going on really but was choosing not to take part.
But now the expression on his face said something different.
He somehow looked to have embraced this new state, a half
smile on his lips evident in amongst the pain and pinkness
still in his cheeks. It almost seemed wrong to disturb him.
Maybe it was too late. I tried to remember what Evelyn had
looked like when she finally gave up on life only a week ago
and looked for the signs in little Johnny. But they were so different: Johnny had wanted to live, to come to Jerusalem with
me and Lucille. Oh God, *Lucille*. Was it too late to do anything? And if not, should I act at all or just let him slide into
the next dimension? Not everyone wants to be saved; Evelyn
told me that.

'Johnny,' I whispered. 'What shall I do? What shall I do?'

But, of course, there was no response.

'Johnny . . .'

I wondered what had brought him to this, splattered
between two sets of airport urinals with such astonishingly
bad timing. Was it suicide? Or murder? Perhaps the murderer
was standing behind me at that very second, hatchet in the
air, waiting. More likely, Johnny had innocently slipped on
the wet floor and hit his head. But there was no blood, no evidence of a struggle even; just a peaceful deadish body waiting
to be rescued or abandoned. I still hated him as I sat down by
his side and began to attempt shaking the boy to life, lifting
his top half from the floor and clattering the floppy frame as
hard as possible, jangling him like he was the embodiment of

everything that had ever thwarted me, fairly or unfairly, in my whole life. I could have killed a healthy child with that shake.

'Johnny, Johnny, Johnny – fucking WAKE UP!'

The limp torso did not respond to my treatment. I punched it. It came to life, briefly, then died again, the only sound a cough. Or was that the sound of my own fist?

'Wake up, wake up, wake up, wake up . . .'

I looked anxiously around the room, searching for something or someone to help me bring Johnny back, but saw only a camera in the top corner of the room, recording events. Evelyn was there with me and the lens, yelling from inside an empty cubicle:

'Help him, help him, you idiot!'

But I couldn't. As much as I didn't want to let her and him down, I couldn't.

'Wake up, wake up, wake up . . .'

I punched Johnny again, in the face this time, collapsing onto his body in the aftermath of the hard crack.

'Fuck, fuck, fucking . . .'

He was still not fighting back. If anything, he was deader than before. I dragged him by the arms out of the toilet and began screaming for help through my tears, his head banging the door as I attempted to get him out of the toilet and into the main hallway. He now lay straighter but with one leg still trapped in the closing door, the rest of his body out in the hallway where hundreds of sleep-deprived passengers were waiting for their cue to go to their gate and get on a plane to somewhere, to forget the ugly things in the world for a couple of weeks – to escape responsibility. Nobody moved to help. They had planes to catch that would not wait for small dead boys to come back to life again. Parents shielded their children, poorly paid airport staff froze in their places; nobody sounded the alarm. My scream rang out through the big room, seemingly endless, until finally a young girl in yellow, not much older than Johnny herself, ran over to me to help. Forgetting

Johnny for a second, I hugged her as if she were my own daughter, clinging, not wanting to let go. She pulled away.

'Have you tried resuscitating him?'

'I . . . yes . . . I found him in the toilet . . .'

'It's OK, you did the right thing. Try and relax. Let me try . . .'

' . . . He's not breathing . . . I listened . . . I . . .'

The girl smiled.

'I'm Colleen. I'll do my best.'

'I'm Abe.'

Colleen set about trying to revive Johnny, alternating repeatedly between blowing into his mouth and applying pressure to that chest I thought would snap so easily. So fragile, so delicate. I imagined me on the airport floor and Gilda and Nas above me, lamenting how far I had strayed from my walk with Jesus.

'Are you getting anything?'

'Nothing at all. Do you know what happened?'

The Rabbi was there now too, shaking his head in disappointment, Evelyn standing behind him doing the same.

'No, I . . . we needed to catch our plane, I was coming to tell him . . .'

By now there was a crowd gathering, Lucille at the back of it dragging the three bags awkwardly behind her. A man was calling an ambulance, airport officials cordoned off the area, and a woman with a walkie-talkie spoke seriously into the speaker. On seeing Johnny, Lucille dropped everything and ran to him, dodging two officials on her way through and smothering her friend completely on her arrival.

'Poor Johnny,' she cried, in shock. 'He was only trying to help me . . . I did it, I did it . . .'

As she crouched down to hug him she heard Colleen say:

'You did well, Abe. If he survives, he will have you to thank.'

Lucille had reacted instantly, automatically, desperately. I had lied. Johnny lay motionless between us.

29

A Guilty Thrill

We rushed Johnny to St Mary's hospital – a quick phone call to his desperate-sounding mother settled the question of where to go – and what seemed like just a few minutes after leaving the airport I was again in the main corridor of Accident and Emergency, going in the other direction this time, accompanied by two ambulance crew and Lucille, she and I gripping a hand each with the boy laid out flat on the slab between us dead or alive – we weren't sure. For now, my own health was forgotten. We followed Johnny and the medics through the building, now so impossibly vast where before, in the escape, it had been so easy to negotiate. We twisted and turned as the terrain demanded, passing patients and loved ones and listening to the medical jargon being passed back and forth by nurses and doctors now appearing all around us. All the talk of needles and theatre thrilled me; the thrill disgusted me – *I* disgusted me. We turned another corner and went past the receptionist on the ground floor, who still had an off-licence receipt on her desk; she gave me a queer, unsure look but said nothing. Moments later we had arrived at our destination.

Actually, Johnny was not dead. Not even close. Not any more. He had started up again after Colleen's mouth-to-mouth and was in intensive care, in a remarkably stable condition. The doctors had said he would probably be fine but to wait for them to give the all-clear before assuming anything. Two hours after our arrival and original panic I was sitting with Lucille in the hospital corridor waiting for news, drinking a cheap, bitter black coffee while she huddled on a hard blue hospital chair, a little calmer but still delicate, hands clasped between her knees, looking at the floor. As I put an arm round her shoulder, now a little calmer myself, I felt us getting closer and was grateful to Johnny for that.

'So . . .'

My granddaughter looked up at me sadly, crying a little. I tried to do something good.

'. . . While we're waiting, why don't you tell me how you two met?'

Her eyes lit up at the question, while mine dropped in disappointment. She cuddled up to me and spoke partly to me, partly to my chest.

'We met at school,' she started slowly, wiping away tears. 'He was in my maths class.'

A nurse came past. We both looked up in hope. She walked on.

'Johnny's fifteen but he'd been kept behind because he wasn't very good at it. It doesn't matter though because he's going to be an artist, and artists don't have to do long division.'

Typical; an artist.

'That's nice.'

'He's a proper artist already you know – he's been in an exhibition at the Town Hall and everything. Johnny's a painter.'

It was hard to believe she was talking about the same tiny boy who had announced his piss so proudly only hours before.

'He has these really clear dreams about all kinds of really cool and scary stuff and gets up in the middle of the night to paint what he remembers. He uses lots of black and red. Usually his paintings have wolves or dogs in them. He's a genius, like me and Granny Evelyn. One day he's going to be famous and I'm going to help him.'

'I see. And what are you going to do to help?'

'He's going to need a manager to organise everything and take care of the business side of things. It's a very important job. And that's what I'm good at – organising.'

241

'I thought you were going to be a teacher, like me.'

'I can do that too – I still might – but I'm not *just* going to work for someone else, am I? Anyway, teaching is boring. You have to keep going over the same stuff every year and you never really get anywhere. With this, it's easier.'

'It sounds like you've discussed it thoroughly already.'

'Well, I did most of the talking, but Johnny definitely agrees. He knows I would never make him do anything he didn't want to do or compromise his artistic integrity, and that's really important.'

'Artistic integrity?'

Sometimes it was still strange to hear big words coming out of such a little mouth. Lucille was now sitting up proudly.

'Yes. He's very principled when it comes to his art.'

'That's very admirable.'

'He says he would rather die poor and unhappy than *sell out*.' She threw the words out of her mouth as if it dirtied her just to say them. 'And that's very rare these days. We think that Israel is going to inspire him to do some great work, if we still get there. Granny Evelyn says the north is really green and beautiful, and that it would be a good atmosphere to paint in. Though I suppose it's usually dark when Johnny works. These are the kind of things I'm going to have to think about.'

She thought about this last remark carefully, and then continued seriously:

'You've *got* to have the right atmosphere.'

'Of course.'

We fell back into silence, holding each other.

'I'm sorry we didn't make it today, Grandpa,' said Lucille finally. 'It wasn't Johnny's fault though. It was mine. You see, I . . .'

'I didn't know Johnny was coming at all until this morning,' I interrupted. 'I thought it was just going to be the two of us.'

'So did I until last night. It was too late to say anything.'

242

'What do you mean?'

'Johnny's mum ripped up a load of his paintings and threw him out of the home – she drinks a lot and goes crazy sometimes – and he had to stay at Uncle Henry and Auntie Beryl's with me. He was really upset and said he didn't ever want to go back home anyway, so I told him about our adventure and invited him along.'

At that moment, Johnny's mother came storming into the hospital and up to the front desk of the ward, demanding to know where her son and his kidnappers were. I introduced myself nervously. A smiling doctor came out into the hall, addressed Lucille and me with a smile, and was just putting this miracle down to my quick thinking at the very moment Johnny's mother was about to throw herself at me in a hail of blind fury. Instead, she was instantly calmed. Even Colleen, it seemed, now back on shift at the airport, had put his good fortune down to me before leaving. Everyone was agreed: there could be no other explanation for the boy's astonishing recovery.

'Mr Stone,' said the doctor, shaking my hand as I had shaken Johnny, 'if it weren't for you this boy would certainly be dead. We are unable to say exactly what happened, though there is evidence that he was attacked in some way – he has cracked ribs and an almighty black eye – but who knows what events may have unfolded if you hadn't arrived when you did. Perhaps we will have a clearer picture soon if there was a camera in the airport toilet. There usually is. Anyway, whatever happened, he and his family owe you a debt of gratitude. And so do we – you'd make a fine doctor!'

We all laughed.

'Actually, don't I know you? Aren't you a neurosurgeon or something?'

'Oh no, I've never been in this building before in my life.'

'Oh well, my mistake,' he said cheerfully. 'Too many hours in this place and you begin to see things!'

The doctor left, passing Ryan on his way down the corridor. I speedily turned my back, only to see Johnny's mother collapse drunkenly on the hospital floor in a fit of relieved tears, thanking Almighty God for his merciful intervention. She was lifted out of the way as another stretcher came hurtling round the corner by two quick-thinking nurses experienced in handling distraught family members. Everything was happening too fast. Lucille looked on in shock, holding firmly on to my arm.

'Truly, you are a saint, sir!' clamoured Johnny's mother, heaving her stinking gin breath all over me. 'I will remember you all my life! Let me look at you . . .'

She held my head in her hands and kissed me many times all over the face and neck. Then she pointed to the sky with a spindly finger and said:

'The Lord has sent you as a messenger, a sign, and from now on I shall be a better mother. Little Johnny, it's what he deserves . . . he's such a good boy . . . please God, let him pull through . . .'

'It looks like he will . . .'

She fell on me and the tears started again, faster this time, dropping straight onto the hospital floor, mingling in with the dirty prints of wet and mucky shoes. There had been so many tears in this one day. With Lucille on one arm and Johnny's mother leaning heavily on the other, I felt like I was being dragged down, literally, into the tiles below.

'Now,' continued Johnny's mother, struggling more with each syllable, 'you two go on home and rest. There's nothing more you can do. We'll let you know what's happening when there's more to tell. Thank you, thank you . . .'

More kisses, this time to both me and Lucille, who did her best to avoid each one, smarting at their sloppy wetness and wiping her face afterwards. Johnny's mother's voice was slurred and now barely audible in amongst the kisses. She looked despicable; I was glad to be sober. Actually, I had hardly thought about drinking since my heart attack. Somehow, it didn't seem quite so essential any more. I resolved yet again to stop drinking; it could only lead to this. We got away from Johnny's mother as quick as possible, almost running out of the hospital as soon as she turned her back.

We left the hospital arm in arm and piled the holiday bags into a taxi, Lucille's childish grip, unceasing since we arrived, almost cutting off the blood to my hand in its fervour. We still didn't know what would happen to her friend, but, feeling the warmth of her small hand on me, dependent, needy, anxious, I supposed it didn't matter any more. Our big adventure had been ruined; a boy was fighting for his life; I was a fake hero soon to be exposed. A gaping silence hung in the air, one that perhaps should have been filled with a reassuring word or gesture. The moment for it passed. The fantasy of the hospital nurse flashed through my mind instead, as my poor, beautiful granddaughter sat with her head in her hands, mumbling about being under too much pressure and nothing being fair and nobody understanding what she had to go through. I couldn't help but agree with her.

It was a quick journey back; the traffic had cleared.

'Arabella's not coming back, is she, Grandpa?' said Lucille, as the taxi pulled up outside our house.

'I just don't know. I wish I could tell you . . . she's not been gone long though, it's only been a week . . .'

I hoped she could hear the honesty in my voice. Though I wanted my lies to remain hidden, the truths I still wanted credit for.

'It's OK, Grandpa, it's not your fault,' said Lucille softly. 'We can do our adventure another time soon. Maybe when all this is over.'

Her voice was weak and shaky, more like the sound of an old woman beaten by life than a smart teenager at the beginning of it. She began crying again. We climbed out of the taxi, paid with the last of the money in my wallet and walked into the house. It was empty.

30

Regret

While Lucille escaped to her room, I went through the post. Amongst it there was another letter from Evelyn, which had arrived the day before.

Though there was no one to hide from I locked myself in the toilet with the letter anyway and tore open the envelope, wondering as I did it if maybe Lucille had been right after all and I should have waited to see what happened at the end of the story before running off into the night. Yes, suddenly it was obvious – I should have. As I pulled the letter from the envelope, I understood the mistake I'd made and felt foolish for my previous certainty, my stubbornness in ignoring Lucille's warnings. It wasn't meant to happen today and that was always clear – I just wouldn't see it. Evelyn knew what she was doing, and until she decided she was done, I was her prisoner. I took another one of my deep breaths and prepared myself for the next shock, but, before I could even open up the piece of paper, the front door opened.

'Dad? Dad? Are you there?'

Nathan charged around the house until finally he arrived at the toilet door, knocking fiercely on it.

'Speak if you're there.'

'Hello,' I said quietly.

There was the sound of Rachel holding Nathan back, and then a struggle.

'I'm going to kill him . . . I swear I'm going to kill him . . .'

'Nathan, don't!'

He crashed into the door, which shook but would not give way. He did it again. Still nothing.

'Don't! Don't! I'll talk,' I gasped. 'Just don't break the door down.'

'You bastard! What the hell did you think you were doing? Is this anything to do with those bloody Christians? Because if it is I'll have them *all* put on the cross!'

Rachel spoke calmly, first to Nathan, whom I could hear breathing heavily, and then to me.

'I'll handle this. Go and sit down. *Go!* Are you all right, Abe?'

Nathan could be heard stomping to the kitchen, opening the fridge and beginning to pack things away. That was a first. Rachel's voice was soothing.

'Yes, I'm fine. The doctors said everything was going to be OK. I just have to take things easy.'

'Good. But you're a fool. We'll talk more about your health later, properly. Now, are you going to tell me what happened? The truth?'

'Where's Nathan?'

'He can't hear us.'

'OK, give me a moment.'

'My father ran away from the hospital to join a cult!' shouted Nathan, banging around the kitchen, sounding very like Evelyn. 'A cult! A bloody cult!'

Perhaps Nathan was still a little closer to the precipice than we'd thought.

The toilet was a small room, with barely enough space in it to stand. I got up off the seat, put away Evelyn's letter and thought about telling Rachel the facts. She went into the kitchen, got a chair, closed the door to keep Nathan in and returned, speaking even more softly. Her head was pressed to the door; so was mine. For a second, I thought I could smell her.

'Right,' she said.

'Lucille was expelled from school on Monday for stabbing a bully through the hand with a knife. We've been looking for a new school for her since.'

'But she's been going to school all week! You said it was all fine!'

'I know. But no.'

'Well, what about the hospital? I *meant* what happened at the hospital, why you *escaped* . . .'

'I left to go to the airport with Lucille and her friend, with the intention of going to Jerusalem. But her friend was attacked in the airport and we never even made it to the gate. He's in intensive care now. His mother thinks I'm a hero.'

'I see.'

'I don't see how you can.'

'I mean, I see what you mean.'

'Do you?'

'I mean, I understand what you're saying. Is there anything else, Abe?'

'No. Just the expulsion and the escape. That's all.'

We paused.

'Do you hate me?' I said finally.

'No, but Nathan might.'

'What do you suggest we do?'

'Tell him what happened, of course. He has no idea. We didn't even notice her gone today – she was at Henry's last night – and we thought she'd been going to school as normal all week.'

'I want to tell Nathan about all this, but I want him to like me as well. I want him to respect me.'

'You may have to wait a while for that. Are you going to come out?'

'Yes. I'm a little old for hiding in the cupboard, I suppose.' But I didn't move. My body wouldn't.

'Any conditions?' asked Rachel.

'Lucille wanted to do her own service for Evelyn. I think we should, today. Now. And I don't want you to punish her for any of this. We should be apologising to her, don't you think? All of us.'

'You have yourself a deal. I'll ask Nathan about the service. And yes, we should. Everything is going to be all right, I'm sure of it. Come out now, we'll get everyone together to talk about this.'

248

And we did. Once again, Evelyn would have to wait. You can't, it seems, control everything from the grave.

31

This Is Also Vanity

Of all the events of the last seven days, this farewell was the saddest, and of all the silences this was the hardest to bear. There was no comedy in our task. We rose from the kitchen table and, without comment, put on our shoes and went outside into the garden still so dominated by Evelyn's willow trees to try and do something together, for her, for Lucille, for ourselves. Of course, it was raining. We shared two umbrellas – one emblazoned with the name of the company Nathan perhaps still worked for, the other a red and white print of Buddy Holly and the Crickets I'd bought at a show about his life – and stumbled unsurely in pairs to a spot near the centre of the garden. Nowhere in particular; we just kept walking until it felt right to stop. Lucille, tear-strewn, broken, clamped her arms round her father and buried her head in his chest, while Rachel and I attempted to start the formalities somehow, certain Lucille was listening to every word.

'What shall I say?' Rachel whispered as we stood there waiting for something to happen.

'I don't know. Anything. Just state why we're here. What does the first page say?'

Rachel and I held Lucille's prepared booklet between us, trying to protect it from God's splashes, trying not to cave in ourselves. Nathan and Lucille shared the other copy – each one A4, folded neatly and stapled, colours bright, words large and clear. Standing, heads bowed, in-between a set of swings and a crumbling rock garden to say a last goodbye to my mother, the whole thing seemed so horribly final. Nathan tried to smile, though not at me; Rachel rubbed his back softly. His expression was the same as at the first service the Sunday before.

Rachel started, paraphrasing from the introduction originally meant for Arabella and still labelled with her name. She stood up to her full height, firmly clearing her throat before speaking. Her hair was modestly tied up for the occasion, a few stray threads flapping in the biting morning air, and she spoke slowly, calmly and gracefully, as if born to lead people in grief. Nathan looked on, proudly stroking his daughter's head. These moments come rarely, pass quickly and are hard to understand, but briefly it seemed we were truly together, a family of sorts.

'Hello, everybody,' said Rachel, 'and thank you for coming, especially Grandpa Abe, who has been unwell, but who we are very pleased to have with us today.'

Rachel winked at me suggestively. Nobody saw. She continued, using some of Lucille's words and some of her own.

'We are here today to say goodbye to Great-Granny Evelyn, who died last week, aged ninety-three. I never knew her but am told she lived a remarkable life. Born in Jerusalem and brought to England during the war, Evelyn was a talented, dedicated fighter for what she believed in, and she had a profound effect on the lives of all those she came into contact with. Us being here today is testament to that; she will be greatly missed. This short service is a small thank you. Also, we would like to take this opportunity to say prayers for Arabella, also missed today, and for Johnny, who is recovering in hospital as we speak, and whose life we give thanks for. If not for the quick thinking and heroics of Grandpa Abe, he might not be alive.'

Nathan flinched.

'And let us say Amen.'

'Amen,' came the chorus of voices.

Suddenly I loved Rachel.

'Lucille has prepared a few things for us to say – Lucille, would you like to read?'

Lucille shook her head, very definitely.

'You do it,' she said to me.

The rain came down harder. I coughed before speaking.

'Everyone, this is a piece from Ecclesiastes that Granny Evelyn chose before she died and wanted us to read. True to her nature, she has seen fit to edit the Bible.'

My arms and legs shook, and yet again I felt the insistent swell of oncoming tears beginning to form behind my eyelids but not come. On the page were Lucille's handwritten verses underneath a crude charcoal picture of Evelyn in her bed: bed, bedside table, lamp and single chair – just like her room – a grinning Evelyn sitting bright and upright. I stood deadened; Evelyn surely hovered disapprovingly above, though she was strangely quiet. I read:

And how dieth the wise man?
As the fool.
Therefore I hated life;
For all is vanity and vexation of the spirit.
Yea, I hated all my labour
Which I had taken under the sun,
Because I should leave it unto the man
That shall be after me.
And who knoweth whether he shall be
A wise man or a fool?

Behind us the willows shook in the breeze as if in reply.

'Thank you, everyone,' said Lucille. 'I don't think we need to do any more.'

I was surprised.

'Are you sure? There are three more pages. You wrote them specially.'

'No, it's OK. It's raining. I want to go inside.'

Lucille came close to me, pulled me towards her, and whispered so no one else could hear:

'I'm sorry, Grandpa. I was just doing what I was told . . . I'm really sorry.'

And with that she ran back to the house.

When Lucille and Nathan were safely inside, Rachel turned to me and touched my hand.

'Thank you,' she said.

'Thank you? I didn't do anything.'

'Well, thanks anyway. For doing nothing.'

We hesitated a moment as the next gust of wind passed noisily through, and I caught a glimpse of the nape of her neck, reddened from exposure to the cold.

'I hope you stay,' I said.

'I will. I think I can make things better.' She smiled deviously. 'What was that passage about?'

'Ecclesiastes? Evelyn's sense of humour, perhaps. Really, I don't know. Maybe she chose it before her revelation. Does it matter?'

'No, I don't think it does. But really – "Therefore I hated life?" I'm glad you didn't give *that* one to the Rabbi at the funeral. I nearly pissed myself.'

Rachel laughed her beautiful, musical laugh, slipped her arm through mine, and together we set off to join the others inside.

32

Sales Pitch

Rachel left the house for a shift at The King's Arms, sending Nathan out with a shopping list before going. We still hadn't heard from Johnny's mother, and Lucille had gone back up to her room. After attempting and failing yet again to console her, I gave up and came downstairs to my favourite chair in the conservatory to read Evelyn's letter, which, I was certain, was to be her last. But, again, life got in the way. The doorbell rang.

It had been months since I'd heard that noise. Hardly anyone uses our doorbell. Henry knocks on the window and everyone else has a copy of the new keys, apart from Arabella, of course. I downed the letter firmly in irritation, leaving it on the table, and went to see who it was.

'Yes? Can I help you?'

A smart man in his mid-forties with shiny, neatly parted, wavy blond hair stood before me, beaming, his locks glistening in the light morning rain. Sharp pinstripe suit, straight white teeth and tasteful patterned tie, this person was success itself and knew it. At first I thought he must be selling something – encyclopaedias, double glazing, insurance maybe – and whatever he wanted to sell me, I already felt obliged to buy; he was that classy. But finally I recognised him as Hagstrom from next door; he looked very different to the pottering gardener we saw occasionally tending the flowers at the weekends.

'Hello there! Have we fallen out?'

'Sorry?'

'Have you received my letters, Abe?'

'What letters? I don't know what you're talking about . . .'

'My secretary has sent you three letters this week, which

should have arrived with you on Monday, Wednesday and Friday, respectively.'

'I'm sorry, Edward, it's been quite a week. You see, Evelyn passed away last Sunday . . .'

'Yes, I know. I was very sorry to hear that, though of course it was no surprise . . .'

'. . . And . . . and I have been ill myself . . .'

I felt like I had to make up a good reason not to have replied to Hagstrom's letters. I couldn't even remember receiving them. The week's post was a sea of wallets and Evelyn and debts that meant very little.

'Well then, never mind the letters. I only sent them because I have been away on business this week and never arranged with Evelyn exactly how we would go about this. I was hoping to make an appointment for an appropriate time . . . are you busy now?'

'. . . Er . . .'

'Abe, do you not even know why I am here? You seem a little confused.'

'That's because I am,' I said, confused.

'Evelyn said she would explain everything . . .'

'. . . Yes, well, she's been telling me that as well . . .'

'I see. Well, not to worry.'

Hagstrom put his hands in his suit pockets, took a step back, looked grandly upwards and said:

'Abraham Stone, I am going to buy your house.'

'But it's not for sale!' I protested. 'You can't!'

'I know,' he grinned, 'but nevertheless I'd like to purchase it from you. And when you hear what your mother and I have arranged, I think you'll want to sell.'

He offered his hand for me to shake and held it there strongly until I finally did so.

'But I live here! My whole family lives here! You've not even seen it!'

'Abe, our houses are the same, right down to the positioning of the toilets. Evelyn let me look around, months ago.

And anyway, it doesn't matter how it looks *now* . . . '

'I don't understand. You've never shown any interest in the house before . . . we've lived next door to each other for fifteen years and hardly spoken! Anyway, how can I sell? I have no idea what this place is worth!'

'There is that, yes, but no matter. Evelyn and I have been negotiating a figure for some time now – and she is a hard negotiator, I can tell you that – so I think you will be pleased with what she has signed her half away for. I shall be offering you half of that, as you clearly don't have the same talent for negotiation. For the whole thing, bearing in mind Evelyn is no longer alive to claim her share, how does this figure look to you?'

He took out his card and wrote the number across the bottom, clear and large.

'What?'

'I said, how does that look to you? It's more than fair, I think you'll agree . . .'

The zeros jumped out at me.

'You're insane!' I yelped. 'This house is a dump! It's falling to pieces! Look!'

I hit the nearest wall with the side of my fist; a few small pieces of brick and dust fell to the floor. Hagstrom continued, unconcerned.

'The lamps and shades business has been very kind to my family and me,' he said, 'and we are simply looking to extend our property . . . onto yours. This is a large house in a fast-growing, increasingly exclusive area . . . Abe, do you mind if I come in?'

He hovered on the doorstep, looking for a way inside.

'Now hold on a minute . . . how can . . .'

'Times have changed, Abe . . . Yesterday's middle bracket can easily be today's top bracket, surely you know that . . .'

'I'm not sure what you mean, but why are you telling me all this? Shouldn't you be bartering?'

'I would happily lie to you, but a brief phone call to your

solicitor would show me up to be a fraud and then there would be less chance of a deal. I think it better if we are honest from the beginning, don't you? And anyway, as I have already said, Evelyn has signed for her half of the house and instructed me to pay it to you. She has already bargained hard for her half, you clearly have no sense of the worth of yours, and hey presto, we have a figure. Abe, surely I can come in to talk about this? It really is very important.'

I leant with one hand on either side of the door frame, trying to clear my head, desperate to understand what was going on. I spoke quietly and distractedly.

'Well, it still seems very steep . . .'

'Perhaps, but that is my figure. Really, Abe, I appreciate the reasons for your hesitance, but if you knew my wife you would understand.'

'Understand what?'

'Why I am offering you such an absurdly high figure to ensure you sell, whether you want to or not.'

'But you just said that . . .'

'This fine piece of land,' he interrupted, gesturing grandly to our bare wooden floor, 'is destined to be my wife's tennis court, and if this is where she wishes to serve repeatedly into the net from, then that is what shall happen. Believe me, it is not worth making her unhappy. The smashed headlights on my BMW are testament to that. Please, Abe, be reasonable. It's cold out here, can I come in?'

'. . . Well . . .'

He stepped into the house before receiving an answer, wiping his feet carefully on the mat outside first, somehow seeming to be polite though he was walking into my house entirely without invitation. I had been young, suave and well-dressed once; no longer. I was wearing baggy trousers sagging at the back and an old hole-filled cardigan that smelt of unwashed male, in stark contrast to Hagstrom, who, though dressed for the office, smelled like he'd just bounded out of the gym shower.

257

'I'm sorry,' I stammered, wrapping the cardigan round me like a shy schoolgirl, 'I wasn't expecting visitors.'

He laughed warmly.

'Oh, don't worry about that. You needn't be well-dressed on my account. A drink, perhaps? You look like you need one.'

'I often do. But I'm not sure – I've just had a bad scare . . .'

'Oh, come now. It's not every day a friendly neighbour knocks on your door and offers you so much money for your house, is it? Just a small tipple . . .'

'Actually, you rang the bell. I noticed that because almost everyone that comes here has a key. But yes, I suppose a small one can't do any harm.'

Whose house was this? Mine or his? Hagstrom was hard to resist. Each of his slick movements seemed designed to persuade me to sell, every nuance, smile and flick of his bouncing quiff more reason for me to say yes. But what about the others? What would they think of this? And if Evelyn had been planning this for so long, why hadn't she told me about it? Was it a test? I poured stiff whiskies for both Hagstrom and I (mine a little larger) and we went through to the conservatory to conduct our business.

'Oh, wow!' he exclaimed. 'What a feature! You should pick this up and put it out the front!'

'Well, soon there may be no point,' I said sarcastically. 'It *is* lovely though.'

I sat at one end of the long table in the centre of the room, he at the other, as if we were a royal couple waiting for the banquet to be brought. How would Henry VIII have negotiated this situation? Of course, he didn't negotiate, he *commanded*.

'I have no plans to sell my home and will not be persuaded,' I said, trembling with sudden determination and puffing out my chest. 'You may bully me all you like but I won't back down. This property is all I have and I shall retain it until my dying day.'

I downed my whisky in one, the smooth liquid slipping effortlessly down, calming me, soothing me, encouraging me to relax. I refilled my glass; Hagstrom had not touched his.

'Let me be completely honest with you,' he began. 'I understand this must be a shock to you, and a difficult decision, emotionally speaking. I really do. But that is precisely why I am willing to pay you so handsomely for this property, which you have already conceded is falling to pieces. Of course you are attached to your family home, and I want to compensate you for your loss – a loss, I might add, soon to be counterbalanced by huge gain in the near future. Just think of what kind of a home you could buy for future generations of your family with the money you are being offered . . . How old is Lucille now? Your mother told me a great deal about her . . .'

'She's fourteen.'

'Lucille is such a pretty name, isn't it? It means "light" you know.'

'Er . . . yes . . . it does. How do you know?'

'It's my own daughter's name, the eldest one; she's married now. As you know, Mrs Hagstrom and I are in the lamps and shades business.'

'Hence the name.'

'Indeed. And just think what a bright start in life you can give your own little light by taking us up on our generous offer. In this uncertain world it is a lucky young woman who can thank her grandfather for a home to be proud of and some money to help her on her way in the world.'

'And a lucky woman who can point to the house next door in the knowledge that her husband will barge in and demand its owner give it up,' I said wryly.

'Perhaps, though I have hardly barged. As I have said, I approached Evelyn about this quite properly. She has been dragging her feet over the deal for months. Waiting for the right time, she's been telling me. She wanted me to keep very quiet about it all.'

I thought for a second.

'I don't understand. If you want a bigger house, then why don't you move to one? Why does it have to be mine?'

'You know nothing about property, do you?'

'I didn't realise I had to.'

'Well, no – and I don't have to justify my reasons to you if I don't want to – but if you want an answer to your own question you should listen.'

I grunted in assent.

'Well, it's simple. Sometimes, Abe, things are.'

'So I keep hearing.'

'My wife and I are happy in this area. It would be more expensive to start again buying a new, large property, and we like the home we have . . . we just need more space. Also, we still have two children at school here.'

Only now did he drink his whisky, shaking his big shiny head in silent amusement, apparently unruffled.

'Abe, children are like trees, are they not? We plant them, feed them and watch them grow. And does not every good parent – or grandparent – want the best for their little sapling?'

He was nodding sagely now.

'Indeed, like the king who plants trees in the royal gardens not for himself but for future generations to enjoy in years to come, is it not the ultimate in selflessness for a senior member of the family like yourself to secure the financial future of the next generation, and the one after? Is that not, after all, what Evelyn is trying to do for you?'

He was right: Lucille *was* a sapling that sorely needed water, and Hagstrom was an angel with a watering can. But my anger at Evelyn for not telling me about the whole thing made it impossible to agree to.

'Anyway, what do you want to stay around here for the rest of your life for?' he continued. 'I'm sure there are plenty of dreams you have, things you'd like to do. Am I right?'

'Well, actually you are.'

'Think of the travelling you could do, you and the whole family. Think of the freedom this deal could give you.'

Hagstrom smiled. If I turned him down, would I ever be able to live with myself? Each time repairs needed doing on the house, each time a bill needed to be paid, wouldn't I hate myself for turning Edward Hagstrom away? If I was clever I could buy a good home, clear my debts and have plenty left over to live on, to educate Lucille at a school she could be happy at, to pay for the rebuilding of the Evelyn Stone Memorial Hall. I could pay all my bills in a single day. If I gambled cleverly I could double the money – it was the kind of thing Henry had made a career out of. Another whisky went down like a rocket, with hardly a thought for my health. But no, I could not make this kind of decision alone. What if I made a mistake? I listened for voices; once again there was nothing. Evelyn had fallen silent. I needed to talk to her now. She wasn't talking to Lucille any more either, it seemed. I missed her, and felt a wrenching in my gut.

'Excuse me,' I said to my guest, 'I must make a phone call.'

He nodded, smiling and taking out his mobile phone. I almost ran for the toilet, adrenalin sloshing around my system uncontrollably, and took out Evelyn's letter on my way into the toilet under the stairs. I locked the door and read. It was written in Lucille's handwriting and there was a distinct change in tone. This was Evelyn hollowed, close to death:

Avraham –

Do not be alarmed by the identity of my new secretary; she deserves to know, as you do, the end of the story. You will not punish her for keeping these letters secret from you or for posting them for me daily after my death; primarily she is writing this because I cannot, and she has been my postwoman because I ordered it. Now, finally, to you.

I have been negotiating the sale of my half of 174 with Edward Hagstrom, who wishes to extend his own property onto ours. He will try to persuade you to sell your

half. If you do, all the money will come to you. If you
don't, my signature means nothing. I have thought a great
deal about trapping you into doing this, in the hope it
would give you some happiness, but I have decided
instead to simply show you what can be yours.

Avraham – a single signature will solve many of your
problems, but if you have done it resenting me, you might
as well not do it at all. I said I would make everything all
right for you, and maybe I still can, but not without your
consent. With the money Hagstrom is offering you could
go to Israel, even live on the kibbutz where you were
born, if you wish. You could pay off all your debts, settle
your third divorce, go on a long holiday, or simply sit and
read your precious royal-history books for the rest of your
life. It really does not matter to me any more.

I am now nearing the end of my existence and am
pleased to report it is not as bad as first imagined. These
pills, I admit, are having a strongly positive effect on my
mood. Though weak, I find myself strangely content: I am
thankful for my life and am, surprisingly, at peace with
my God, who, against all previous indications, has turned
out to be merciful. Everything is in place now and I am
satisfied, choosing my own time to go, my own way.
Thank you for not taking my pills from me.

You are free now.

I love you.

Mama.

I folded the piece of paper, put it back in the envelope and,
with steady hands, picked up the mobile phone and punched
in Henry's number.

'Henry?' I whispered. 'It's me, Abe. Listen . . .'

'Abe? Abe, you *bastard* . . .'

'What?'

'I came to see you this morning and they told me you'd
checked yourself out. Are you insane? Do you want to die?'

'No, I want to *live* . . .'

'Then what in heaven's name are you doing? Time and time again you . . .'

I interrupted in my most authoritative voice.

'Listen, Henry, there will be plenty of time for you to tell me off later. Right now I need you to listen. I have my next-door neighbour in the dining room. Evelyn has signed away her half of the house for a fortune and he wants me to sign away my half. Do you understand what this means?'

'How much has he offered you?'

'Enough to make me a very rich man . . .'

'Then what are you calling me for? Do it, you fool! Can he hear you now?'

'No, I'm in the toilet. I just thought I should check . . .'

'Listen, Abe. Where is this man from? Is he a northerner?'

'I'm sure he's foreign.'

'Hmm. French? German? American?'

'I'm not sure. But definitely European. His English is perfect. Damn it, he's been living next door to me for so long . . . but we never talked. I never thought I would need to know.'

'Mmm, yes. We rarely talk to our fellow man any more, unless we want something from him. That's the modern world for you. Cold and unneighbourly. What does he look like?'

'Very tall, blond hair, blue eyes, named Hagstrom . . .'

'Sounds like a Swede – good. Swedes can be trusted.'

'Is that how you do business? *Henry, that's crazy!*'

'It's how *everyone* does business, Abe. Trust me. Count yourself lucky you didn't get a Finn. Finns – now *there's* crazy. Norwegians, they're crazy too, crazy as you like . . .'

'All right, all right, enough! I'll call you after I sign.'

'No, wait! Never sign on the first meeting. Shake hands instead. Say he has your word on it but that you must consult before signing. You never know what might happen. You could fall down dead any minute. In fact, you probably will.'

'Good thinking.'

'And Abe?'

'Yes?'

'You're an idiot. A real fucking idiot.'

'Thanks.'

'And a lucky son of a bitch. I've never known anyone like you. I'm coming round right now to discuss your health, if you live that long.'

'Cheers, Henry. Goodbye. I love you.'

I put the phone down and returned to the dining room.

'Right, Edward,' I said, brimming, 'you have yourself a deal. We'll shake on it now and I'll sign once I've checked the details.'

'Fine,' he said, beaming once more. 'I've got the contract right here in my pocket. The address to send it to is across the top, along with my phone number if you want to talk about it.'

Actually, the contract was already out of his pocket and on the table, pen lying on top, waiting for my official surrender.

33

Dear Nathan

Edward Hagstrom lifted his glass high and cried:

'To the future! *Your* future!'

We shook hands. Then, the deal done, he poured and drank a second whisky down in one, retrieved his suit jacket from the chair and made to leave.

'You've made the right decision, Abe, a *brave* decision,' he said earnestly, stopping in the doorway. 'You will not regret this, and my wife will be *delighted*! For a minute there I thought you weren't going to see sense . . .'

And then he was gone, my guardian angel, out of the door and skipping off down what I supposed was now his wife's cracked pathway, withered front garden, bus-stop entrance, and then back up the one he already owned. I stood at the entrance after Hagstrom had gone, door still open, letting the biting spring blast in for a good couple of minutes before having to forcibly bring myself out of the daydream. *To the future!* It was all too delicious. Now, accidentally, luckily, I had one once again simply by disposing of the house so tightly clung to for so long. My whole existence, so happily abandoned. How queer life was. I tapped my heart for good luck with one hand while closing the door with the other. I was left alone again, without even the mumble of Lucille's now expected prayers. It was my turn to write a letter this time, to Nathan. Things were really going to change now.

'Thank you, Mrs Hagstrom,' I said to the escaping draught.

Returning to the house with a secretive laugh, I poured another drink – a large one, why not? – and settled in my favourite chair, revelling in its worn but comforting softness. As I cleaned another glass out I felt, all at once, so much pressure fall away, like a plane tumbling out of the sky, the brittle tension in my shoulders slowly evaporating, the itch and tightness in my throat disappearing, the pains in my limbs subsiding. I was like jelly. Another drink and I fell back into the chair, vindicated. My mind raced. 'You cannot run from what you are, Abraham, no matter how ugly the truth – and, by *God!*, how ugly it is!' I let a crafty smile creep across my lips and felt another wave of relief and childish excitement swell around my insides. A little of the old Evelyn still survived, then. Yes, I would go to Jerusalem, on my own terms, and this time I'd do it properly. I was going to do everything properly now. I picked up the pen and wrote DEAR NATHAN in clear block capitals proudly covering the top of the page like a title. And then I stopped, tried to continue, but couldn't.

Sitting there, head spinning, I imagined it all spilling brilliantly, spectacularly out, everything that needed saying. But not yet. Soon. More shuffling in the armchair, another drink poured. I was drunk now; shouldn't have been. I looked down at my shaky handwriting – DEAR NATHAN – and tried to focus on the name, wishing I'd insisted on Isaac. *Abraham and Isaac*, like in the Bible. I'd even tried to call him Isaac for a while, but he ignored me, said it was stupid and wished it wasn't even his middle name. What were we thinking anyway, he'd say – but, of course, only to me; his mother was dead. Everyone's mother was dead now. In the final draft of this letter I would start DEAR SON; it would be better that way. But for now DEAR NATHAN could stay. The empty page dared me to continue. Through the window I could see the rain had stopped and the sun had come out brightly. The clouds had all disappeared. A clear blue day posed the question, what are you going to do next? If you could just say everything without having to articulate it at all; if only I knew what that everything was to be able to say it. The familiar fuzz of drunkenness began to take hold and I tried to think of what I would tell Nathan if I was on the brink of death right now and knew it; if I was Evelyn, setting everything straight, just in time. Would I say anything? There need not always be talk. Not all father–son relationships had to be like friendships. Looking at the cream emptiness on the page I was ashamed, but then quickly angry too that the words wouldn't come. I wrote: 'THERE IS SOMETHING YOU MUST KNOW,' and then sat growling at the clumsiness of the sentence, its melodrama, its silliness. I would change that bit too. I toyed with a few phrases in the fug, trying to crowbar Nathan's name into each one, playing with the sound of the word, still so unfamiliar, but couldn't write anything down. The bald opening – DEAR NATHAN, THERE IS SOMETHING YOU MUST KNOW – remained; it was all there was, so far.

Overcome with tiredness, I had to rest before doing any more. I folded the letter, slipped it in the envelope, marked it NATHAN and lay back, closing my eyes suddenly to find the Rabbi crouching beside me in his long black cloak, smiling peacefully, surrounded by a small gaggle of prune-like faces. Their presence alone was a comfort, their warm-heartedness something I wanted to wrap myself in.

'Hello, Abe,' said the Rabbi. 'Have you decided yet?'

'Decided? Yes.'

A look of pleased recognition came over the Rabbi's face, as if he had been waiting for something unspoken to plant itself in my mind, and it just had.

'What is happening?' I asked.

I wanted to make him happy.

THERE IS SOMETHING YOU NEED TO KNOW.

He, and the prunes, disappeared. The pen fell from my hand.

As the vision of the Rabbi ebbed away I found myself swept speedily off into a kind of curious half sleep, a deep calm, different to anything I had ever known. My arms came down to rest on the chair. I couldn't move. I began to claw desperately for wakefulness. The biro on the floor below wanted to be picked up, but when I tried to reach down for it

I found myself only imagining the motion, my hands still clamped onto the large chair, unable or unwilling to move. Over and over again I reached for the pen in my mind, but found that with each imagined grab I became less capable of actually opening my eyes and getting it, instead feeling myself slipping easily, happily away from reality. Now the glass in my other hand fell. There was no hope of retrieving it. My eyelids were unbearably heavy, as if weighed down with anchors.

Outside in the real world our doorbell rang for the second time today. It rang on, the loud sound piercing my very being, but I could not rise to stop it. Somebody's voice now, familiar, calling out from the haze. Gladly trapped in my new state, I wondered who it was, what they had come for – perhaps it was Edward Hagstrom, returned to tell me his wife had plumped for the house on the other side instead – but strangely I felt no anxiousness. Instead, a giddy satisfaction swam all over me. The voice was calling louder now. It was a woman's. The bell sounded again, for longer. The woman was annoyed or confused and was banging on the door.

Once more I attempt to rise, but fail. The bell has stopped. Now somebody else is at the door, another, deeper voice. Nathan's. Talking to the woman. Getting louder now, both of them; the sound of a key struggling with a lock, then a door giving way. Nathan and Arabella walk inside, disagreeing on something. Nathan is screaming at her now. She puts her suitcase down on the floor and I can feel the vibration of the floorboards in the soles of my feet. It is a very determined sound; Arabella is going nowhere. Nathan is spluttering, he doesn't know what to say.

And here we are. They're getting closer; I can hear them through the wall. They can't be more than a few steps away. I still can't get up; I feel even more distant than a few seconds ago, but their voices are cutting through clearer – it's almost as if I am between them, above them. Nathan is talking; the sound reverberates all around. The doorbell rings again;

that's three times. Nathan gets up angrily to see who it is and lets Henry in. He stomps towards the hall. Surprisingly, all this is calming. It makes sense that it should be like this. A chaotic peace. And now, suddenly, I am certain of everything. I know what I have to say. The door opens. This is strictly secular, free of all guilt, obligation, higher knowledge. Free of everything, yet somehow unaccountably lucid. I fall fast and gladly into the arms of this mysterious thing I cannot resist and know I will never open my eyes again. A lukewarm trickle spills down the inside of my trouser leg. This is it, and I am on the brink of yet more tears that will not come, in my mind at least, at the joy of it, though it means all that it means. And then Henry appears in front of me, sees my limp body in the chair, the half-empty bottle of whisky by my side, the pool by my feet, the letter addressed to Nathan, and cries out in pain. Cries out so loud that Nathan and Arabella forget their argument and come running, so loud that Lucille comes bounding down the stairs to see what's going on, so loud that I feel the hotness in every part of me. Is this just another trick? If I can feel and see and know, it must be. The horrifying thought flashes past in a whisper: more games perhaps, more unfathomable play. But no, it can't be, isn't, won't be. Everything is ruined, scattered to the four winds. Out of existence and out into the sprawling great warmness on the other side. It is the end, and I am alone in it.

Acknowledgements

A novel is a joint effort. Without the people below this book would not be.

For practical help with *No Fireworks* and all that lead up to it, thank you to: Andrew Cookson, Anne Donovan, Barbara Glass, Georgina Glass (my good omen), Jo Glass, Alasdair Gray, Jacqueline Kelleher, Robert Alan Jamieson, Danny Leigh, Willy Maley, John Marshall, Eilidh McCreadie, Mhairi McClymont, Ken Roberts, Hymie and Lily Summers, and everyone at the Glasgow University MPhil course (especially Editorial Group 4 2002/3).

Special thanks go to: my ever-supportive agent Jenny Brown, Gemela Nagi for putting www.rodgeglass.com together, my inspirational editor Hannah Griffiths, publicist Kate Burton, Kate Ward, Stephen Page, everyone at Faber who has backed me through this project, and my large, wonderfully supportive family in all its forms, especially my parents. Also, to friends: Paul Carlin, Scott Stainton Miller, Ross McConnell, Haim Shalom, Steven Turner, you all know what for . . . and, of course, AJC.

Parts of the story the Rabbi tells Abe were inspired by *Zeidlus the Pope* by Isaac Bashevis Singer. The book Abe reads by the German aristocrat is *Diary of a Man in Despair* by Friedrich Reck Malleczewen. Schiller's passage regarding friendship in old age is paraphrased from an interview Aldous Huxley conducted with *The Paris Review*.

The author gratefully acknowledges the continuing support of the Scottish Arts Council in helping to finance the writing of this book.